CORPORATION OF CANES

*There are five women sitting near you. I am one of them.
Which one of them do you want it to be? Choose wisely.*

He starts taking sneaky looks around his desk, does a
one-eighty from the waist. When he looks in my direction,
I make sure I am peering at my computer screen.

A new message arrives from him: *You'll get us in trouble.
But I am curious. Tell me which one you are.*

This makes me smile. I write: *I'm the one wearing no
panties.*

Ha, ha! he replies. *I know your name is Lizzy from the
mail address. It won't be hard to find out more.*

I start to reel him in: *Sure, but then you'll miss out. You
won't be able to make enquiries until after work. And I want
to suck a cock during lunch. In fact, that's what I want for
lunch. I need to know if you're going to provide it today,
otherwise I'll shop elsewhere. The window of opportunity is
closing.*

CORPORATION OF CANES

Lindsay Gordon

This book is a work of fiction.
In real life, make sure you practise safe sex.

First published in 2002 by
Nexus
Thames Wharf Studios
Rainville Road
London W6 9HA

Typeset by TW Typesetting, Plymouth, Devon

Printed and bound by
Clays Ltd, St Ives PLC

ISBN 0 352 33745 1

For Hanna

Career History: Part 1

Demotion

Working hard on a smile, you stand before her desk. In the room the blinds are drawn. The only light comes from a table lamp which creates an icy circle on top of her desk. Her hands are inside the glow. The fingernails are long and painted scarlet. They look sharp and wet. Between her thumbs, there is an open file. Her face is angled down to study the contents.

As usual, her suit is dark and well cut: the jacket is worn over a simple white shirt and her breasts are made insolently hard by constricting foundation wear that you can sometimes see as an impression through her tight clothes. She always has that chic, streamlined look and never wears more than two colours. Usually black and white. Her raven hair is pulled from her forehead to form a tight bun on the back of her head. In the neat bundle of hair she wears a silver spike.

She frightens you. More than what she says to you, because she rarely ever speaks to you, it is the way she looks at you that makes you feel hopeless, inferior and self-conscious. There is no compassion in her arctic glare, and the fine lines at the side of her mouth and eyes weren't made by forty years of smiling either. You imagine this beautiful, cold face has never done anything but frown and control a terrible rage. And the rumours about her temper and the sadistic delight she takes in humiliating staff just contribute to this sinister-sexy aura that commands an instant silence in any office where she appears. So when Mrs Raker wants to see you first thing, on the final day of your probationary period, you suffer an acute anxiety.

You clear your throat. 'Good morning, ma'am.' You are still uncomfortable calling her ma'am and it's been a month since you started working for her.

There is no response. The silence stretches until you become aware of an ache in your lower back. Straightening your tie, you try to breathe easy and slow your pulse. It's really chilly in here too. How she likes it; the heating turned off and the air constantly conditioned. It makes you wonder if there's any warmth in her pale fingers and cheeks.

You look around her office and hope to see a family photo or patterned scarf on a hook; anything to suggest the everyday. But there is nothing. Other than the desk and chair, there's no furniture in the office. The creed of the corporation is well represented in Mrs Raker: minimal colour and clutter, everything kept scrupulously clean and simple. Paper has virtually disappeared from the working environment. All of the managers' offices are the same. And the hard, uncompromising interior design extends into the communal areas of the vast building: into its corridors, elevators, conference rooms, restaurants and bathrooms. Everything in monochrome, steel, mirror and marble. It's a place of right angles, straight lines and total silence punctuated by abrupt announcements. You always feel cold and exposed here. And no one will talk near the lights or the sprinklers in the ceiling; apparently they're bugged. People whisper, if they talk at all.

When Mrs Raker switches her attention from the report to you, the look on her face makes you want to apologise. Though still beautiful at forty, there is nothing in her expression to offer warmth or welcome.

2

Above the frames of her glasses, perched halfway down her nose, her dark blue eyes blink twice, deliberately, and then fix on you. There is a shake of her sleek head. She says, 'You have hurt me.'

'Hurt?' you say.

'Yes.'

'I am sorry.'

Her answer is quick. 'For what?'

'What?' you ask.

'Yes, what are you sorry for?'

Your mind fills with a dozen things you could have done wrong, or that might have upset her. It's so hard to tell. Your start for the company has not been easy and there are so many rules here. You try to smile again, but the look on her face straightens your lips. All you do is shrug helplessly and when you open your mouth no sound comes out.

'You have no idea why I arranged this meeting, have you?'

'Well . . . I supposed . . . I guessed it was . . .'

'Yes, you suppose and you guess. But supposing and guessing is not precise. It is woolly, indecisive, weak. Just what we have come to expect from you.'

You swallow and hate that she's seen such an obvious sign of fear.

'A great opportunity was provided for you here. Such patience we have shown. Am I right?'

Your voice sounds too high; wants to break into a falsetto. 'Yes, you've been very good.'

'Consider the investment in you. Is it not too much for us to expect something in return. For us to stay competitive, our staff need to be competitive. I think I'm right' – she has to look at the report again to remember your name – 'am I not? What do you think?'

'Yes, ma'am.' Despite the cold, you're sweating; it's all over your back and on your top lip. Your mind is just racing: they're laying you off. After relocating from across the country to take the job, the company apartment and the car, they're sacking you. Dead man standing. What will you tell your wife? What have you done? Think, man. Think. Think.

But what do you actually do for the corporation? It's never been clear. Has never been made clear to you. And the corporation's business here, on this floor of the building, what is it? What do they do? How would you define it? Not exactly IT, or finance, more of a consultancy, or was it? You try to remember back to the interview and then the job specification in the advertisement on the internet. Something was said about creativity, about loyalty and dedication, about flexibility. But nothing more specific comes to mind. Been the same since you started. Maybe you're stupid, or never paid enough attention at those first meetings, or read enough of those ambiguous email circulars. Nobody else in the department seems troubled. Mrs Raker must have spotted you skulking around the office, playing at being busy, at being knowledgeable. Maybe you made a mistake with all that fumbling on the computer and it's been traced back to you. And your CV was full of lies too, not to mention the one fake reference from your old roommate at college. You don't really know anything about anything now and her eyes are reading your thoughts like subtitles. You feel like a fraud.

'In a way, it's fraud,' she says.

Time to wipe the face and loosen the shirt collar. Maybe beg her to keep you on? 'I have a wife,' you say, out of desperation, without really thinking and it sounds like you're desperate and not thinking. Or did you say it? Was it just a thought that sounded audible? It feels like an enormous sound and pressure has filled your head. You hear loud, rushing sounds in the silence.

Mrs Raker nods. 'A wife, yes.'

'Responsibilities,' you add.

She agrees, her face hard to read, at best indifferent.

'It was a simple mistake,' you blurt out, grasping for sympathy.

'But a significant one. And under a more rigorous scrutiny there appear to be irregularities in your career history.'

'Yes. But I can make it right. Fix it. I can fix it all.'

'We're not so sure.'

'Give me another chance. You'll see. Everything will be good again. Everyone deserves a second chance.'

'Tell me precisely what you did wrong for this matter to be brought to my attention?'

'I don't know.'

Disgusted, she shakes her head. 'You don't know?'

Speaking quickly, you feel like you are drowning and that every excuse is an arm flailing for wreckage. 'Maybe it was the system. I'm not totally familiar with it yet. There was something on my desk one day. The next day it was gone. It looked ... important. And I have been asked to do things. Things I couldn't understand. I mean, the instructions. They never made sense. Never seemed to fit into the other things I was doing. So I ignored them. And the charts. The figures. Hard to work out what ... No one seems able to put me right. I was just waiting for it all to become clear. I don't know what to say. I'm sorry.'

'You are incompetent?'

'I'm new.'

'So you admit you don't know what you are doing?'

'Only so far as –'

'Only so far as you mislay important documents, do not follow instructions and are incapable of grasping the broader horizons of our vision?'

You feel giddy and think of running through the miles of white corridor to find the miles of flat, black tarmac in the carpark. You want to run until this terrible pressure is released from your skull, run until you can breathe again, run away from those searching eyes and the long nose.

5

'Further more, you are a perspirer.'

'Yes.'

'I make you nervous.'

You giggle but immediately feel stupid. 'Yes.'

She crosses her legs under the desk. They make the sound of a knife being sharpened. 'You have good reason to be nervous.'

You nod.

'You are incompetent, you sweat, you are dishevelled. And yet you have a wife. She must have low expectations.'

You are stunned. Nothing forms into words. You feel disembodied, lost, abandoned.

'We can only use the very best in their chosen fields. In all matters must they excel. Their personal lives must be as immaculate and successful as their professional lives. Statistically, failing professionals soon lose their spouses in such an environment. It is only natural, and in this environment everything happens sooner.'

'My wife . . .'

'Yes, your wife, your responsibilities can so quickly become someone else's wife and responsibilities. Do you follow?' The preposterousness of what she is suggesting seems to have stricken you dumb. You can't even feel your legs. Smug, she continues, 'Once settled into a corporation apartment and the attendant lifestyle, we find wives prefer to remain here when offered the choice. I mean, who wouldn't?'

You lean on her desk.

'Remove your hands from my desk!'

As if electrocuted, you withdraw your hands and step back, losing your balance.

'Sit on the floor! Losers sit on the floor!'

You sink to your knees and wipe at your face. This was a trap. They would take your job away and then your wife. But is that such a terrible thing? a little voice says inside you.

'Divorcees are well taken care of in our business community. Their every need is addressed. I myself am a divorcee. Statistically, a divorcee can expect to begin a new and wonderfully fulfilling relationship within one month of an unsuccessful partner's removal from company property. She is often impregnated within six months by a far more suitable companion. I need not remind you of the very precarious situation in which you presently exist.'

'No.'

'Yes. You stand to lose everything.'

'God, no.' You can picture every single thing she describes. Your wife was so happy here; loved the apartment and garden, the retail development, the fashion, the golf course, the lake, the night life, the smiling fulfilled faces, the men who paid her compliments. The slut! She's in on it. What does she know?

You sit in silence, knowing Mrs Raker is watching your facial expressions change from the panic-stricken to the despairing. Through your trouser legs, you can feel the cold floor tiles. You feel worn out from emotion and the beginnings of nausea.

From the back of the dark office, Mrs Raker rises from her chair. On the marble floor her high heels click and clack, drawing circles around you. Ever-decreasing circles. 'A man in your situation should consider all of his options, few as they may be.'

Unable to look away, you watch a pair of long, slender calves appear before your face. Her stockings are black and sheer. The light that spills from the desk makes the top of her feet shimmer. The heels on her patent leather shoes are spikes tipped with steel. Around her left ankle you can see a thin silver chain. It seems tight on her leg; you can almost feel it around your throat. Everything she wears is flawless, expensive, co-ordinated, smart, professional: symbols of a world speeding away from your clammy grasp. And she's

7

caught you staring at them before. Waiting for your interview, when you were sitting in reception, she saw you ogling her bottom and legs. But how were you to know she was going to chair the interview? And then when you were offered the job, you even flattered yourself with the thought that she hired you because you admired her.

Cold fingertips touch the top of your head where the hair is thin. 'Look at me.' You look up into the hard lines of her sculpted, shadowy face. 'The time has come for you to redeem yourself.'

Blackmailed into sexual favours? You can think of a fate much worse. And with Mrs Raker? All she had to do was ask. 'Thank you. But please, my wife . . .' You want to ask if she can be left out of things.

'Your wife?' She frowns, then laughs. 'Oh dear. No, no, no. It's not what you think. These' – she raises one of those great legs in front of your face – 'are not for you. Did you really think I'd . . .?' She laughs some more. 'You really have no idea, do you? What I'm talking about is a new position.'

'New position?'

'A reassignment. To a place more suited to your . . . abilities.'

She's not sacking you. You overcompensate to show your gratitude by making light of this situation; pretending to be a slave you bend over and kiss the pointy toes of her spiteful shoes. 'Thank you. Thank you. Thank you –'

The kick is swift and takes you by surprise. Sprawled on your back, not sure which direction you are facing, which way is up and which way is down, her glossy shoes materialise before your face again and stand close to your cheek.

'That is the very last time you touch me,' she says in a stern voice. But when you peer up, you can see right inside her skirt; the top of her stockings, the pale inner thighs, the naked sex.

Your mouth dries out. 'Sorry.'

Her voice could crack ice. 'You will be if you ever so much as look at my legs again without prior written permission. Do not forget the gravity of your predicament.'

'I won't. I promise.'

She takes a deep breath and then exhales. When she speaks again her voice is softer. 'And be grateful the corporation's approach to career realignment is flexible. You are a very fortunate man.'

'Yes, ma'am. I am. I know it.'

'Before you are escorted to your new place of work, you will be required to participate in a corporate seminar, designed for management. I cannot stress how fortunate you are to be present in such an exercise, considering your recent performance in our employ and the liberties taken with our selection procedures.'

'I'm sorry I touched you. I was . . . just . . . overwhelmed. Relieved. How can I thank you? I don't deserve this.'

'No, you really don't.' She walks back to her desk and depresses a button on her phone. 'Take him,' she says into the cool silence of her office.

Career History: Part 2

Seminar

You have no idea which part of the building you are in; the two women have marched you through so many bare white corridors, tugged you inside elevators, clattered you down fire escapes that lurked behind reinforced fire doors, before leading you into this padded chamber. The floors and walls and ceiling are coated in white rubber. Once the door has closed its outline disappears into the padded surround. In the centre of the room is a large plug hole.

And these two women you have never seen before: dressed identically, their tailored white coats remind you of a cross between laboratory smocks and the overalls heavily made-up women wear behind cosmetic counters in department stores. Each woman's waist is cinched and her breasts are pushed up into a pale cleavage that smells wonderful. Patent leather boots with a square heel are zipped up to their knees which then shimmer with flesh-tinted nylon beneath the hem of the dress-coats. You've seen the same uniformed staff elsewhere in the building – as doors were hurriedly closed in the lower service areas, or occasionally you've seen them marching through the corridors with faces frozen by what appeared to be severe disappointment. The wearers of the white coats were always women and the shiny hair styles never differed from the taut and stretched buns perched upon the rear of their heads.

And in the rubber room they begin their business in a quick and methodical style. Thin white rubber gloves are stretched and then snapped over their fingers. Legs kicked apart, arms pulled outward, head tugged back, your jacket, trousers, shoes, tie and shirt are stripped from your body. 'Remove your socks and underwear,' the older woman says, her green eyes and lacquered eyelashes close to your cheek, her minty breath cold on your mouth.

You hesitate. 'What? Why?'

'Remove your underwear! This is no time for reticence.'

You comply and stand naked under the harsh light from the overhead bulb, feeling foolish but obliged because Mrs Raker has not fired you. And when the hose is turned upon you, they never even hear you shout 'No!'

Freezing water blasts against you, forcing you into a huddle on the rubberised floor. Protecting your face with one hand, you try to deflect the arctic cannonade with the other. But you slip over and squirm in the abrasive torrent; become undignified with cock and balls on display.

Mercifully, the water gets warmer by increments. The relief is brief. A soapy brush with long hard bristles turns your skin pink in under a minute. Choking and floundering on the streaming rubber, you catch glimpses of shiny boots as the women skip and splash in the puddles, delivering the water and the swift, violent scrubbing from every angle. Your head is manoeuvred by unsympathetic fingers that are placed under your chin or spread across the back of your skull. Every part of your body is thoroughly cleansed. Close attention is paid to the genitals.

You keep asking, 'Why? What is this for?' but the questions go unanswered. Hauled to your feet, you are

11

then assaulted with rough white towels. The exfoliating fabric further punishes the skin until you become dry but tender from toe to scalp. Pushed to your knees and held face down, you then hear the sound of an electric razor buzz into life. A slippery knee is painfully inserted between your shoulder blades. 'Is this really necessary?' you shout. But as your head is shaved by the older woman, the younger woman shoves your suit inside a black plastic bag and tags it with a 'Refuse' label.

'My suit!' you cry out.

The older woman pulls you away from the discarded hair gathered about your feet, and douses your body with a powder that smells milky. 'You won't need it again. Not just anyone can wear a suit here. Your unworthiness for the formal attire of business has been proven. Put this on.' A plain white boiler suit is shoved into your hands. Flip-flops are kicked towards your feet.

The older woman checks her watch. 'We have four minutes and thirty seconds to deliver him.'

'Deliver? What do you mean? This is outrageous!'

Catching you unawares, the younger woman snaps steel cuffs around your wrists. Held in a headlock, you then watch the next set of stainless steel manacles being clipped around your ankles. Gleaming chains then shackle your hands to your feet so your movements are restricted. 'For your own safety,' she says, without looking you in the eye, as if this is all routine, as if they have done this before. Weakened by humiliation, you stand still and ponder how swiftly the last of your freedom just diminished within steel. Confusion over your alleged incompetence has led you this far; your growing sense of insignificance in the eyes of the company enabled them to lead you even further away from what you had previously thought of as normal and reasonable behaviour by an employer. But that was not the only reason you are allowing these uniformed disciplinarians to do as they wish. Mixed in with the

12

embarrassment, guilt and fear, you are giddy with arousal. While they dried your body with the stiff towels, you experienced the first swelling of excitement between your legs. During the haircut, you stared at a booted leg, shining with the promise of something warm and soft inside, and your crotch began to feel weighty. Now, inside the boiler suit, your cock has set hard and shows no signs of softening. You are excited enough to put your fate into the manicured hands of these two unpleasant strangers, to allow yourself to be led into an uncertain future. Inexplicably, you even feel liberated. The pretence of knowing what you are doing in the department is over. The illusion of being professional has gone. The fussy managing of thinning hair about your crown is a thing of the past. The gnawing anxieties have been replaced by other things they have given you to consider.

Stumbling behind the orderlies, and watching their firm curves, corseted inside their white uniforms, you are led down another corridor and into an annex. The older woman approaches a second door in the chamber. She peeks through a peephole. 'Nearly time,' she mutters to her younger colleague, who holds you by the elbow with her elegant but strong fingers.

'Where am I?' you ask again, beseeching the younger orderly's face.

'You'll see soon enough,' she whispers. 'Just do as you're told and you'll get through this.'

The older woman turns and nods to her partner. The second door is opened. You are pushed forward and out of the annex.

Shackled, you stand at the front of a conference room. Behind you, the two female orderlies wait with their feet together and hands clasped across their stomachs. To your left stands a lectern. Behind the lectern, Mrs Raker peers through her spectacles at the assembled female executives. 'The subject's performance was well below average. He was unable to complete even the most basic tasks. Everything from his appearance to his attempts to acclimatise into the company creed were mediocre.' A spotlight partially blinds you. You can see little besides the silhouettes of the watching women in the front row. 'But our streamlining process,' Mrs Raker continues, 'has weeded out this inferior material within the probationary period. And our investment in what was originally perceived as an asset will not be wasted. The corporation will regain the debt and penalty payments at its leisure, although not in the usual monetary sense. This subject is another prime example of our revolutionary techniques in human resource management.' Mrs Raker turns and nods to the orderlies. Behind you, you hear their heels click-clack away to the far corners of the room.

From a control panel on her lectern Mrs Raker widens the spotlight over you until you have the sensation of standing on a small stage. 'Research has shown that our methods of resettlement and ideological realignment are fool-proof.'

Looking over your shoulder, you catch a glimpse of something made from steel being wheeled behind you. It is made from tubing and looks like a machine astronauts would train on. And yet, the sight of the device scares you; it suggests a far greater surrender of control and will. There are harnesses and straps attached to the uprights, and cuffs at the bottom. This is not the kind of apparatus that requires volunteers.

Mrs Raker struts across the dais to stand beside you. Her perfume seems especially sharp. Again, she nods to her assistants. Working swiftly, the women remove your shackles. When the older woman reaches for the zipper on your boiler suit, you begin to struggle and shout, 'Enough!' But your hand is seized and your thumb pressed painfully into the palm of your hand until you stop moving.

14

The boiler suit is stripped down to your ankles by the younger orderly and then yanked free from your feet. Before the assembled elite, your erect penis is unveiled. A moment after your total exposure, you detect a stirring in the crowd.

Proudly, Mrs Raker raises her face. 'As I said earlier, do not be squeamish about inflicting pain. Intimidation always plays a vital role in maintaining order.'

'What the hell –' you begin to cry, but are quickly silenced. Jaws forced apart, your mouth is filled with rubber. Then you feel an assistant buckle a strap around the back of your skull. Against the nape of your neck her hot breath quickens with excitement. Any further struggle is neutralised by the painful grip inflicted upon your thumb, so you allow them to arrange your naked body within the gleaming frame.

Feet spread wide and arms tied above your head, you are stretched into a star-shape. Mrs Raker strides across the stage and stands beside the apparatus with one hand at rest on a tubular strut. 'This appliance is effective for purposes of communal humiliation, but can be unwieldy in an impromptu office situation. A foot stool or backless, orthopaedic chair will be sufficient. Such correctional functions were taken into consideration when the corporation's own furniture was designed. Now if you'd like to gather around the working area, you can better observe the correct procedure.'

From behind the ball gag, you salivate. Your eyes bulge. The female executives gather in a neat semi-circle around the apparatus. Lowering your eyes in shame, you see the legs of the female executives gather to become a forest near to the uprights of your stocks. A forest that grows from roots of elegant stiletto shoes and painted toenails to many slender limbs, sheathed in fine nylon stockings.

'Note the genital area. Feel free to observe it closely.' About your thighs and legs pretty faces jostle. Steely

15

eyes scrutinise your girth and length. Glossy lips part. Some of the women whisper.

'See the close kinship of pain and pleasure, the blurring of distinction,' Mrs Raker says. 'Note the twinship of humiliation and sexual arousal in the male psyche. Exploit it tactically. Take control.' The women nod their approval.

Mrs Raker's voice then rises above the mutterings. 'And now for an introduction of the crude into the sophisticated. The interface of manual and technical expertise.'

Hot-faced with embarrassment, dazed by this confusion of your own impulses, you still maintain enough presence of mind to notice the mood of the conference change. Soon there are 'oohs' and 'aahs' at something Mrs Raker, or one of her assistants, is exhibiting behind you.

'Due to its long-standing effectiveness, I must ask each of you to limit your strokes to no more than three. With the subject gagged and rendered immobile, it is important to check levels of discomfort at regular intervals. You can read it in the face. Too much discomfort and the exercise is wasted. Our sadism is best employed in a controlled and limited capacity. Sustaining the brevity of pain is vital.' All around you there are mutters of agreement. 'Keep strokes sharp and short. Avoid breaking the skin. And don't worry, he really does deserve this.' The women laugh. 'Now, my assistant will now demonstrate the ideal method of delivery.'

Never have you felt so naked, so utterly revealed, so mentally exposed. But curiously, the sight of so many attractive, well-dressed women staring at your naked body and unclothed sex supplies its own thrill. And you want to be punished by their long, pale hands; you want the clean, hot pain of punishment to obliterate the anxiety and pretence of your time at the corporation. Had they ungagged you, you wonder if you would have

16

begged to be set free or asked them to be hard and thorough with such a miserable creature.

The cane falls.

Three strokes descend from one of the orderlies, interspersed with commentary from Mrs Raker. Most of what she says is lost on you because the sting and heat from the caning distorts your senses and even lessens your awareness of the public nature of the humiliation. Each blow sends a titillating judder through your abdomen to further stimulate your already swollen cock. It protrudes, thick and tender, from your body as if reaching for the pretty executive closest to you, who absent-mindedly watches your sex and wets her top lip with the tip of a slender tongue.

Mrs Raker speaks again: 'My assistant will now pass a cane to each of you. Before you strike the target, I suggest you practise your swing. Remember to keep the distance between hand and buttock close. Not to draw your elbow too far back. Our subject has to last for all of you.' There is more laughter before the women begin to find their own patch of space around the dais. Soon, the conference room is full of smart executive women whipping the thin canes through the air. Some of them joke and giggle, some appear heavy-handed and make you wince in advance, others just stare at the stick in their hands with faces transfixed by the power it seems to give them. Most of them shed their jackets; two older women roll up their sleeves. A beautiful brunette with a short bob and straight fringe looks you in the face and sneers.

Then, one at a time, they walk behind you and begin to strike your buttocks. One or two miss the target area and hit the back of your thighs. It makes your eyes stream with tears. You lose count of how many times you are hit after the first dozen strokes. Mrs Raker encourages and corrects throughout the session. Only once does she assess your condition by examining your buttocks with a hand gloved in rubber. The assessment is swift and the punishment commences.

Most of the women seem to approach the caning like a tennis lesson. Their strokes are fastidious and repeated if flawed. Points of technique are discussed and those who draw an interesting sound are applauded.

When one woman strikes you especially hard, your muffled cries are heard over the gag. 'A little too firm,' Mrs Raker corrects. And when the next blow smarts just as much, she says, 'Better.'

As the thrashing continues you begin to imagine every misdeed and indiscretion of your life. You begin to believe that you are being publicly punished for each failing with the women in your life. The harder you think this way, the more you realise just how much you deserve to be caned. And as the body's natural painkillers rush to your striped rump, you begin to feel dizzy with pleasure too. Without being aware of it, you begin to say 'Yes,' or 'Oh yes,' after every lash.

While the caning occupies the attention of the crowd, a curious and unexpected event occurs. A young executive woman with short red hair has moved to the side of the frame. Gently, she touches and then begins to stroke one of your cuffed hands. And instead of watching her colleagues whip your backside purple, she turns the focus of her attention to your penis. Discreetly, she then reaches out with her cane and begins to stroke the length of your cock. Your body screens this delicate caress from the rest of the women who stand behind the frame. The ticklish pleasure makes you dizzy. You begin to push and gyrate your hips forward to encourage the brush of wood.

Pleasure is obliterated by the pain of a cane-stroke from behind. Then the physical joy returns, stronger and embellished with endorphins, as the woman's gentle ministrations on your sex continue. You look her in the eye but your attempt at a smile is turned into an oafish clown-grin by the ball gag. Smiling back at you, she pinches one of your fingers until you shriek. Another cane falls from behind and you think you might soon faint. Gently, but firm enough to give a jolt, the woman then begins to tap your penis with the tip of her cane. The first few strokes are light, then more severe. This vandalism of your privates combined with the humiliating exposure of your naked rump, and this total absence of sympathy from these cold and suited bitches, reduces you to an overwhelming condition of powerlessness. You imagine them all stamping on you, and pulling your hair in a big playground, removing your trousers behind a tree to inspect your willy. You weep, but know that a single stroke from a painted fingernail on your shaft will lead to an eruption between your legs.

Faint from emotion and pain, your body finally loses its tension and swings loose within the frame. Prideless, unwound, sore, reduced, you hang like an executive toy from the rear-view mirror of a performance car, in whose glass is framed a pair of beautiful arctic eyes. You have given up. All resistance and ambition has been flogged from you. Self-respect has drained from your mouth and dripped from a ball gag. You belong to them now. They are your new masters. You welcome their firm handling.

'Check his condition,' Mrs Raker says to the redhead who has taken such an unusual interest in your genitals.

'Yes, ma'am,' the girl says, her smile reflecting her obvious delight.

She moves to the front of the frame and faces you. Looking you right in the eye, her face alive with devilish mischief, she says, 'Oh, he's good for a few more, ma'am.' You shake your head. No, you cannot take any more; it feels like the skin has been flayed from your rump.

Discreetly, the cruel woman with the red hair then removes a tissue from the cuff of her blouse and holds it in the palm of a hand. With her other hand, she holds your cock with a firm grip and begins to stroke it in an up-and-down motion. You try to look down and see those red nails on your skin, but she corrects the position of your head by forcing your chin up. She's eager not to draw attention to what she is doing with her hand – with what she has in her palm.

As the canes continue to fall from behind, her hand shuffles and tugs at your meat, determined to draw the gravy. And she does. That cool hand massaging your girth and now the tissue wrapped around your phallus is too much to withstand. Crying out, the muscles of your cock contract and pump, contract and pump, contract and pump, contract and pump. Your eyes roll back. She kisses your cheek quickly and stands back. 'That's enough now,' she says, over your shoulder, to Mrs Raker.

'Enough!' Mrs Raker calls out to her fastidious pupils. 'Well done. All of you. A fine performance that you can repeat with confidence where you see fit in your working lives.'

The women applaud Mrs Raker, each other, themselves. Their pinky faces beam and shine from the discovery of a new channel for their power. Gathering their jackets and slipping their canes into black velvet bags that are closed with a sash, they then depart from the room in groups, talking and laughing.

You only see the woman with the red hair who milked you into her hand, one more time, and only briefly. Alone, she teeters from the hall on thin heels and holds a hand to her face; to her mouth or nose, you can't tell. But in that hand, she holds the tissue that absorbed your ejaculation.

Soon, you are alone with Mrs Raker and her assistants. 'Take him back to Hygiene,' she says. 'Then drop him off at the reassignment.'

As the younger girl unshackles you from the frame, the older woman rubs an ointment into your punished

20

rump. It feels cold and mentholated. You can smell peppermint. Then you are reclothed in the boiler suit – all the time supported by the strong hands under your arms – before being taken from the conference room and back the way you came, back to the rubber room.

Career History: Part 3

Back to Grass Roots

It appears the corporation needed another gardener. But when you realise the full extent of your demotion, while kneeling on the flat grass beside the west wing of the building with a weeding tool in your hand, you feel nothing; there have been so many shocks for you today. You wear strong gloves and pull out the weeds and longer clumps of grass that grow between the pavement and the wide, immaculate lawn. Then you drop the off-cuts in a wheelbarrow. Slowly, you shuffle about and weed one section at a time. You can't sit down and tend to wince after every movement of the thigh. Four hours before, you were a corporate executive on the eleventh floor. The last time you worked in a garden, you were a child helping your parents.

Above you, the sky is cloudless and blue; the sun warms your body through the white suit. In the distance you can see another two figures in the same boiler suits. One drives a mower, the other looks for litter and loose pebbles on a path. Shaking your head in disbelief, you realise these men are also fallen executives. Every day, you have seen men in white suits at work on the grounds and in the town, but never realised the truth of their predicament. You wonder what the likes of Mrs Raker had done to them before reassigning them to Environment Services. And there were many, many lockers in the changing room of your new department; the place they took you while you hopped from one foot to another with a ball-gag between your teeth. Tonight, you will also be fed in the cafeteria on the wooden benches and you will meet the other men who sleep in the barracks full of bunkbeds under the building. This is your new home. Your new job. Your new life.

In front of you, as you weed the path, the vast corporate building rises into the stratosphere. Like a giant alien sculpture, it sits silent and mysterious amongst acres of flat grass and straight paths that seem to go on for ever around the building and the attendant carparks. All of the glass in the building is dark and acts like a giant mirror. Chromatic clouds move across the windows. But the people inside can see out. You wonder if you are being watched from an office window. Near the foot of the building, a CCTV camera turns on its mounting and peers at you. Immediately, you look down and concentrate on your weeding, but silently hate yourself for doing so, for being afraid of the consequences of failing again. 'Your work will be checked, thoroughly,' your new supervisor said, the frowning woman with the big chest and red lipstick, who ran Environment Services and called all her employees 'boys'.

Behind you on the path, you hear the sound of high heels. Fastidious in your work, you still manage to peer sideways. A young blonde woman is walking towards you. She wears sunglasses and a black suit. Her legs are long and slim. To one ear she holds a cell phone. In her other hand she holds a smoking cigarette. As she approaches you, she slows down and raises her voice. It's like she wants you to hear her conversation; like she wants you to know how important she is. 'Yes,' she says. 'I need you to do something for me. Get every file on the A14 account and give me a summary of last year's performance. I have a meeting tomorrow, so I need it on my desk first thing. Yes, yes. I know you try.

But if you were more organised, it wouldn't be so difficult, would it now? So don't be such a silly boy. Get it done.'

Looking at the grass, you see her long feet stop walking before your hands. She wears patent sling-back shoes with spike heels. Her black stockings are all shiny in the sunlight. 'Just can't get the staff,' she says, to you.

You look up, so grateful to hear a voice that is not shouting at you for a change. 'Yes, ma'am,' you say.

She sniggers. 'But you know that, don't you? That's why you're down here with a spade in your hands and I'm up there, on the forty-second floor.' Her breasts are hard and make her white blouse tight across the front. She is beautiful, successful, wealthy; she is rude, unpleasant and cruel. You want to please her; you want to tell her she is a bitch.

'Do something with this,' she says, holding her cigarette butt out to you. Then her phone rings and she answers it, dropping the burning cigarette in the palm of your hand. You wince and drop it. Then you quickly pick it up again.

'Charles. How lovely,' she says into the phone. 'Yes, it was wonderful. Wonderful . . .' You hold the cigarette butt between your fingers and feel like you are about to choke from all the things smouldering or exploding inside you that come up your throat with a scorching sensation. The woman continues to walk down the path, away from you, chatting to Charles.

They have to be stopped, you say to yourself.

But the part of you that enjoyed the caning also wants to be treated badly by these girls. You watch the shiny legs and tight backside of the executive teeter away. Come back, that part of you says. Come back and kick me. Stamp on me with those beautiful shoes. I am worthless. But instead, you shout something inarticulate into the sky. The woman with the phone turns and looks back at you. Then you hear her laugh. She walks on.

In the distance at the front of the building, in the mouth of the carpark, you see a second woman. Wearing a leather suit and high-heeled boots, she walks quickly and pulls something behind her. At first you think it is a big, white dog with a black head. Then you see that it is a naked man on all fours with a hood over his head.

'Outrageous,' you whisper, but are no longer sure it even seems outrageous. The woman opens the rear door of a BMW hatchback and the naked man climbs inside. Sharply, she clouts his buttocks with the back of her hand. Then she slams the door. You hear the sound with a delay.

Blind with rage and bewilderment, you stand up and begin to run away from the path and the building. Despite the pain in your buttocks, you streak across the grass and head for the trees in the distance. 'Bitches! You bitches!' you scream into the sky, in between the laboured breaths you take. But when you near the trees that grow on the other side of the perimeter fence – the one that hums with a high voltage and is curved with evil razor wire at the top – a black Range Rover is waiting for you. The tinted driver's window lowers slowly with an efficient sound. From inside, a pale face peers out. It is a woman with a thin face and dark lipstick. She wears sunglasses. You also see the black shoulder of a security uniform and one hand in a black glove. The leather glove is clenched around a rubber baton. She stares at you without speaking. You stop running and bend over, your hands on your knees. When you get your breath back, you think of her fine, soft hand inside the leather glove. And you wonder whether she is wearing boots. The thought of the damage that such a woman's hands and boots could do to you, makes your cock stiffen against your thigh.

'Go back to work,' she says, in an emotionless tone of voice.

Without another thought of resistance, you do as she says.

25

Company Profile 1

Initiative

In Sales the desks go on for ever. Columns and columns of chairs and desks in neat rows. Everything identical, like the people that sit at them. And in the distance, I can see the supervisors carefully moving through the rows, like predators in the middle of a heard of docile animals. They are the only people who ever stand up in here during working hours. No one else would dare. The supervisors have desks at the front of the hall where they listen in on your phone calls and check your productivity in an endless time and motion study. Those employees who lag behind their targets are picked out. Then they are punished in front of all of us. We either see it with our own eyes or up on the giant video screens. If you're really bad, you are corrected during the company assembly that starts each day. If your performance does not improve after a public humiliation, you disappear. Never to be seen again. But then some people claim to have seen the disgraced working in the kitchens or on the grounds, sweeping and cleaning and chopping, or in the town either collecting rubbish or going through bins, but I'm not so sure. It's just best to meet your targets.

I'm doing well this morning – three sales – so Mrs Shank, my supervisor, does not stop at my desk to give the usual icy glare. I still look down when she passes and still shiver with a feeling that is both excitement and fear. Her perfume is sharp, her shoes polished so you can see your face in the toes when you are on your knees with the collar around your throat. Her stockings are black and so sheer they make her legs look like they have been cast in glass. Up the back of her calf, a seam runs and disappears inside the dark skirt of her suit. It makes you wonder where it leads. But I know where it goes; I've been forced to put my face up there. She never bothered me after the time she punished me, but sometimes she looks at my breasts and legs and I can tell she wishes I would underperform so she can get me up on the stage at the next assembly. It's tempting just to let my work go to hell again – what she did to me with the ropes and cane was amazing – but the better you are at the job the more money you get, plus there are apartment upgrades and special privileges to be enjoyed with the junior staff. We all like money and nice things here.

The only thing that could mess things up for me is the pretty guy who started two weeks back. I have my eye on him and I'm so bored with this job and all the cold-calling to retired people that I ache inside.

Anyway, this guy sits two desks in front of me, in the next row. He always looks so shy; perfect for this place. He almost runs to his desk first thing in the morning, like he's worried he might fall behind if his computer is not humming at nine sharp. By the end of the day, he must be weak with hunger, because he mostly skips lunch. This attitude of his just makes me want to misbehave.

In very sly ways, I've watched two other girls from my row start to look in his direction also, but I intend to get there first. They'll waste time trying to get him to look at them, and they'll be all cold and pretentious and professional, hoping he'll chase them after work. But forget it, girls. For this type you have to be direct.

I send him an email: *You should eat lunch. You could make a mistake in the afternoon if you're hungry. And someone is watching you. All day, every day.*

His reply comes back real quick: *Yes, ma'am.*

I have to put my hand over my mouth to stop laughing; he thinks I am a supervisor. In his chair I see the poor boy blush red and then fidget.

I send another: *Relax. I'm not a supervisor, just a girl in this crazy world who wants to look out for the new guys. What's your name?*

He writes back a bit abrupt for my taste. *Thanks for the thought. My name is Tim. Sorry I can't talk. Too much work to do.*

To which I reply: *Goody two shoes! Don't you even want to know who I am? I could be cute.*

He does not reply. Wants to play hard to get.

I should be more careful, in case I'm being monitored, but the supervisors can't watch every one of us all the time, and I don't give up easily on the things I want. *I want to suck your cock*, I write.

He pauses at his work. I see his back straighten. *Who are you?* he writes.

I reply: *There are five women sitting near you. I am one of them. Which one of them do you want it to be? Choose wisely.*

Now he looks frustrated. He starts making sneaky looks around his desk. Yawning, he does a one-eighty from the waist. When he looks in my direction, I make sure I am peering at my computer screen.

A new message arrives from him: *You'll get us in trouble. But I am curious. Who wouldn't be? Tell me which one you are.*

This makes me smile. I write: *I'm the one wearing no panties.*

Ha, ha! he replies. *I know your name is Lizzy from the mail address. It won't be hard to find out more.*

I start to reel him in: *Sure, but then you'll miss out. You won't be able to make enquiries until after work. And*

I want to suck a cock during lunch. In fact, that's what I want for lunch. Do you have a big cock? I need to know if you're going to be my lunch today, otherwise I'll shop elsewhere. The window of opportunity is closing.

Now he's really getting into this. The back of his neck is red and he's typing really quick: *Yes! Yes! Yes! I want to be your lunch. But it's not fair to make me guess who you are. Give me a clue.*

I do: *OK. I'm wearing a black suit, white shirt, shiny flesh stockings and sling-back heels. Oh, and no panties.*

His reply comes fast: *Oh, you're killing me! That's not fair. Every girl wears the same thing.*

I get carried away: *Ha, ha, ha! Yes, but do they love to suck cock? Really worship big cock? Do they suck to completion? The other girls are so up themselves; they wouldn't look at you unless they think you're important. But I'm different. I look for talent in ordinary places. Time is running out. You have ten minutes before I leave for my lunch.*

He's getting desperate: *I want you. Please give me a clue. Are you blonde?*

I don't want him to think I'm easy, so I play with him: *Like blondes? Pity.*

He panics; I can tell by his movements. This new boy wants his cock sucked. *Not necessarily just blondes.*

I giggle to myself, then write: *Just teasing you. I am blonde, but that only narrows it down to three.*

He looks at his watch. *Another clue.*

I'm the one with the red toenails.

As soon as he reads the mail, he discreetly lowers his eyes to the floor. The first place he looks is behind him, under my desk. A good move; this impresses me. He wanted it to be me. Under the desk I have slipped one high-heel shoe off. I snake my foot around in a sexy way and he sees my red toenails. He looks up at me, his face all shocked. I see him swallow. One of his eyelids twitches. When he looks at my face, I hold his stare and

29

begin to slide my pen in and out of my mouth while pushing my tongue into my cheek. He takes a deep breath and shifts around in his seat on account of the big hard-on he's nursing. Then he tries a nervous smile.

Maybe you're disappointed, I write.

No. You are lovely. I wanted it to be you. I really did, he replies.

I know, I write.

Where can I meet you?

Wait ten minutes. Go to carpark G, space 42. You'll see a black Saab Cabriolet. I'll be in the driver seat putting lipstick on.

He's changing his mind about the job. I can tell. He's been having second thoughts about the regime: the rules, the strict discipline, the hostility, the terror, the pressure. Been here two weeks and he thinks he's made the biggest mistake of his life. But now he's getting his fat cock sucked in the back of a car by a pretty, blonde office slut, I can sense him reappraising his opinion of the corporation.

This role I like to occasionally play to alleviate stress and to do something to relieve my heart-burning boredom. My job is so monotonous. I feel like I have indigestion all day.

He's looking down at my head in his lap, like he still can't believe this is happening to him. And he's stroking my hair while I eat him, which is nice. 'Oh, you're good. You're so good. That feels so good. You are so beautiful,' he's saying, and I get the feeling he doesn't get much excitement. I've pulled my skirt up to the top of my thighs so he can see all of my legs in stockings and my trimmed fur. Sometimes I move my head on an angle so he can see his cock sliding between my thick lips too. They're painted a reddish colour called Daylight Massacre. This lipstick is not supposed to come off but it's given the top third of his cock a pinkish tint.

30

'Can I fuck you? Oh, I need to fuck you. I really need to fuck you,' he says, getting so excited when I circle the tip of his phallus with my pointy tongue.

'Mmm,' I then say, when my mouth is full of this salty, savoury lunch-meat. If he shoots into my mouth, which I like, I wonder if he'll recover in time for me to ride him. We only get thirty minutes for lunch. Sliding my lips back up to the head and off, I look up at him and lid my eyelids. 'I want you to sperm into my mouth,' I say. 'Then you can fuck me.'

He comes the moment my face is snuggled in his lap again. I feel the pressure of a hand on the back of my head, like he's determined for me to collect every drop of his seed. Then he raises his buttocks off the car seat and makes a whinnying sound that comes from behind his nose bones. And into my mouth he floods. There's lots of it. Real hot with a strong taste. He's so uptight about work and has been neglecting self-pleasure. Even with his cock gone, my mouth is still full of salty cream. Some of it leaks over my bottom lip and runs down my chin. I swallow and then wipe up the spill with my index finger. Then I pop the finger into my mouth. 'Mmm,' I hum. 'You taste great.'

Resting, with his flies open and eyes closed, his head spins through the post-coital moment.

'It's supposed to take a man nineteen minutes to recover,' I say. 'But we don't have that long.'

'OK,' he says, and stares at my lap.

Sitting beside him and leaning into his shoulder I open my thighs.

'Oh, boy,' he whispers, when he sees me slip my fingers on to my sex. 'Oh, you are so sexy,' he adds.

Closing my eyes and rolling my head a bit on the back seat, I tickle the outside of my pussy-puss. Using the pad of my middle finger I then massage my little spot, like I'm at home in my room and under the duvet. He stares at that red fingernail moving between my nude stocking tops that are all shiny now because the sunlight is flooding into the car through the side window.

'Is that good?' he whispers in my ear, before kissing the outside of my face and my eyelids.

'Mmm, yeah.'

'You still want me?'

'I want a cock.'

'Really? Will mine do?'

'Mmm, oh yeah.'

'You like it?'

I nod my head. 'It's big. They have to be big. I like to be stretched. I don't have patience with small ones.'

Breathless, he can hardly speak. 'You get many?'

I smile. 'Big ones?'

'Yeah.'

'Maybe.'

'At lunch time?'

'When I'm horny.'

'How many?'

'Lots.'

'Oh, you're too much. I'm hard again. You made me all hard again.'

'Mmm.'

'Stop it,' he says, rubbing his cock with one hand.

'Mmm. I like to have that bruisy feeling inside, all afternoon. Where a cock has been. Pounding me. Pumping me.'

'In the car?'

'Mostly. Sometimes on the grass. In the toilets too. But I got caught in there once.'

He has heard enough. With his rough, grasping mouth he smothers my lips and barges his tongue into my mouth. Holding my face with both his hands, it's like he wants to devour my whole head. I remove one of his hands and resettle it between my legs. Then I moan directly inside his mouth when he slips three fingers inside me. We break from the kiss. 'That's it. Fuck me with your hand. Fuck me.'

'Then with my cock.'

'Oh, yeah.' This makes me want to come; just the thought of that swollen, shiny, purple head splitting my pussy apart and forcing itself deep. I wonder if he'll be hard.

He's losing control, which I like. 'Now. I'm gonna fuck you now. You lovely slut. You lovely blonde slut. I'm going to put my cock inside you.' Together, we manage to wrestle and roll about until I am lying underneath him with my high heels pressed into the ceiling of the car.

'There, there. Can you feel it? Is it big enough?' Against the lips of my sex he presses and slides his meat up and down. It feels huge between my legs. I just have to have it now. I claw the back of his head and trap his buttocks against my body with my calf muscles.

'I won't fuck you until you tell me. Is it big enough?' he demands.

'Yes! It's big. Oh, so big and beautiful. It's gonna hurt me.'

When I say that he suddenly pushes his cock inside me. I shout and feel like coming straight away. My eyes have gone all white and rolly under my eyelids and my mouth opens. Stuffing my sex full of his thick beef isn't enough for him; he jams his tongue deep inside my mouth also, almost choking me so I have to breathe through my nose. Plugged in the pussy and mouth I relax under his weight; give myself to his animal fury, his lust to mate with me. 'Fuck me so hard. Fucking hurt me. Slap me,' I cry out.

He doesn't slap me. Instead, he clenches his hands on my shoulders and directs all of his weight through his arms so I am pinned down on the seat. Helpless and under his control, my sex turns to liquid. Through the squelchy and loosening flesh of my little entry, he begins to thrust himself. Deep, hard, followed by a grindy circle with his crotch which presses my little spot and makes me choke and cry and whisper bad things. 'My ass. Put your finger in my ass,' I say.

One of his hands disappears from my shoulder bone and forces itself under my buttocks. A middle finger, wet with saliva, pokes and pushes until my ass has taken the digit to the last knuckle. Now I will come. I always do. Pinned down, plugged in the ass, filled to the womb with rock-muscle, my dirty, smudged mouth stoppered with his tongue; it's all I need. It's my addiction. I think of all the other strangers I have given myself to in this car. It's like I can still smell their after-shave and sweat and hear their desperate breathing in my ear. I swoon and black out and grunt like a little piggy with something on its back, thrusting.

Rubbing our bodies together, grinding our groins, clutching handfuls of hair and skin, we climax at the same time. Pulsing, contracting – I feel his organ ejaculate inside me. Filling me up. Pussy and tummy full of his creaminess. I break from the kiss to moan and catch my breath; he pushes his face into my hair and inhales me.

And then there is a movement close to the car that blots out the sun. 'Oh no,' I cry. 'Oh shit.' The car seems to get colder.

He lifts his chest off my body. 'What is it. What is . . .' Then he sees the two supervisors peering through the windows on either side of the car. They look angry. I'm used to that look and I know what it will lead to. But this poor boy is new to all this and has a long afternoon ahead of him. 'Shit. Shit. Shit,' he says. Making the whole car rock, Tim struggles to free himself of my legs. He starts to belt himself up and tuck his shirt away. He looks like he's about to cry. I almost feel sorry for him. Slowly, I swing my feet into the footwell, pull my skirt down and apply a tissue to my lips like it's a napkin and I have just eaten lunch.

The supervisor with the glasses speaks first: 'Get dressed and step out of the vehicle.'

The other supervisor is Mrs Shank, who punished me the first time I got caught doing this. She just stares at me in an odd way. Looks like she's admiring me. Or maybe she's pleased. 'You are coming with me,' she says, when I step out of the car.

They had monitored the entire email exchange between Tim and me; I guessed they might. The risk of being caught was half the thrill for me; I never forgot the ropes and the cane from the first time. At night I often dream of the knots and constriction, the helplessness and the pain. But for poor Tim, I guess the whole experience has probably changed him. He's sure to remember the doggy parade for the rest of his life.

I don't feel too guilty; they were bound to get him sooner or later. I'm sure they give everyone a taste of the corporal discipline at least once after they start work here. But he did get the full works, though, first time out.

In the afternoon following our lunch-time liaison, as soon as everyone in Sales was back behind their desks, Tim was given the strap at the front of the hall. For ten minutes we were instructed to watch. After the compulsory viewing, all the heads lowered once again to read their computer screens and make phone calls, but you could still hear the giggles and whispers throughout the hall as his ordeal continued. The supervisors must have had him down there for at least an hour. Completely naked, he was bent across the leather horse and received the strap around his buttocks, over and over again. In the end, we even got used to the sound as we worked. But that wasn't all; while his long, white body was strung over the leather saddle, we could hear the taunts from the supervisors as they began his re-education.

Fraternisation during the working day is forbidden. But sometimes I think we women are made to look so sexy while the men are deliberately denied an outlet, so their frustrations are taken out in extra productivity.

'This little doggy,' they called him, 'thinks he's better than everyone else. The rules don't apply to him. He knows better. Yes, we found this naughty doggy with his trousers down in the carpark.' And then one of the supervisors read out the emails we wrote to each other as he was slapped down into the leather saddle. The strapping was really hard too. You could feel the impact in your stomach. And there were long pauses between the wet lashy sounds. That's when you could hear Tim's whimpers.

After a thorough leathering, he was then led around the hall on a short leash, so everyone could witness his disgrace. On his hands and knees, he was pulled behind a supervisor. She even wore a special leather glove for the silver chain attached to his little studded collar. I thought he looked so cute, but Tim probably didn't feel so good about himself. And the girls near me just couldn't stop staring at his long cock when he was brought by. They tried to pretend they were looking at him in a disapproving way, but I knew what they were staring at. It was so hard and long and hung beneath him the way it does on a race horse. Everyone saw it. And you could see the long red marks on his buttocks and thighs from the leather belt-thing they had whipped him with.

The supervisor kept him pulled tight against her legs on the choke chain, so he would walk at her heel. At least being so close to her spike heels and stockings must have been a thrill for Tim, even with everyone watching. And down on the floor, as he was led past the desks, he could also look up the girls' skirts. I opened my legs when he was brought by and saw the two girls in front of me, who had their eyes on him since he started work, slowly cross their legs at the thigh when his red face was paraded by. Slap, slap, slap, went his paws on the floor tiles.

In fact, he got overexcited. Was unpredictable. Surprised everyone. No one expected him to just go off like that, but the supervisors had debased him so much, he stopped caring about everything. You could tell by the wild look in his eyes when he was brought by your desk. And everyone cheered when he mounted the supervisor at the back of the hall.

I heard her shouting, 'Get down! Get down!' Followed by the sound of her high heels clattering on the tiles. And you could hear his grunts too, as she lashed at him with her hand. When I peered up to the top of the row where all this noise was coming from, I saw Tim on his knees pushing the supervisor against a desk. Her skirt was up around the top of her legs so you could see her garters and stocking tops, and the white skin of her thighs. And between her legs, Tim had stuffed his face. No one would have thought quiet little Tim would have been capable of something like that.

By the time the other three supervisors had run down there to help their colleague, he had lifted her bottom on to a desk top and was standing up straight between her thighs while she was pulling his head around on the leash, trying to shake him loose. I'm not so sure he got inside her, but her legs were kicking in the air and her hands in the tight leather gloves were slapping his shoulders while his little buttocks pumped in and out. Supervisors hate to look foolish.

Tim wasn't on his feet for long. With three supervisors soon striking him all over the arms and back with the little crops they carry in case of a situation, Tim soon sunk to the floor with his head covered by his hands. And for a while the women also kicked at him with their pointy shoes. Then they put the cuffs on his hands and ankles, a black hood over his head, and dragged him out of the hall by his feet. The things you see in this place! Three women wearing black Armani suits and leather gloves pulling a naked man across the floor: you never get used to things like that.

At the end, when he disappeared from the hall, Tim was just laughing through the hood. But it wasn't happy laughter. It was hysterical, mad laughter. I've heard that in Sales before too. But what happened to him after that is a mystery. He didn't return to his desk for three days. And he looked different when he finally came back to work. Less nervous. In fact, he had no expression on his face at all. And his walk was different; a little straighter and stiffer than before. He seemed to have lost all interest in the people around him too; never looked at me once, or answered any of my emails that day. He needed a cushion on his chair for a few days also, so I guess they were really hard on him. And when they moved me out of the long room, they gave Tim my desk. I heard they made him keep a photo of my face as his screen saver.

I've heard there are cells under the complex where they take the worst people. No one is sure about the cells, because those people who they say go down there never get out. So all we have are rumours and myths. I wasn't taken down there, but I should have been; this was my second major offence. What happened to me was really surprising.

Mrs Shank didn't use cuffs on me like the last time. No restraints at all, and there was no escort. She never shouted, or glared, but she didn't really smile either. She just asked me to follow her back to the building. So I stayed quiet and followed her to her office, all the time thinking I would have preferred her to rage at me and then cuff me. This attitude of hers was far more worrying; it made me assume the corporation had completely given up on me. There would be a discharge, or I would just disappear like the others.

But nothing of the sort happened. Instead, she led me into her office and politely offered me a chair. What she then said stunned me. 'Well, Lizzy, besides a little motivational problem at the beginning of your time with us, and the indiscretion with that silly boy in your car, I can tell you how pleased we are with your work.'

'You are?'

'Certainly,' she said, and slowly crossed her long legs in front of me so they made a whispery sound. 'And you are obviously capable of more than tele-sales. You can achieve much more with your latent talents. What I'm saying is, we like your attitude.'

'Thanks,' I said, feeling real bad about sucking a cock at lunch time, but how was I to know they liked me so much?

'In fact, we would like to offer you an opportunity, a trial if you like, for a far better position with superior benefits.'

'Wow,' I said, and then felt stupid for saying it, but she didn't seem to mind.

'It's an opportunity for a young lady who is not squeamish. Who can act with initiative, courage and guile to get what she wants. Who overcomes every obstacle to achieve her targets. Who can give herself to her purpose wholeheartedly.'

'Is this still in sales?' I asked.

Mrs Shank paused, then smiled for the first time since I've known her. Not a pretty smile; more of a sly one. Maybe it was a bit sexy too. 'In a manner of speaking, yes, it is a sales position. It certainly requires motivation, confidence and an ability to think on one's feet. And the salary is based on a commission system, which is very generous also. For the right candidate, there will be travel and an expense account too.'

'I'm in,' I said, and then went all tittery.

'I hope so. I'm rarely wrong about a person's character and potential.'

'And I thought you were going to cane me.'

Her face hardened a bit when I said that, and it kind of darkened also. I noticed her knuckles go white around a pencil. 'Yes. Perhaps you should have been.'

I casually pouted my lips and made my eyes go all half-lidded and sultry. There was an awkward silence in her office and I could see her looking at my legs and breasts like she wished they were hers to have and to hold. 'You are not afraid of such experiences,' she said. 'You have never found your limits. And an office is no place for your curiosity. Am I right?'

'Guess so.'

'I am. I know it. And I'm anxious to see how you will perform during the trial.'

'I'm ready. What's the test? Theory or a practical?'

She laughs. 'A practical. Most definitely a practical. But you have to be a thinker also, to be any good. And that's why I want you to try out. You have the right kind of intelligence, Lizzy. A sexual intelligence. We can always find work for that.'

I giggled and blushed.

'But what I need to know before we go any further, is just how flexible you are. I am fully aware of your predilection for youths' – and she said this like the words tasted sour – 'And there are plenty of malleable men in this world. But what are your feelings about girls? A far more discriminating and cautious gender.' She raised her chin and it was an effort for her to not look embarrassed.

'Guess I like them too. Not known many in that way, though.' This is true. But there have been girls I met in bars and clubs on holiday, when you could get away with it easily.

'Don't worry. You're a natural. Maybe a little guidance would do no harm. I believe in my powers to instruct.' She stood up and moved around to the front of her desk so her knees were nearly touching mine. Her voice went all whispery. 'I have to be sure, Lizzy. The new position I have been speaking about involves a certain flexibility. More than a passing interest. An enthusiasm, if you like, for other girls.' She took the grips from out of her hair and then shook it around her face. It made her look younger and softer. 'Sometimes the company needs the custom and co-operation from very important, influential ladies. Ladies in business who need additional encouragement about where to invest their business interests. Ladies who need persuading. Ladies who need to be spoiled.'

'Ladies who want pretty girls to suck their pussies,' I said, getting carried away and not really thinking.

This made Mrs Shank swallow and say, 'Quite,' in a delicate way.

'I can do that really well. Once I made a girl in Spain cry. She fell in love with me.'

'I bet she did,' she whispered and seemed to get all lost inside her head for a bit. 'Now I want you to imagine a scene. I am a prospective client and we have just finished dinner in an excellent restaurant. And I am a lady who likes intimacy with other girls. You know this. Maybe we're looking over a contract in the privacy of a hotel suite. What would you feel? How would you approach her? Reassure her? Convince her the corporation is the best place for her business?'

Immediately, I just slipped on to my knees in an easy, graceful way. Holding her stare, I smiled sweetly but still looked a bit shy and flushed in the face. With interest, Mrs Shank raised an eyebrow. 'I'd probably make the first move,' I said. 'Especially if she had pretty legs like these.' I smoothed my hands up her calf muscles and behind her hot knees and made her stockings slip over her shaven skin. Slowly, I pushed my long painted fingernails up inside her skirt, and on to the inside of her thighs. Then I withdrew my fingers before pushing them up again, but higher on her legs this time. 'I can be quite forward,' I whispered. 'When I've had my eye on someone. You know that. It's why I'm here, isn't it, ma'am?' And I thought of the first time she pulled my arms and legs around and fastened metal cuffs real tight on them. I recalled the hard look on Mrs Shank's face – the mouth tense, almost spitting. And so

41

this exercise of hers became a challenge for me. I wanted to have my way with her – to make her go all warm and soft inside whenever she looked at me. I like having that power. She's in charge of me, but I have the power. She doesn't know it. I love that. It sounds mean, but it makes me feel really good. Maybe my sexual intelligence works things like this out.

'But I often reach a point when I can't stop, even if she told me to stop. Because I know her pussy is close,' I added. 'Under a few layers maybe, but only a few inches from my mouth.' Spreading my fingers I stroked her stockings some more and then caressed the white skin between her garters.

Closing her eyes, Mrs Shank leant back on the desk. From down on my knees I could see she had clenched her teeth, like she was trying to hold something back, but was failing and enjoying the failure. With one finger, I then tickled the damp fabric of her panties. At the front where the black material was see-through. Her sex felt so soft underneath my finger, and moist too. It was hard to believe that such cold, hard women have this special softness. But it's such a thrill to find it.

Slipping my hands back down her legs, I then reached around her bottom to find the zipper of her skirt. I wanted this bully-bitch-dyke in her skimpies, begging me to suck. So I got aggressive, my fingers more sure of themselves. I rushed things.

She sensed this; me getting carried away, over-confident because she had let on about how much she liked me. She was angry with herself but took it out on me. I was never supposed to take the dominant role here and she had ground to recover. The mood changed. She changed. I suffered. 'You little slut,' she suddenly said, with a sneery mouth, and I immediately realised my mistake, quickly remembering what she was really like; mean and unpredictable and sadistic. Her expression altered so I hardly recognised her any more. Chiding myself for believing I could seduce special treatment and finer feelings from her, I began to realise she wanted to beat me. Had wanted to beat me all along. There was no way I was going to escape punishment for being in the car with Tim, even if she wanted me for this new job. Why can't I ever be humble?

She pushed me away and slid off the desk. Using one hand, she then unzipped her skirt, shook it loose and then stepped out of it. She did this with speed like she couldn't wait to free up her movements and get on with the correction. With her other hand she gripped my hair and pulled it so hard I cried out with my eyes all watery. 'Oh, you're good, my girl. But not that good. Never fuck with the big girls unless you want to be fucked back, twice as hard.' She stuffed my wincing face between her thighs and pushed her sex down on my nose and mouth. 'But you'll learn, my girl. You'll learn. Strong women don't like little tarts getting above themselves. They must stay on the bottom. Make no mistake.'

It was hard to breathe and she wouldn't let go of my head, but I managed to move my face sufficiently so the hard parts of my mouth and jaw were rubbing her pussy all over. She let out a 'ugh, ugh, ugh' winded sound, and loosened her fingers in my hair. I pushed my face deeper into that pinky sex with the shaven skin and got it all wet, smearing my lipstick and make-up all over my mouth. Then I looked up her body and right into her glacier eyes to see if she was softening. Nearly there, I thought.

She lay back on the desk and pulled my head up by the hair, keeping it clenched between her thighs. She draped her legs over my shoulders so I could feel the spikes of her shoes in the middle of my back. Feeling a bit confined and needing air, I tried to pull back and slap her hand away from out of my hair. That is when things really changed.

Throwing her head back, she laughed out loud and sat up on the desk. Helpless, I remained on my knees with my mouth trapped against her sex. 'Flexible, girl. Be flexible. There are times to resist and times to comply. And you are always in a foolish, impetuous hurry. You must learn to pace yourself. Or I will be forced to teach you the hard way.' Her face was all wild and mad-looking now; her black hair was all shaggy around her cheekbones. Kind of scared me a bit and made me feel like I didn't know so much about girls after all.

'It's coming,' she said, and stood up. 'Ooh, it's coming. It's so . . . so . . . so hot.' And before I realised what she was talking about, my face and mouth were suddenly drenched with hot piss. Clear, kidneyish, salt-water piss was spurted all over my face. Spluttering and choking, with my hair gripped between her skinny fingers, she lowered me to the floor and squatted over me. Spraying my neck and face and blouse and jacket, it just kept coming out of her. Then she slapped my wet cheeks really hard. Just pulled her arms back and beat me. I never thought a woman could be like this.

Rolling me over, she stripped my jacket down my back until it hung around my elbows and prevented me from using my arms. With the sound of stitching being torn apart, she made quick work of my skirt and slip too. 'Stay there!' she shrieked at me, like the Mrs Shank I know best. Skipping away from me, her long legs in the seamed stockings disappeared around the other side of the desk. Then I heard a drawer open. Something was taken out of the drawer and I knew my experience of institutional pain was about to be revised.

Before I could get to my knees and shake the wet fringe out of my eyes, her long shin bones were shimmering before my face again. Feeling the smooth sole of her shoe on the back of my head, she plunged my face back down to the piss-spattered tiles.

'You bitch! You bitch!' I screamed, losing my mind.

But the first stroke of that stick shut my dirty mouth. It hurt so bad I sucked in air and felt my eyes bulge. She kept her foot on my head, even ground my face into her ammonia swamp. 'You think it's easy money, girl. That you'll take charge and have them falling for you. Am I right?'

'Yes,' I said, but would have said yes to anything at that moment.

'Different league, girl. Pussy-sucking is for the dormitory. I'm sending you to women that would go to prison for a vacation. Tough girls. Women who like pretty things, but like to slap the sluts around. They eat corporate sluts. Eat them alive. Especially those too big for their boots. Back-stabbers and wannabes. Young, ambitious things. They love girls like that. Girls like you. They'll take a cane to your back at supper time, that would go through the silk camisole they brought you before lunch. Do you understand who I am talking about? Big girls in designer suits. Bad girls with nasty tempers. The girls I am going to give you to. Mmm? As a sweetener to close a deal. You could be wined and dined in Paris or have your face down the can on Concorde. You have to be prepared for whatever they want. And they want sluts. You, my girl, are the most sluttish individual I have ever met.'

'Yes, ma'am.' Somehow, I knew all of this punishment and the hard words were because of the cock I had taken at lunch time. She was jealous. Despite my current situation, this pleased me. After realising how pliant and soft I was the first time she disciplined me – after admiring the clean, neat strokes her cane made on my pale flesh, and looking deep into my watery, vulnerable eyes – she knew she had to have me for her own; to keep me but brutally punish me for still admiring others. My wayward habits with others gave her a special brand of pain; a sweet, jealous anguish that was only eased by the

45

quick fall of a cane in her hands. She must have been biding her time until she could catch me out again. I imagined her excitement when she discovered the email exchange between Tim and me. And strangely, the first time she put a stick to me, I knew she was going to be a big part of my destiny, of my career.

'Now this is going to hurt. Really hurt.'

'No.'

'I have to, Lizzy. To see if you can take it. If you are right.'

'Bitch!'

'Exactly! And the worst kind of bitch you have ever dared to mess with. I'd brand you if I had the right tools in my office. I'd listen to you sizzle, you pretty, little fool. And I'd come while smelling your little chickadee arse on fire.'

But that day I was to feel a different kind of fire. Five strokes; that was all. But five strokes I could still feel a week later whenever I sat down or stood up too quick. Five strokes I took to get that job. And five strokes I thought about fondly whenever my fingers were getting busy under the bed sheets in the privacy of my corporate condo. I'm a strange girl, I know, but being all straight about sexy things makes life less intense.

And Mrs Shank is a madwoman, so close to going too far. That's why she's so good at her job. You have to be clever but also a bit mad to get anywhere in this company. I know this. And although she made me come after the caning, by manipulating my little pussy-puss with three fingers and another a thumb in my arse, I silently vowed to bring Mrs Shank down, because I have found her weakness. With my face turned away from her, my face on which her briny water was drying, I whispered an oath to destroy her.

Her judgement is beginning to slip – she's spoilt and needlessly wicked and extremely vain – and must make room for someone younger and hungrier and stronger.

I can only despise her for loving me. I understood it all as I climaxed; this is the creed of the corporation.

After the flogging I cried a bit in her office and she stroked my hair and wiped my face. Then she let me shower in the executive facility, and she had a new suit and underwear sent down to me. It was a Gucci suit and see-through lingerie. And over dinner that night, she told me more about my new job. Although I would stay in the long office and carry on with my usual sales work for the time being, she would train me after hours. She had contacts. She would help me. Eventually, I would be tested in the field, as she called it, and if suitable, moved into the Client Embellishment wing of Acquisitions and Mergers.

I never thought that sucking a cock could do so much for my career.

Company Profile 2

Personal Assistance

Waiting for my mistress, I draw the blinds in our room. Outside the windows of this hotel, the sky has bruised from purple to black and the definition of the city buildings is disappearing. Their presence is now marked by thousands of pinprick lights that will shine until the sun rises and we depart for the next destination, the next hotel room, the next meeting, working breakfast, power lunch and evening appointment.

I turn the wall-lights on and adjust the dimmer switch so her tired eyes will be soothed when she returns from her final meeting in this city. Her bags are mostly packed – I saw to that earlier – and her meal has been ordered from room service. On the last night on a trip she usually prefers to dine in her room. When things have gone well, we often celebrate together with champagne. When the trip has disappointed her, there are usually strong words and tears in our room. Her words and my tears.

Certain things are used on my soft body to wet my eyes; devices and tools she likes to put to me. There is a cane – my favourite – and cuffs and the rubbery things she slips between my teeth. And as this trip has not gone to her absolute liking, I expect to feel the stick many times tonight. She will bend my supple shape and set my skin alight with her secret, invisible fire that I can only just withstand. Between my legs, things are getting warm when I think of this treatment – some would say mistreatment, but nothing else has ever brought me so close to another lover. If I slipped a hand against my sex right now, I'd expect to get my fingers wet.

This morning, I even cleaned her correctional equipment and then replaced it inside the metal case that once caused such a fuss in an airport. My employer's name is Mrs Kruck and she is Austrian. A very powerful woman who stole me from my old tutor, Mrs Shank. I was taught well by Mrs Shank and under her strict guidance learnt to like certain things that occur between ambitious women in private. Mrs Shank liked to broaden horizons, cultivate taste and complete a young working woman's education. But ultimately it worked against her; she couldn't help herself wanting me to be a bad girl, while also loving me at the same time. So it wasn't long before she made a fool of herself and I found someone else. Although most people would say I was head-hunted. It was during my trial for Acquisitions and Mergers, set up by my former tutor, that I met Mrs Kruck. She works for the same company, but in a different department and was the examiner for my trial. And on my very first attempt at client embellishment, Mrs Kruck decided I was better suited to personal assistance. Or rather, I was to become her personal assistant. Mrs Shank was furious and there was a nasty incident – a fight – and security was called. Now, I belong to Mrs Kruck. Or so she thinks.

When I see my outfit laid out on the hotel bed, I get a little giddy too. So much of my power is in those clothes. People's eyes change when I wear them. Some men lose their ability to speak when they see my spike heels catching the light. Some women want to destroy me with their claws when they study my figure coated in such a tight second skin of rubber. And those I have been given to always take the time to just stare before

49

they touch or unwrap. Zipped inside my new flesh, there are times when my mistress claims she doesn't even recognise what I become.

Dropping my bathrobe to the floor, I continue with the transformation. In the bathroom I have already applied my lavish make-up, so now all I have to do is begin the careful dressing. I start by sliding the garter belt around my waist. It is made from a thin rubber that always looks polished. Falling from the waistband that covers my womb, there are four garter straps with heavy silver clips. They feel cold against my shaven thighs. Then I sit down on the end of the bed. From a flat packet I unravel the black nylons with the new smell and then ruffle them over my long fingers. Making sure the seam runs straight up the back of my leg – all the way from the reinforced heel to the very top of my leg – I smooth the stockings over ankle, calf, knee and thigh. Making final adjustments to the seam alignment, I take extra care not to ladder the fine gauze of pure, virgin nylon with my longish fingernails. My mistress won't touch me unless my hosiery is fresh (she sends my used stockings as gifts to a colleague in Japan; my panties go to a gentleman in Switzerland). After the stockings are tight on my legs and shining like polished glass against my moisturised leg skin, I attach the dark, silky tops to the silver clasps.

Next, I put on the boots. The pointy toes of the boots press my own toes together and squeeze the flesh of my leg all the way up to my knee when I zip them closed. Feels like I'm walking on air when I stand up.

In the long mirror of the wardrobe I look at my reflection. I'll probably be wearing this much – boots, stockings, garter belt – when my mistress first gets busy with her straps and sticks. But when she fucks me, she usually likes me to unzip the boots. It makes me smaller and more vulnerable and without the elevation of spiky heels I feel more submissive too.

Standing up, I step into the sheer panties and then pull them up, close against my pussy. They are so fine I hardly know I'm wearing them. All of this slipperiness makes me feel as if I'm as heavy as a spider's web with a few drops of dew hanging from the fine strands. It also makes the lips of my sex glossy.

Leaving my small, natural breasts bare, I squeeze my arms and torso into the rubber dress. Takes a long time to work a seamless and crease-free membrane of black rubber over my body, from my throat down to just above the knee. When I'm zipped up tight, my skin moistens and the delicate girlish wine that seeps out of my pores starts to gather inside certain parts of the dress. A German man once told my mistress she should put the precious moisture from the inside of my rubber clothes into a fancy bottle; men like him would have bought it up. But mostly, after I have peeled the rubber from my body, when my mistress has finished with me, she likes to wash the damp off me in the shower. Only the men she gives me to prefer to lick it from my skin – especially off the toes and breasts.

Over the sleeves of the dress, I put on a pair of matching, clingy gloves to add another super-thin layer of rubber all the way up to my elbows. Turning from side to side, and taking short, teetery steps in front of the mirror I admire myself. Make-up perfect, clothes immaculate, hair lovely. My long, blonde hair is arranged into a ponytail that starts at the top of my head and fails all the way down to my waist. When I wear my hair loose the ends of my hair get stuck under my bottom every time I sit down. Easier to move about and see things with it tied away.

Now that I'm all dressed up, my body looks like it has been air-brushed with black paint; like I'm a really shiny plastic doll that is normally hidden in a special place and couldn't run away if it tried. I finish my dressing with the mask. Matching the material of the dress and

51

gloves, it only covers the top half of my face, but there are eyeholes cut in an almond shape so that all of my blue eyes and thick eyeliner is displayed. My mistress likes the mask because everything I am feeling is emphasised by my eyes. The mask also makes my red lips look even bigger and the white flesh of my jaw seems paler when framed by the shiny black rubber.

Checking myself out in the mirror, I begin to hope my bum looks big enough in this dress to provide a tempting target.

Then I wait.

'How was your day, ma'am?' I say as I welcome Mrs Kruck into our room.

'Had better,' she says in a quiet voice. Her face looks dark and tired, but something sparks in her eyes when she takes in my outfit.

Standing behind her, I remove the long woollen coat from her shoulders. Without a word, she walks into the bedroom. I follow her into the room. As I hang her coat up she sits on the end of the bed and stretches her legs out. Yawning, she closes her eyes. Immediately, I move to her and then sink to my knees. As I do this my boots and dress make little squeaky noises. Taking her ankles in my gloved hands, I slip her shoes off. Today she is wearing the sling-backs she bought in Florence. They are made from a supple black leather. The heels are long and sharp; each toe looks like it could go right through meat.

With her shoes removed, I begin to gently kneed and caress her tired feet. Lying down on the bed, she keeps her eyes closed while I massage. I move my hands on to her calf muscles where the puddles have splashed little droplets of water on to her stockings. They are Italian stockings and the colour is called mink. She wears them with the black pinstripe two-piece suit, a white blouse, designer bra and black panties. I know all of these details because I dress her too.

Moving herself further up the bed, she takes her legs out of my hands. 'Pleasure me before dinner,' she says without looking at me. Her eyes are still closed.

Oh yes, I want to cry out loud, but am careful not to show my excitement. But the feel and taste of her pussy so soon!

She rolls on to her side and allows me to unzip her skirt. Slowly, I inch the skirt down her legs and pinch it from her toes. Folding it carefully, I place it on the chair beside the bed. She sits up and allows me to remove the jacket and shirt and bra. Her breasts are tanned the colour of unbleached sugar, except for the nipples which look almost black. I'm desperate to pop those little suckers into my mouth. Instead, I fold her jacket and shirt and put the clothes on the chair with the skirt. When I make her comfortable between the fat pillows, she opens her legs.

Using only my parted lips I brush her labia. Up and down and side to side my head moves, sometimes drawing little invisible pictures with my mouth until she starts to sigh and her pupils grow big up there on the pillow. Sometimes I think she is frightened of me because of the way I make her feel. My power intimidates her.

Propped up on the pillow, she watches my eyes through the holes in the mask. Maybe she thinks I am a big cat washing its mate.

After a ten-hour day involving three meetings, her pussy has a strong but not unpleasant smell. This odour lessens as her sex moistens beneath my mouth. Soon it's hard to tell my saliva apart from her rich waters. Widening her lips, I probe my fingers into the slippery pinkish folds and gently brush the tender flesh with circling finger tips made slippery by her dew. It makes her bite her own hand and arch her back. When her legs lock, I apply my mouth to her sex again, speeding up the motion of the side-to-side caressing, but maintaining a light pressure – the way she likes it.

Making her little doggy-coughing-sounds, she soon clamps her thighs together and pushes me away with her feet, as if annoyed that I have guided her to this peak, or perhaps she is like a selfish child refusing to acknowledge her benefactor. Maybe she is just lost to everything but her own shudders of climax and wants no interference.

Reapplying my lipstick, I then wait for her to rouse from the tousle-headed, curled-up creature of the pillows she has become. 'Water,' she says. 'Bring me water.'

When I return with a glass of spring water, she has covered her body with a silk robe and is sitting up in bed. She watches me carefully as I hand her the glass. Her red fingernails clink against the glass. 'What have you been up to today?' Her tone of voice is tense. She hates it when I go outside unaccompanied by her. But what am I to do? Sit at home all day waiting for her to return?

Raising my chin, I say, 'I went to the gym.'

'And?' Her fringe has fallen across her eyes. I'm glad of this; it's too much to look into them.

'Shopping.'

There is a silence. She drinks a mouthful of water from the glass. I sense something dramatic about the swallowing. The way she raises the glass looks posed and unnatural. 'Were you not told to stay inside today? There was packing that needed doing.'

'Done it, ma'am.'

'And arrangements to be made.'

'Did them all this morning. Everything is ready for tomorrow.' In the morning we fly home to the corporate town.

'Shopping,' she says, looking up at the ceiling. 'Hmm.' Her mouth is smiling but her eyes are not. Then her accent gets stronger. 'Bit of shopping, eh?' She always does this when she's angry. 'Just a bit of shopping, eh? I am aware of what can happen when my personal assistant goes shopping.'

I look at my hands and begin to sulk.

She stretches a hand out holding the glass. 'Here.'

I pretend I've not heard. I'm so sick of these jealous episodes. And I only strayed once on a shopping trip; how was I to know the man in the store was going to follow me into the changing room and make me get down on my knees?

'Here,' she repeats. 'Here. The glass. Take the glass.'

I turn to face her but am blinded by the water thrown from the glass. It's been lashed hard across my face and I didn't have time to blink. I shriek with surprise, but am silenced when she seizes my ponytail. Pulling my hair, she moves me up the bed until my wet face is pressed against her mouth. The skin of her face has gone all tight. Her voice comes in a whisper that is worse than shouting. 'Do you think I am stupid?'

'No,' I answer.

It's as if she hasn't heard. 'Do you think I am stupid?' Her voice is louder.

'No.'

'Do you think I am stupid? With the MBA, and the PhD, and a sales force of two thousand under my control, I wonder if you think I am stupid.'

I hate it when she gets like this; spiteful and boasty. Sometimes I can't take it. Like tonight. 'Maybe you are,' I say.

There is a silence so deep I suspect every air molecule in the room has stopped moving.

'Pardon?' When it comes, her voice is deep enough for a man.

Now I'm getting a bit jumpy. 'All I did was go out shopping.'

She pushes me off the bed. 'Get out of that dress. Maybe you wore it to the shops. To catch someone's eye. Can you last a single day without flattery? You're

55

pathetic. Or did you think you could just dress up like a little tramp after disobeying me and assume everything would be all right? You know me better than that.'

I start to remove the dress. Her face flushes when she sees my body in the underwear and boots. 'Oh yes. Oh yes. Now I see it all. Now I see.'

'See what?'

'Never you mind. Never you mind. Get the case. You know what's coming. I've had a hard day and I'm not going to argue.'

'All I did was –'

'All you did was not do what you were told. You know better and I'm tired of justifying myself.' She starts to laugh in a hideous way. 'I don't have to. You forget. I don't have to, my love.'

I collect the case from the dresser and drop it on the bed. Then I step back and fold my arms.

She opens the case and her smile gets so broad it is accompanied by a devil-giggle. If she thinks I am amused she is mistaken. I even think of slapping her, but manage to stop at the thought of where that will get me (I really have no idea, but it wouldn't be nice).

My mistress throws her robe off and stands in just her stockinged feet, holding the black cane. She's chosen the hardest wood in the case that always leaves the strongest marks. In the past when she used it, I could even feel the evil stick in the middle of my bones. 'I'm hard, girl. You know that. But I'm fair. I'm fair, girl,' she says.

'No.'

'No?'

'No,' I repeat. 'Not tonight. I don't want to,' I lie. 'I've been working hard too. It might not be meetings and things, but I've still been getting everything ready for you. And I dressed up nice because I knew you were going to be in a bad mood.'

I just have time to flinch before she bends me double and then force-marches me to the bed. With her hand spread on the top of my head, she pushes me to my knees so the top half of my body is lying flat across the duvet. Then she moves the hand from my head to place it between my shoulders. She kicks my knees apart then steps back.

Clenching my vulnerable, naked buttocks, I then look over my shoulder, fearing the first stroke to be imminent. But rarely is she predictable with a cane in her hand. She stands behind me, rotating her shoulders and taking deep breaths. Taking her time, making me wait, she talks to herself in a quiet voice, but it's really meant for me. 'It's taken three days to close the deal. I played hard. I always play hard. That's what I'm known for. I'm hard-core, if you like. And all she wants when she comes home is peace and quiet. Some food and a glass of wine. Not much to ask. Not much at all, really. But what she doesn't want is lies from a silly little girl whose idea of work is playing dress-up. What she really, really doesn't want is lies!'

The cane hits me, on cue with the word 'lies'. It makes me do the hot-potato-mouth and I try to clamber up on to the bed, try to get my legs up there so I can crawl away. But she gets a hand on my left shoulder and holds me in place for the next four strokes. They fall hard and seem to take all the air from my lungs and the energy from my limbs.

My buttocks go all warm after the blinding sting has melted a bit. And now, unable to control myself, I realise this evil bitch has turned me, summoned my true nature into this room. It's why I am connected to her. Panting from the pain and the arousal that makes me giddy, I push my striped buttocks back at her wanting to feel more pain. And I struggle against the firm hand on my shoulder; I want the hand to press down harder or to get into my hair so my eyes run with hot water.

'Had a cock?' she whispers, as if ashamed to speak those words.

I give her a coy look that can only mean one thing.

'You ... little ... slut.' She looks really angry, but is secretly exalted by my betrayal. She reminds me of Mrs Shank. I've never seen my mistress taken by a man – she likes young, feminine girls – but she loves and hates it in equal measures when I am given to a client or associate of hers. Especially when she sees me writhe and squeal with enjoyment on the end of a thick cock. She only lets me go with the big ones. That's her sweet pain. Since I have worked for her, I've learnt that everyone has a pain they enjoy, no matter how secret or subtle. And me riding a long cock knocks the wind out of her. 'I work hard all day and you play behind my back,' she says, barely able to speak for the anger that threatens to close her mouth down into bared teeth.

'I only did it once. Quickly. And not in my arse this time.'

That's all she needs to hear. She stoppers my slutty mouth with a rubber ball-gag, and cuffs my delicate wrists together with stainless steel. She changes the cane for a leather flail that she can use for longer and with much greater force than a cane. With wood, I wilt early and take days to heal.

As the blows rain on my upper thighs and my buttocks, across my back and over my shoulders, I slip into a realm of pure sensation: of heat and pain and tears that empty me and then crazily refresh me. My only thought for the outside world is that someone in the next room can hear the pretty blonde girl being put to the lash. I want them to hear my cries and hear the wet 'placky' sounds of leather on soft flesh. People knowing it is happening makes it better for me.

My mistress stops to wipe her hair from out of her eyes. Breathing heavily, she throws the flail down and looks at me as if she's only just begun to recognise me. She unbelts the ball-gag and lets me breathe. 'I think you've had enough,' she says. 'Think I've made my point.'

She's tired after such a long day, but I'm not satisfied. This bitch will not stop until I let her. 'Had enough of you maybe. But I wish I'd taken more cock this morning.'

A high-pitched whinnying sound rises from the back of her throat. She throws her head back and I see her squarish face suddenly come alive; more than it has been in three days. And that beauty spot makes her look so handsome. Go on, bitch, show me your teeth.

She dips one hand into the case. 'A cock, you say? You sure about that?'

I sneer at her through my tears and then look at my punished rump. The skin is criss-crossed with thin purple stripes. This fills me with pride and satisfaction. I open my mouth and sigh. Just the sight of the damage pushes me closer to a peak that has been building since I slipped that garter belt around my waist. 'Mmm. A big one.'

'I'll fix you, my girl. I'll fix your craving for a dirty big cock. For some dirty bastard's big veiny cock. I'll give you the biggest cock of your life.'

'Oh, yes,' I say, growing faint with pleasure. I've upset her and aroused her so much she's saying things she'll remember with shame for the rest of her life.

Around her waist, she fastens the last buckle on the harness. Between her fist, she holds the thick latex penis that looks and feels so real, but is much bigger than a real one could ever be. Pressing my face into the duvet again, she then mounts my body like a dog. With her thighs, she crushes my legs together. Against the zip of my boot, her stocking runs a long ladder that shows the tanned skin beneath. Added to the wild red face and messy hair, this makes her look dishevelled and a bit mad. That's good because I know she'll be hard.

And she is.

Deep, plunging strokes broaden my sex until I'm sure the head of the giant false cock is touching the back wall of my womb. The stretching sensation of the initial penetration makes me come. And as she rides and thrusts that thing through me, while calling me such filthy and disrespectful names, I come again and again and again.

Career History: Part 4

'Hi, Honey, I'm Home'

You never expected to see this: so many cars outside the house you shared with your wife before the demotion. Sleek, gleaming, sporty cars. Confused, you check the number on the little white post box at the end of the drive to make sure this is your house. All the houses look the same in this neighbourhood: wooden colonial-style buildings, perfect square lawns, neat paving on the drive. An immaculate recreation of a past idyll. But yes, the post box reads number 15. This is the right address and it seems the corporate elite have descended on your home.

It's been a month since you've seen the place; in Environment Services there is only one day off a week for the servitors and you are not permitted to leave the commercial compound. When the working day is over you go to a barrack full of bunkbeds and other disgraced men who wear the white boiler suits. They have also been taken away from their homes and wives and now spend their free time with card games and regrets.

Hiding inside a catering van, you made it here tonight by concealing your body under bales of paper napkins as it drove through the main checkpoint at the end of the carpark that is so vast it looks like the runway of an international airport. When the vehicle stopped to refuel at a gas station you continued on foot in your white boiler suit, carrying a broom and bin to avoid raising the suspicions of the security vans who constantly patrol the neighbourhoods of the corporate town.

And things have changed since you've been away from home. Music pours from the ground-floor windows; songs you don't recognise. Some kind of electronic music; it sounds youthful. Every window is bright with light too. Some are open. From the bedrooms laughter competes with the music from below. People are in your house; strangers are upstairs in the bedrooms. So where is your wife? Her car is not on the drive. Has the corporation expelled her from their town because of your failings? You think fondly of her; you imagine her confusion when you never returned home from work that day; the lies they must have told her to cover your disgrace, humiliation and subsequent imprisonment. Has she been sent back to your old life to live with her family? You feel so angry it makes you grind your teeth and press your fingernails painfully into the palms of your hands. You begin to sob with rage and then muffle your mouth with your forearm so none of the neighbourhood dogs can hear you.

Hugging the deep shadows that are created outside the yellowy circles of the street light beams, you run at a crouch, up past the side of the house, along the gravel, then the grass, past the hosepipe and into the back garden. You crouch in the flower beds and look across the lawn where you once had a barbecue and spent Sundays gazing at the perfect blue of sky. You fold yourself into the darkness around the bushes and shrubs that grow just inside the fence. Your overalls are bright and could make you conspicuous. Perhaps that's the point.

Certain no one has seen you, you stand up and are about to take the next step toward the house so you can peer through the patio doors when they suddenly open.

Music and male voices made loud by drink, and female laughter made loose and shrieky by drink, are forced through the aperture to fill the garden with the sounds of life. You retreat and duck down behind the foliage again. You hear the door close and the sounds of the party dim. Huddled into a crouch behind an ivy bush, you glance through the prickly leaves. Two people have come out of your house. A man with a red face pulls a giggling woman behind him into the garden. You hear her high heels scrape on the patio paving. 'They can't see out,' he says.

'They can!' she says, shouting and laughing at the same time.

'No, they can't,' he insists. They move on to the grass and their shoes become muffled. 'Because the lights are on. All they can see are their own reflections on the inside of the glass.'

'Oh yeah,' she says. 'But –'

'But what?'

'Someone could open the door.'

'Well,' he says. 'That's half the fun.' She laughs and spills some of her wine on to the perfect lawn.

Kissing with wide apart mouths, they sink to their knees. Discarding his jacket and tie, he begins to eat at her neck, her cheeks, her ears. Through the thin pink dress you can see her body shivering. Around his shoulders and back her slender arms fold, but not tightly. Gold flashes on her fingers and wrists in the faint light. She looks helpless against his broad torso.

'Don't you want to save yourself for later? For her?' she asks in a challenging, sarcastic tone of voice.

'No,' he says. 'I can't wait.' This pleases her.

Now lying on the grass, their hands pull at each other's underwear and then greedily stroke the flesh that is exposed. From under the straps of her dress her pink bra straps show on her narrow shoulders. He pushes the front of her dress up to her chin. Through the sheer

63

fabric of the brassiere cups he begins to massage her breasts; they look smallish but hard and he concentrates on them, his brow smoothing with wonder as if amazed they are actually in his hands. And, without blinking, you stare open-mouthed at her long thighs and narrow hips. You can see her shiny stockings and white suspender straps and then the tanned skin of her tummy.

Her whole body moves in the grass under the hard caresses of his hands. 'Oh yes, you remembered. Be hard there,' she says, and then moans as his hands pull at her nipples through the gauze of the brassiere cups. Blonde hair fans across her face, hiding her eyes and falling inside her open mouth where the red lipstick is smudged. She moves her head from side to side and then grinds the top of her skull into the earth; she goes beyond feeling conscious of exposing herself on a lawn outside of a crowded party.

With one hand the man then presses his hand against the triangle of white panty satin between her thighs. Pulling the teeny wisp to one side, he then pushes a thickish brown finger into her sex. She bites his shoulder and her body begins to jerk about as if electrocuted. Slowly and carefully he slides another two fingers inside her before withdrawing them back out to the first knuckle. Again and again this rough hand slips in and out of her delicate parts while you sit there, stunned and terrified of being discovered. You feel you shouldn't be here intruding on their private and intense time. But damn it! It's your home. You shake off those feelings of decorum; being polite and apologetic and civil got you into this mess, allowed you to be manipulated. It was easy the way the corporation took you down. And how dare these strangers have sex like cats on your lawn, when you've been imprisoned in a military-style dormitory under the skyscraper and had to creep home like a fugitive? You'll watch if you like; you escaped and will go anywhere and do any damn thing you please. As if you had just swallowed a hot drink, the warmth of your excitement at being free and able to think independently spreads through your body; it's been so long since you've been able to act on your own volition.

Clawing his back and shaking her head, the woman starts to inch her body along the grass. It's as if she's trying to escape the hand inside her and the weight of the body on top of her, while pulling it all along at the same time, unable to let go. 'I want you inside me. Now,' she says loud enough for you to hear. Her lover begins to breathe heavily and his fingers become frantic with his belt buckle and zipper like it's the quick release mechanism of a parachute and he's falling towards the patchwork of land below. Under him, the woman begins to push the disturbed silk of her panties into his groin – the softest part of her seeking a hard surface. Even if someone were to walk out of the house and on to the patio, you feel she would still continue pushing her hips to encourage a thorough penetration.

She moans, ecstatic, when something dark but reddish, at once shocking in its raw beastliness, appears between his legs, cradled in his fist. He picks the strip of silk off her sex like a hair from his soup and nudges the thickish purple head against her lips. She lets out a little cry and then says, 'Fuck me.' She repeats it with teeth clamped together. 'Fuck me.' Her face is obscured but you are sure the expression is fierce.

Leaning over her body, supporting himself with one arm, the man eases his fat sex inside her. There is a sharp intake of breath from the woman and then a long moan as all the length slips in. At once her frail arms tighten around his shoulders and her hands grip the white cotton of his shirt. Her legs cross around his waist. You can see the spikes of her heels waving in the air as the man withdraws and plunges, withdraws and lunges inside her. Placing his hands on her shoulders, he then presses her body into the grass to contain her wriggling and to create the stability required for his uncompromising thrusts to the back of her womb. 'Oh yes. Oh yes. Oh yes!' she says with the hands on her shoulders. She likes to be handled, to be controlled and dominated by the man she has chosen after all that flirting with a wine glass in her fragile fingers. She starts fires in men and likes them quenched in the most assertive manner.

When the man leans back and rests on his knees, he places her legs on to his shoulders so her high-heeled feet are next to his jawbone. Momentarily, he pauses to look at these wonderful feet in the strappy sandals, before thrusting his sex into her twice as hard as before. She makes an 'ugh' sound that gets louder and louder with every stroke until he is forced to put his fingers inside her mouth to stifle the sounds. Immediately, she hungrily sucks on his fingers and all the blonde hair that has become wrapped around them.

'In your mouth,' he whispers in a hoarse voice. 'I'm going to put it in your mouth.' She begins to climax, the moment he speaks. Despite the illusion of class created by her chic dress, perfect hair and designer underthings, the rough sex in the grass and now this talk has made her climax. He takes his fingers from between her teeth. 'You're going to suck my cock and swallow every drop.'

Shaking and almost choking from her climax, she does not answer him. She doesn't need to. His realisation of her wanton, tipsy, salacious nature – this woman who will take him on the grass near a room crowded with people – has already overwhelmed him and makes him ejaculate. Suddenly, it's as if he is emptying every ounce of vitality from his body; his arms shake with a palsy and his mouth opens to mouth a single, silent word. He withdraws from her sex. 'Now,' he says.

Little tremors pass through her body from the climax, but she still manages to open her mouth and shuffle her body down between his thighs. There is an urgency to her movements; she must have it.

The first thick bolt of cream hits her chest and she whimpers with disappointment. But then, stretching her head upwards, she seizes his sex between her lips. Immediately, he pumps it through his fist. Like little fleshy bellows her cheeks move in and out. Her throat starts to gulp and he pushes his cock further inside her mouth until half of it has disappeared into the painted O of her lips. Every one of his grunts signals an expulsion of hot seed inside her head. For a moment, they are a fleshy, animal machine – he pumps, she sucks. And even after his groans stop and his head falls across his chest, her cheeks keep moving and her body wriggles as if this writhing in the grass will extract more of him.

Eventually, she releases his softening sex from her mouth. Gasping for air, it's as if she has just emerged from the depths of a chilly swimming pool. She starts to giggle and he collapses on top of her. They kiss and then he nuzzles the side of her dishevelled head. Whispers pass between them but you can't hear what is being said. Soon, clothes are being rearranged and a cigarette is lit. Moving more slowly than before, they re-enter the party. As they pass through the patio doors, he uses a hand to swat at the back of her wrinkled dress.

You stand up from behind the bushes and stretch the cramps from your legs. You breathe out with relief and push your erection to the other side of your boiler suit. Its presence makes you feel ashamed, as if you are complicit in this intrusion on your property.

You creep along the inside of the fence and get closer to the house. Crossing the tiny path that runs between the side of the house and the fence, you lean against the wall by the patio doors. Your body tenses as you inch your face further and further towards the glass. Holding your breath, you are about to steal a peek inside the living room when the music inside stops. And the laughter, and the excited voices cease also. Your house becomes silent. And then dark.

Panic grips your insides and you are too afraid to even breathe. Convinced the party has stopped because the people in your house are aware of an intruder, you withdraw from the patio door and stand with your back pressed against the side of the house, listening but ready to bolt.

When nothing happens, you speculate that it is more likely that the party has finished early and the guests have retired. Even worse, they may have all gone upstairs to the bedrooms.

There are no further sounds and the French windows remain shut. Your body begins to stiffen in the cold. All over your skin goose pimples rise. You have no watch but guess you wait, shivering out there, for over fifteen minutes before you hear a muffled voice from inside the living room – a man's voice, raised as if calling for attention or making a speech. One or two faint but distinctly feminine voices call out in what sounds like encouragement and there is a small round of applause. Gradually a faint bluish light seeps through the glass of the French windows. Curious, you creep back on to the patio. Confidence growing, and remembering what the man said about the occupants not being able to see outside while the living room is lit, you linger to stare.

Candles encased in greeny-blue glass have been lit high up on shelves to cast an ever brightening glow over a tight circle of people who stand around the edges of the room. But what immediately preoccupies you are the clothes the women wear. Party dresses have been exchanged for shiny second-skins that glisten in the flickering light. Rubber dresses, or skirts complemented by clingy shirts with tiny zippers to push their breasts up and outwards, are now worn by every woman. The top half of their faces are masked too with more of the thin rubber. It makes their hair – mostly shoulder length

68

and blonde – look more resilient. Through the eyeholes of the mask worn by the woman closest to the window you can see a pair of wild, drunk eyes. She seems eager to misbehave, desperate to be free of the tight controls in her working life, if only for a short time. Yes, there is a real sense of expectancy in this place, of barely contained excitement amongst the gathered women. But what you find most alarming but also compelling are the short, hand-held whips they each grip in their gloved hands.

The only man now present in the living room stands in the centre of the circle of women. He wears a long red robe, like a graduation gown, and his silvery head is uncovered. You recognise the face – the lean tanned features and strong jaw are instantly familiar; he is one of the senior managers from your old department, a member of your original interview panel, but junior to Mrs Raker. Under the hem of the cloak you can see that his feet are bare. When he finishes speaking the women applaud.

And around this mystifying scene certain features in the background of the living room begin to look more familiar to you. The red chair under the tall lamp belongs to you and your wife; the hardback books on the long shelves are yours; her yucca plant stretches up the wall behind your television set; the three small landscape paintings under the wall lights were given to you as a wedding gift. So this is still your home full of your possessions, but where is your wife?

From the doors that lead to the dining room, another woman is brought forward. Wearing a long black robe with her entire head covered except for the eyes and mouth, she is escorted by two women wearing spike-heeled boots that are zippered up to their crotches. They stand on either side of her and gently hold her elbows as if she might try to escape. But the captive woman is smiling and there is something familiar about that mouth, even though it is thickly covered in red lipstick.

There is a similarity, a connection, that you cannot accept and refuse to pursue.

This robed woman kneels down on the floor in the centre of the living room. Her two escorts leave her side to join the circle. Compliant, she raises her face and her lips part. Allowing his scarlet robe to fall from his broad shoulders, the tall man who gave the introductory speech now stands completely naked before the kneeling woman. Slowly, this gathering of giant rubber dolls begins to slap the whips against their thighs, in time with each other. This is no longer a game or theme party; any illusions you may have harboured about the playfulness of its nature vanish. Outside in the cold, you find it hard to believe that such a thing is happening in the room where you used to read a newspaper and eat toast, but are still unable to stop looking and, despite the cold, you enjoy a thick erection. Never in one place have you seen so many women made tall and magnificent in spike heels and thigh-length boots, or glimpsed so many stocking tops with taut rubber suspender straps pulling the black gauze high on their legs, or seen so much soft, pale flesh exposed and hidden in turn by this new skin of wet-looking rubber. And the attitude of total subservience of the kneeling woman before these giantesses adds a sexual charge that makes you feel giddy. You want to see this creature well-used; the idea just overwhelms your mind. It's her compliance before the group that both seduces you and makes you feel angry as if personally betrayed.

Between the legs of the naked man, you can see most of her body but little of the face of the captive. But despite the obstruction of his naked buttocks, you realise his sex has been inserted and greedily received by the captive's painted mouth. The clapping of the rubber women begins to speed up and they sneer under their masks. Some of them whisper, or shout at the kneeling creature whose body rocks back and forth as she feasts.

70

With his hands, the naked man holds the captive's head by the ears and begins to thrust his buttocks towards the masked face you cannot see. Around the coupling, the women tighten their circle and begin a slow approach. Some of them crack their whips in the air. Limbs and spines tense inside the supple rubber. All are impatient.

Throwing his head back and unleashing a long groan, the tall man then steps back from the captive, the tension suddenly passing from his muscles. And, for a moment, before the circle of women move in and cover the captive, you see her engorged face. Eyes full of lustful adoration for the man who has just ejaculated on to her mouth, the woman grins under her mask. Around her red lips the rubber is wet.

The sight of this shocks you, nearly makes you cry out; baffled and aroused and frustrated all at the same time. What kind of woman would allow this to happen? And to actually enjoy it? But there is little time for reason – to force your imagination to stretch and encompass such a display of gross submission – because the assembly of women have suddenly surrounded her. Teetering but agile on their stiletto scaffolding, they flay the captive with their whips.

Crouching and writhing amongst a forest of slender legs, all bound in nylon and rubber and leather, the captive makes no attempt to struggle or escape. Amongst the thin heels of so many boots and the black rain of the leather whips, you catch glimpses of her masked face, and interpret the expression to be one of sensual euphoria. You can see it in the lines around the wide-open, dewy mouth: her gratitude for the stinging shower.

And then the tall, naked man claps his hands above his head and the women withdraw in unison, stepping back to the fringes of the room to resume their original positions. Their pale breasts rise and fall from the recent

71

excitement. Only one of them hesitates and still stares at the captive as if she has not been punished enough. The master of this perverse ceremony then reclothes himself in the red robe. He calls out another command. You think he says, 'Wet her,' but you cannot be sure as he stands with his back to you on the other side of the thick glass of the French windows which are designed to insulate the house against the cold.

From the dining room, the men enter. Huddled together, looking nervous but excited as if about to start a sporting event, they file into the room and form an inner circle around the captive with the rubber women behind them. They are completely naked save for the masks. All their heads are covered in plain red head-pieces that stretch over their skulls like latex swimming caps. None of their bodies are overweight. Even those with greying chest hair have bodies cut with a tight musculature from regular and vigorous exercise. Already, most of them have erections.

Following the next command from the master of this ceremony, the men move forward and jostle around the captive. She unhooks her robe and lets it fall from her shoulders to the carpet. Between their hairy legs, you can see the curves of her pale flesh and the sheer dark underwear she wears – a see-through brassiere, black stockings, transparent panties and a suggestion of a gauzy garter belt: pampered and prepared for sacrifice.

You hold and begin to stroke your sex. Slut, slut, slut, you say to yourself in time with the new rhythm slapped out by the whips against the leather boots of the masked women.

And the captive raises her masked face again. Only this time she receives ten erect cocks to worship. Sucking them in turn, sometimes three at the same time, and always holding two within her caressing, plump hands, she gives the hooded men pleasure. The women draw closer and try to peer between the men's elbows, in order to see the sluttish captive working on so many erections.

Three of the men come in quick succession, perhaps the last two ejaculations are summoned by the first creamy expulsion on to her lips. Soon, her rubber face glistens and a thick trickle slides off her chin to fall into her large cleavage. Beating the cocks more vigorously through her fingers she hungrily sucks at anything hard that touches her lips. She becomes freed of everything but the desire to be adored and to give pleasure; nothing else matters to her. Grinning, she laughs as her face is spattered by another two long, ropy draughts of hot seed. Soon, it is dripping from her chin and running in rivulets on either side of her nose. It washes and bubbles on her slick face and her little tongue darts out to taste and then draw the salty food into her mouth. Three of the men, who have still to wet her, arrange her on all fours while the other seven men work on developing their second erections. Man-handled, assertively arranged like a dog, pulled into position, she crouches on hands and knees in her stained black lingerie and begins to mouth encouragement at the two men who kneel down at either end of her. Panties moved to one side of her wide buttocks, the first man thrusts himself into her sex while his partner fists his cock into her grasping mouth. The third man looks down and massages his length directly over her arched back.

And the women continue to slap out their rhythm with the whips against their leather boots, their eyes wide with passion, some of them eager to rejoin the use of this captive. One woman in knee-length boots and seamed stockings begins to lash at the floor with her whip, and another with nipple rings starts to shriek something into the air as she flogs the wall.

Soon the power of thrusts from behind the captive drive her deeper into the crotch of the man she eats. Climaxing, he then falls away and you catch sight of the

73

captive's gleaming face, tilted upward and savouring the rich soup on her tongue as she is rutted hard from behind. The man standing over her strokes four strings of cream on to her lower back, soaking her garter belt. And it is not long before the last of her lovers, who sweats and thrusts into her sex, holds her buttocks hard against his crotch to empty himself also – the first to come inside her.

But the ritual is not over. Far from it. Three of the other men who previously climaxed on to her masked face, have recovered the solidity required to begin working again on the supplicant. Rolled on to her back with her legs apart and feet reaching towards the ceiling, you are then compelled to watch her taken by two of the men in turn as she sucks the third deep into her throat. Gradually, other men move back to where she lies and take their place between her thighs, or push themselves back between the lips now sponged of paint but glossed with a more natural cosmetic. Soon, the skin of her thighs is recoated with the seed of at least five men. Another three of her anonymous lovers fill her sex until it overruns, and two even venture inside her anus to penetrate thoroughly and at length.

Physically and emotionally exhausted by what you have seen and by the vigorous stroking of your own sex until you fertilised the pot plants at your feet, you lean against the wall of your house. And over your shoulder, behind a thin layer of glass, the captive continues to take cock after cock inside her body. You cannot watch any more; if you do you may be forced the break the glass with a garden chair before rushing in and take your turn between the stocking-clad legs of that insatiable woman in the mask.

Of course, you know full well, have known the minute she was escorted into the room, the identity of the hooded captive. Indeed, you too have been between the legs of that creature. And many times also, but in different circumstances. Despite the mask and cloak and flimsy black underthings and the depraved behaviour – something you have never experienced in years of marriage – you knew all along that your wife was the woman in the mask. She has crossed to the other side; she has eagerly betrayed you; she belongs to the corporation now; has been ritually accepted as one of their own. Numbed, you acknowledge that you never really knew her.

In a daze, you move away from the French windows and sit down in the centre of the lawn. When your wife has exhausted all of the male executives in the red masks – the last few being finished off individually in the centre of the living room by her mouth and pumping hands – you watch the living room empty of the guests. The smiling captive is then helped to her feet and led away from the scene of carnage by her smiling female escorts.

Some time later, the guests return to the living room. But their clothes and their behaviour have changed once again. All the female guests have removed their rubber uniforms and changed back into the informal disguises in which they arrived at your house to desecrate your wife. They fluff their hair out and take sips from champagne flutes. It's as if the previous depraved scene had never occurred. All the guests now laugh and talk. Champagne is poured and food is passed around on wide platters. But they were far better suited to the masks and spikes and rubber dresses; like demons, you saw these corporate fanatics as they truly are. Wearing slacks and short-sleeved shirts and satisfied smiles, the men mingle and top up glasses. You cannot hear what is being said but you know the discourse of correctional punishment, of group sex and of housewife debasement has altered with the outfits. Again, the excesses the corporate regime creates have gone back to ground. The music is turned on and the party continues.

Scanning the faces in the crowd, you recognise all of the senior executives from your old department. You also see a blonde woman you often noticed marching purposefully through a nearby office. Beside the dining room doors, two of your senior female colleagues appear to be holding hands. They never liked you. On several occasions you caught them whispering when you returned from lunch. And there is the personal assistant also who used to make you feel giddy with excitement whenever she passed you in a corridor before the demotion. You begin to smoulder with resentment. Their presence in your absence is an invasion. You begin to wonder how they think they can get away with this: to remove a man from his home and job and wife and force him to work as a manual labourer on a chain gang while they use her as a sexual plaything. You clench both fists and want to punch the lean and tanned face of the executive who made the speech. It takes a great effort of will to restrain yourself from charging into the living room and wielding a sun umbrella like a battle axe. And yet, you instinctively know that this is not an isolated incident. It must occur all over the suburbs and involve all of those who fully integrate with the company creed. And this depraved ceremony, this executive black mass, must have been the fate of all those wives of all those silent, nervous men with whom you share the barracks in environment services.

But then you see something that makes this fleeting spirit of defiance die. Your wife has rejoined the party and is now standing in the centre of the room. Her new friends make a fuss of her; her cheeks are kissed, her glass is filled, and her mouth accepts finger food. It's as if the garden is moving around your head. The faint voices become louder and the music seems to have been specially composed to torment you; the drums thump between your temples as if controlling and accelerating your raised pulse. So much with her appearance has changed. It took a moment for you to even recognise her, to even associate your wife's old figure and style and face with the woman now standing in that room. It's as if you imagined the whole marriage. Shoulder-length brown hair has become short, spiky and blonde; an aversion to make-up has been replaced by a predilection for dark rouge, thick red lipstick, heavy black eyeliner, long eyelashes and dramatic eye-shadow; her plucked eyebrows now arch over her green eyes in two thin lines; a tight leather pencil skirt has been worn in preference to comfortable trousers, and her flat mules have been neglected for spike-heeled sandals; the tan tights are gone too and a new pair of seamed, black nylons cling to her pale legs. She has been overwhelmed, captured and transformed by the ruling tribe of corporate conquerors.

Between your thighs something begins to firm. Looking down, you see your sex is harder than it has been in weeks: bigger, prouder, more determined. Instinctively, you hold it. It contracts in the palm of your hand and wants so much to come home to your transformed wife. But she has other ideas, new clothes, new friends and tastes you can barely comprehend. And now, to your horror, you watch her trail her long red fingernails down the shaven cheek of a man who is standing far too close to her. He is half her age. She then whispers to another young man and he slides an arm around her body to begin a slow, casual stroking of her backside. Your heart seems to have stopped. It's an effort to swallow. This casual show of affection and its potential for intimacy seems like an even greater injustice than her central role in the prolonged orgy you witnessed earlier. She is gone. You know it. For ever lost to you, but made all the more appealing because of it. And why could she not have dressed like this when you were married? Why did she wait until you were gone?

Numbed by the sight of your wife – these tastes you never detected through so many years of marriage – you are helpless to do anything but sit on the lawn and watch. And wait. Even if you are destroyed in the process, you vow to damage the corporation, to destroy it if possible. But first, you intend to confront your wife, this corporate whore who once shared your bed.

Career History: Part 5

Outbid

Entering the bedroom, you see your wife sitting on the bed, removing her high heels. Amongst all the other changes, she has lost weight too; now that no one is obscuring your view you can see this through the sheer black robe she wears over her lingerie. 'Oh, it's you,' she says, as if you have just been down the road to buy milk and she never heard you come back inside the house. 'I was only wondering this morning when you'd show up.'

Emotion – so much emotion and confusion – blocks your throat and stoppers your mouth. You just stand still and stare.

'I wouldn't stay too long if I were you,' she says, without even looking at you as she unclips a suspender from her stocking top. 'I don't think you're supposed to leave where ever it is you live now. And Michael will be back soon.'

You find your voice again. 'Michael?' But it trembles.

'Yes, he's just saying good night to the guests. We had a lovely evening.' She peels the stocking off her foot and begins to unfasten the next one. 'And he won't be very pleased if he catches you in our room.'

'Our room? Michael?'

After placing the hosiery on the bed beside her, she removes an earring. 'Oh, don't start making a fuss.'

'Are you out of your fucking mind?' you say.

'No. Never felt better, actually.'

Your voice is subdued but tense. 'They have me imprisoned at the corporation. I sleep in a fucking bunk bed. I spend my days picking up litter and dogshit.' You shake your hands in the air, before your face. 'Don't you care? Did you ever think about what happened to me? Does any of this seem fucking insane to you?'

'Self-absorbed as usual. Everything was always about you. What you want. What you need.'

Dropping to your knees, you claw your face to make sure this is not a dream.

'In case you haven't noticed, quite a few things have changed,' she says. Her voice has become impatient; you are an irritant. 'Our marriage needed a shake-up. And it couldn't possibly survive in this town. And anyway, I like my new life. I'd never go back.'

'Go back? What are you talking about? What's got into you? Did they brainwash you? Give you drugs?'

She laughs. 'Oh dear. Oh dear me. I like that. You can be funny at times.'

Outside the bedroom window, you hear raised voices. Someone laughs. A car door slams shut. You cross the room and part the curtains. The street outside your house is nearly empty. Down on the drive, the tall man who gave the speech is waving to the last of the guests: a couple in a black sports car as they reverse away from the kerb. This must be Michael. 'Where's your car?' you say. 'We're going to need a fucking car. Get what you can carry. I'll deal with Michael.'

'You most certainly will not. I'm going nowhere. And if you'd like to excuse me, I need to do my face. It's been a long day.' She yawns. 'I'm tired.'

You turn and stare, dumbfounded, at the woman you used to wake up with. She unclips her bra as she pads across the carpet on barefoot towards the en-suite bathroom. 'What about our marriage?' It's all you can think to say and it immediately sounds banal to you.

'Ha!' she says. 'What about it?' she then shouts over the running of the taps in the bathroom.

'I'm your fucking husband!'

'Oh, for goodness' sake, stop dwelling on the past. Move on with your life. I have.'

'Move on ...' You groan and slap your forehead. 'Have you any idea who you're mixed up with? These people are insane. You let them into our house. You fuck them. Dozens of them in our home ...' You cannot finish or feel angry like you want to. You feel blocked, useless, stupid.

She rubs a foaming lotion into her cheeks. 'Oh, you saw that. Peeping through the window, no doubt. Why do I sound surprised? I think it's best you don't come here again. I don't think you'd fit in. It's not your scene.'

Who is this blonde robot with this pre-programmed responses? You look at the ceiling. 'Not my scene!' Clenching your fists, you begin to laugh. You sit on the bed and slap your hands against your thighs. 'Not my scene. Not my scene.'

Your wife opens the bathroom door. Despite the moisturiser she has rubbed over the top half of her face, her expression has altered; at last she looks more familiar to you now. Two lines at the top of her nose deepen and her frown lines show. You saw this face a great deal when you lived here, and never much cared for it. 'Now listen –' she says.

From downstairs, a deep voice calls out, 'Darling. I'm going to tidy up.'

'Yes, dear,' she calls towards the open door of the bedroom and then returns her attention to you. 'I haven't liked you for a long time. I must be honest. My friends were right. You were high maintenance. And you stopped making an effort before the honeymoon. God knows I was a fool for ever marrying you in the first place. I realise this now because things are so good for me. Better than they have ever been. I'd forgotten

81

how good, how passionate, how intense life could be. I've rediscovered who I really am.'

She sold you out at the first opportunity for more attention and money. Even now she fails to sound convincing. Like everyone involved with the corporation, what she says sounds rehearsed to you. Something pre-prepared, learnt from a personal development seminar, a tyrannical discourse that can accept nothing but itself, an attempt at legitimising gross self-interest. A creed you have to adopt to fit in. You have to deny it, resist them or go crazy thinking you're unworthy. She's one of them now and you stopped trying to fit in the day you were first caned. 'Yes, you rediscovered yourself,' you say. 'As a cock-sucking slut who takes it in the ass. A corporate whore.' This sounds churlish to you, but you have to say something hurtful. 'You never had a single ambition or creative thought of your own. You are better off with Michael and his, his, his fucking plastic face. And you call me selfish? It was your fucking self-esteem issues that soured everything. You were always impossible to please. So carry on deluding yourself that everything is perfect in this fantasy world until you realise how dangerous it really is.'

She snorts derisively. 'Have you finished?' She turns her back on you but you can see her face in the mirror of the bathroom cabinet. She is smiling in the unnerving style of someone with no conscience. 'I have my conception exercises to perform,' she says through the door. 'Maybe tonight I got lucky. You see, we've all been trying for a baby some time now. Children are the future of this town.'

Staring straight ahead, but not seeing anything, you leave the bedroom and descend the stairs. In the kitchen you pass Michael. He stops drying a plate and stares at you. Glassy-eyed, you pass him and walk back into the garden. Behind you, he hurriedly locks the kitchen door and begins calling out to your wife.

82

Career History: Part 6

Virus Alert

They must have called their allies in security because the sirens begin to wail and the searchlights began to sweep the fronts of the houses almost as soon as you leapt the fourth fence and dropped into another garden. Out in the street, you can hear shouting. Dogs are barking too.

Running across the perfect lawns of your old neighbourhood, you pass identical patios and lines of shrubs. Vaulting another fence, you find yourself on another square lawn, near another red-bricked patio. Strong yellow searchlights shine down the side of the house and make the holly bushes look artificial. Over another wooden fence you go and into another immaculate garden. Keeping level with you, you can hear the paws of dogs on the pavement and the ripple of car tyres on the asphalt of the street. Someone shouts something through a loudhailer. A window opens behind you. A woman's voice says, 'Who's there?'

In the sixth or seventh garden, you get increasingly breathless and your knees bang together from adrenaline and fatigue. Your vision has gone jerky and you have bitten your tongue. And yet it's like you haven't even made any progress, as if you're still in the backyard of your old house. Indifferent French windows watch you sweat and tramp through another orderly flower bed. For a moment you suspect the whole town was originally planned and constructed just to defeat and demoralise you, that every garden has been waiting for this opportunity to trap the last of the town's rebels.

'There he is!' someone suddenly calls from the street and you hear the paws of a dog skittling down the path at the side of the property you currently trespass. Frantically, you vault the fence but fall face-down in the soil and shrubs on the other side. As you lurch back on to your feet, a branch of a tree whips across your cheek and breaks the skin. Against the fence you have just leapt over, the weight of a dog crashes, bending the timber. Snarling, its claws then rake the wooden planks as it tries to follow you over.

Back on your feet, you sprint across another two lawns and vault another two fences. Vainly, you try to remember how many houses are in this street. Eventually, it must come to an end. The fences are slowing you down and if another dog comes up a garden path you could become cornered. You imagine yellow teeth sinking into your forearm. How long would it then be before a dog handler reached you to pry the black canine gums from your flesh?

Behind you, the beams of torches now whip about the taller trees at the base of the gardens, more dogs bark and growl in the near distance and out in the street someone is shouting through a loudhailer again.

Changing tack, you race down the side of a house and peer into the street. Seven security vans are parked outside your wife's house. The dogs and officers are still searching the backyards you have just run through. This gives you hope; there is still a small distance between you and them. Now you run at a crouch across the front lawns of the houses. Your feet are bare and one big toe has been badly stubbed. Sweat runs down your forehead and stings your eyes. Blinking, you peer towards the end of the road. A desperate cry escapes you. There is a roadblock; one car parked sideways in the mouth of the street with its roof lights directed towards the centre of the road.

Scuttling sideways in a crouch, you begin to sneak across the exposed grass of the last front lawn. Watching the patrol car, you see it is unoccupied. You begin to grin. The grass looks golden under your feet. If you can turn the corner of the last house and get into the main road, you have a chance of rapidly changing direction and leaving the police further behind. And you can discard the boiler suit to beguile the dogs.

'I prefer to run first thing in the morning. In the dark you never know what you might run into.'

You flinch. Your chest feels fit to burst. All over your body sweat turns to shivers. You look up to find the origin of the voice. What you see kills the exhilaration of escape in a heartbeat. A female security officer is leaning against the garage door ten feet in front of you. Most of her dark uniform is swallowed by shadow. And you were too busy looking over your shoulder and at the parked police car to notice the gleam of her knee-length boots in the thin light.

'It's dangerous,' she says. 'You could have an accident.' She steps out and into the yellow light from the nearest street lamp. Tall and slender in the black shirt and riding trousers, she takes a casual step towards you. There is no emotion in her beautiful face. She has dark eyes and thin features. Bright red lipstick draws your eyes to her mouth. 'Better get in the back of my car where it's safe. Lot of dogs behind you. I've seen them shred those suits like paper bags.'

Frightened and confused, your automatic reaction is to nod in agreement. She turns on her heel and nonchalantly walks down the driveway towards her patrol car. Under her peaked cap, her hair is tied into a bun. As she walks she removes her black leather gloves from her long white fingers. Again, you think of wet dog's teeth and velvety snouts ruffled into snarls, while loops of saliva fall from muscular jaws. You follow her into the road on your grubby, bloodied, bare feet. She waits for you by the open rear door of her patrol car. Without looking at you, she chews her gum and nods towards the back seat. You look inside the car and emit one loud sob, and only one. The cushioned seat and the metal grille, separating the front of the vehicle from the back seat, suddenly makes you think of the bunkbeds in the barracks. Whatever vague but excitable plans you had of escape and of hurting the corporation are over. Soon, the soles of booted feet pound off the asphalt behind you. You hesitate on the road before the rear door of the car. You look into the eyes of the female security officer. Smiling, she reaches out and flicks some dirt from your wet cheek. Her fingernails are painted red. 'Better get in. Or I'm going to shoot you.'

The female officer then gently presses your buttocks as you duck into the back of her car.

Career History: Part 7

Entering the System

This unreal, preposterous night will not end.

Naked, legs kicked wide apart, arms spread out so the palms of your hands press the cold tiles of an interrogation cell, you are helpless as two female police officers stretch and snap rubber gloves over their hands. The beautiful arresting officer who drove you to the station is a captain and will not sully her manicured fingers with a search of your grimy, smelly body. She sits on a stool, her posture casual, long legs crossed, her face indifferent to your blushing and sweating. Patting her shiny brown hair flat, she then replaces the peaked cap.

You are being entered into the system. They took fingerprints and made you piss into a small plastic cup. A photograph has been taken and now the search is about to begin.

The two officers with latexy hands turn you around. Through the whitish rubber skin on their fingers you can see the plum nail polish they wear. Their touch is firm. Small and muscular with short black hair, you suspect the younger officer never smiles. There is something of the military instructor about her, but her face is attractively square with even features and clear hazel eyes. Her legs have been blessed also with the tight and shapely musculature of the athlete. The older woman has white hair and a matronly figure, but there is nothing masculine about her. Despite her uniform, her size, the frown, she has a handsome face. Only the slate-grey eyes are mean and you avoid them. In another situation you insist on imagining that she could be cheerful and feminine in a maternal sense.

The scent of their perfume is sharp and both women have applied fresh lipstick. They don't wear the combat uniforms of black shirt and riding trousers. They are dressed in the formal blue uniform: a cotton shirt with buttons and a tight black skirt with a utility belt. The hems of these skirts are cut above the knee and you try to avert your eyes from the glimpse of black nylon between skirt and leather boot as the women swish about you. Old habits die hard.

The older woman checks your mouth; puts her fingers inside your cheeks and looks under your tongue. Your palate is overwhelmed by the taste of hot water bottles, condom rubber and dry talc. Then she ruffles your hair and peers inside your ears. Against your chest, shoulders and back, her large bosom presses. Warm and soft, the gentle contact puts you more at ease; it makes you think of a school nurse. On her knees, the younger guard runs her hands up the inside of your legs. As if innocently opening the top layer of a sandwich she lifts your scrotum and peers underneath. Looking down at her smooth face is a mistake. The head of your sex is no more than a few inches from her glossy red lips. Your cock begins to enlarge. She looks up at you with disgust. You open your mouth to apologise but no words come out, just a rasp. Desperately, you look at the captain for understanding, but the glare from her cold eyes forces you to lower your eyes. 'Bend over, sir.' The command was issued by the older woman.

'No. Enough,' you say and try to step away from the guards. The smaller woman is on her feet in an instant and places one hand on her hip. She fingers an implement on the utility belt. The older guard holds

88

your elbow and digs her fingers into your flesh; hard enough to let you know you will be unable to pull away. With her other hand, she too grips the handle of something on her belt.

'Bend over, sir. So that we may complete the search,' she says, in a louder but still controlled voice.

'No. What do you think I've got up there? I have nothing. Everything was taken when I was demoted. I demand to see a lawyer. This is obscene. Inhumane.'

'Bend over, sir. This is procedure. I will not ask again.'

Again you look at the captain and beseech her with your eyes. 'Please,' you say. 'This has to be a joke.'

She doesn't even blink.

With all your strength you hurl your body away from the two guards, desperate to increase the distance between them and your most private cavity. But you are unable to pull your elbow from the vice of the older guard's fingers, and now the younger woman has seized your other arm and pulls it behind your back. Tugging and twisting and swearing at them, you fall forward and away from them, on to your knees. Down on the floor they won't be able to get between your buttocks, you think, and a proper doctor will have to be called. Looking up at the last second you catch sight of the captain on her pedestal. There is still no emotion in her face, but she nods at her officers.

From each belt, a small black tool is unclipped. It looks like the handle of an umbrella. In unison, with a quick downward flick of the wrist, the two officers extend the curved handles into long, thin canes. Holding your elbows, they yank you back to your feet. Flicking and switching more than lashing, they then pepper your buttocks and the rear of your bare thighs with the thinnest end of the canes. From one foot to the other you dance and tippy-toe, crying out as every blow registers as a fine line of gunpowder lit on the skin.

Glancing over your shoulders to let forth a stream of expletives, you see that the faces of the guards are flushed with the hot blood of excitement. And in their eyes you see passion and aggression and a sinister delight, but you do not see mercy. They begin to nick and slice at your calves and ankles. Twisting your arms, they then force you down and on to all fours so they can get at your back to stripe you red. Blinded by tears of rage and pain and humiliation, you feel the thin wood cut against your shoulders and down the side of your ribs. Beside your face, you see two pairs of leather boots. They stamp and shuffle as the women move about to regain control of the situation.

Both women then begin to steer you across the floor into the centre of the room by nudging your flanks with their knees. When they step back to make room to strike you, the clips of their suspenders press against the tight cloth of skirt and you see the fine, enticing creases of nylon at the back of the knees; reminders of femininity, of a tremendous female power, a sexual aesthetic. As they raise their legs, it gets even better. You are able to catch sight of their shaven thighs shimmering in police-issue nylons. Then you see a stocking top and a plain black garter strap. You wonder if the thighs are hard. In the past, you always found yourself staring at the female police officers as they directed traffic or patrolled the streets about town. What you always wanted was a glimpse up their skirts. Now you have it. But it makes you realise how foolish you were to allow your lust to obscure the obvious menace. Tough women in tight skirts and knee-length boots and sheer stockings are now flogging you raw on a cement floor. But between your legs your sex seems to revel in the pain and embarrassment. It poles out, juts upward, as if anticipating an even greater pleasure.

As ever in this town, there are other motives at work behind your resistance to the strict and clinical discipline. Blinking the tears from your eyes, you turn your head from side to side trying to see more, maybe to even press your face against a leather boot or slippery inner thigh. The experience at Mrs Raker's seminar has stayed with you. Being caned by female strangers carries its own specific and overwhelming thrill. Every time you have masturbated since, in the showers or stealthily beneath the sheets of your bunk, it is Mrs Raker and her pretty executives you think of. And yet, despite this powerful impact the original experience has had upon your inner life, you are still not comfortable with admitting that you enjoy it. Half of you creates a mental resistance; ashamed to be the victim, the humiliated, the submissive. Nonetheless, the muscles in your sex clench and contract with every stroke from the cane. You feel an urge to cry out. To say, Hurt me. Harder. Just do me. I'm a weak and hopeless bastard and I need the cane. You bite your tongue but stare up at an officer's breasts, straining at the blue cotton of her uniform, as she prepares a back-hand swing.

'Enough now,' the captain says and the caning stops.

Weakened by pain and drained by the massive surge of adrenaline and emotion, you say, 'More. Give me more. I can take it. You bitches will only make my cock harder. Then maybe I can put something in your ass.' Sweat runs down your face and over your top lip. As a final act of defiance your spit on the toe of the smaller officer's shiny boot.

The captain yawns. Then she nods at her girls again.

Again the canes fall: faster, harder, the sting spreading out to cover more of your skin. Wrists, knuckles, forearms, biceps, neck, ears, you are covered in a fire that leaves no ash or smoke, only welts. Long thin welts. You go limp in their grip and expect to pass out. Your head slumps against the thighs of the younger officer. Then it slides down to her knees where your cheek slips across nylon and then the slick leather of her boots. The caning stops. Steel chains clink and tinkle and chink. Hard, cold bracelets close tight around your ankles and wrists. A rubber ball-gag forces your jaws wide and makes you salivate like a dog near a bone. Pulled on to your hands and knees, you then feel a cold sensation around your rectum. Your chilly anus contracts and a prickling sensation spreads up your spine to crackle behind your ears. Your whole backside feels wet. Must be a lubricating gel. A finger that feels as big as a night-stick goes through the puckered door of your last hiding place. It's like you want to take a shit, scream and hide at the same time. The finger is removed. 'He's clean,' someone says, and you hope you are.

Back on your feet, naked and in chains, you are dragged from the interrogation cell. As you pass the captain, you see she has removed her gloves and is inspecting her nail varnish.

Career History: Part 8

Staff Reappraisal

Cuffed hands clasped together, knees shaking from the cold and the fear of what happens next, you sit on a bunk bed in the little cell. All over your body the welts have gone warm. You dare not move in case jostling air molecules make them sting. Beside the bunk that hangs down from the wall on chains, there is a stainless steel toilet with no seat and an electric bulb inside a cage that is suspended from the ceiling, nothing else. On some of the white stone walls, shiny bands of fresh paint cover graffiti. You lift your feet off the floor and tuck them under your thighs. Beneath your new boiler suit the sweat has dried and makes your skin feel gritty. The cloth of your suit is coloured the orange of death row.

About an hour ago, the pair of female police officers who processed you into the system left you here with only your thoughts for company; thoughts of what might happen next and who might decide on your punishment – the managers in Environment Services, or the corporate executive that first demoted you? Maybe each will have something to say about this breakout. And the police may also step back in; you imagine they are always eager to oblige. There is always punishment here for anything that differs from the status quo, for anyone unable or unwilling to join the consensus. You think back to your caning at the seminar and guess things will be different this time; longer, more painful, a greater humiliation to be endured. Or perhaps it will be unendurable. Your will may finally be broken; you might become a different person. You think about those quiet, nervous faces in the barracks. Most of them have white hair.

But even if you were reinstated in your old job with your entire life back the way it was before that morning in Mrs Raker's office, you know you could never go along with the stifling, competitive nature of the corporation. And these people are clever; they know that you will never be able to accept the choices they made for you. So maybe you will disappear. Be made to disappear. It seems far more likely that this will happen.

The clanging of cold steel draws your eyes to the cell door. You see the locking mechanism move. Then the thick door swings open. The two female police officers who processed you enter. The door closes. The younger one carries a tray. There are sandwiches and coffee on the tray. Saliva fills your mouth. Never has coffee smelled so good. Nobody speaks.

They walk across the cell towards you, their faces cold. The tipped heels of the boots make loud noises on the cement floor. Standing so close to you, the pepper spray on the belt buckle of the older officer touches your nose. You swallow and fight the desire to back into a corner. Nervously, you eye the long fingers in the black leather gloves that hold the tray. The younger officer offers you the food.

'My name is Officer Dudley,' the small athlete says. 'And this is Officer Smith.' But the way she says it brings you no comfort. Her tone is spiteful. Perhaps there is unfinished business between you and them.

Officer Smith now speaks to you. 'After a discussion with our superior, you are to be charged with an unauthorised absence from your department. There is also a matter of an inappropriate use of company property, trespassing, indecent behaviour, breaking and entering and resisting arrest. Your ex-wife wishes to press charges.'

'The bitch,' you say.

'She says it's the only way you will learn. And we're in agreement with our public.'

Tasting little, you eat and slurp at the coffee.

'Soon,' Officer Dudley adds, as she stands with her shiny boot heels together and arms folded, 'you will be asked to sign a confession and to make a verbal admission of guilt. It will be filmed and broadcast on the company channel. After that you will leave our jurisdiction and be returned to your department. There may be further questioning from internal security.'

'There's a fucking surprise,' you say.

'Don't ever swear again under this roof. This is a civilised place.'

You sneer. 'I'll admit to nothing until my concerns are addressed.' You are surprised by the strength of your own voice. The mention of your wife has made you sullen and angry.

The two officers exchange glances. 'Concerns?' Officer Smith says, raising her voice as if offended by an unexpected and preposterous comment.

'Mmm, that's right,' you say, chewing bread and ham and cheese. 'Issues with imprisonment. I've been held against my will. Forced into manual labour on the company grounds. That was after being caned in public. The company appears to believe it can do as it wishes. It cannot. People have rights. Freedoms. And now you've mixed my wife up in your sordid rituals. Illegally removed me from my home and marriage and inserted someone else. A character called Michael. If that is not enough, you then chase me with dogs and threaten to shoot me before whipping me raw in the station house. Now that is what I call criminal behaviour. I am a reasonable man, not a criminal. You are the criminals

95

and I do not respect or recognise your powers. You are supposed to protect and serve the public and not sanction or contribute to this kind of tyranny. Now, if you will take me to the nearest pay-phone, I would like to contact legal representation.'

Again they exchange glances. This time they begin to laugh. It is the older woman who speaks first. 'We hoped this was going to be easier.'

'Now, the phone, please. I have a call to make.'

Officer Dudley looks at you with a mixture of pity and loathing. 'There will be no call. According to the law in this town you are a criminal. When the evidence against you is overwhelming and there are sufficient witnesses, legal representation is waived. Indeed, we have surveillance footage of you performing a lewd and indecent act on private property. Your behaviour is socially unacceptable.' Her eyes narrow into slits. 'And the public we serve must be protected from you.'

At first you are shocked. Unknown to you, a camera must have filmed you masturbating outside the French windows of your old house. You must have been watched from the day you moved in. Then you begin to laugh humourlessly at the situation, at the charges, at the impossibility of this system, at your wife.

But the young and tight-bodied Officer Dudley thinks you are laughing at her. She takes a step towards you with her little fists clenched. Her colleague seizes her elbow and holds her back. 'You're making matters worse for yourself with this attitude,' the mature guard says.

You laugh again; it's all you can do to prevent yourself from screaming. You close your eyes and swallow. Then take a deep breath. 'This is beautiful. Just beautiful. You people. Do you honestly think this will stick? That you'll get away with it? Any of it? All I ever did was lie on a CV and spin a few tales in an interview. And because of that, I'm down-town listening to this bullshit from a couple of fascists. This fucked-up company and its fucked-up town are facing the biggest law suit in legal history.' The guards take a step closer but you carry on. 'Not to mention the bad publicity nationwide, no, internationally. I'm not the one who should worry. You guys are going to look like a crazy religious cult when it's all over.' Two perfumed shadows fall across the bunk.

Both women begin to finger their utility belts. Their lips have gone thin and tight, their faces stiff. Only now do you decide to keep quiet. Your appetite for the rhetoric of freedom and civil liberty was temporary. Each officer seems to be summoning every reserve of self-discipline to prevent herself from lashing out. There is a long tense silence. Finally, the older woman sighs, tilts her head to one side and pretends to frown in concentration. 'Officer Dudley?'

'Yes, Officer Smith.'

'He mentioned the F word. Will you please keep look-out, I don't want to be disturbed when I'm in the middle of a discussion about the company rules with this clever gentleman. It seems he may have forgotten the stipulations of the contract that both he and the wife signed.'

'I do believe he has.'

'Back when they came here to make it big.'

'You mean to say he has forgotten that he's no longer protected by national or international law?'

'Almost certainly. By working for the company, it's slipped his mind that he has opted out of every legal system except our own. Which, I add, has been rightly enforced and is a great success.'

You remember skim-reading page after page of complex jargon about private law in the original contract that you signed, but never imagined it would ever affect you. You shake your head. 'It won't stick. You just can't do these things to people. Don't you see how wrong this is? That your whole system is a lie?'

97

Both women are smiling; they seem pleased with the desperate edge to your voice. Officer Smith nods to her partner. Smiling, Officer Dudley leaves the room and locks the door behind her.

Your food tray is removed from the bed. Gripping the chain between your cuffs, you are pulled to your feet and turned around to face the wall. Her strength surprises and alarms you. Hot lipsticky breath fills your ear. 'It never ceases to amaze me that some people still complain. Considering the average standard of living in this town.' Officer Smith brings her knee into your stomach while pressing something at the side of your neck that paralyses your arms and legs. Quickly, your face is then slammed into the mattress.

'And let's not forget the wages and career opportunities,' she says in an excited voice that warns you of imminent danger. 'And the health-care. The education system.' Your ankles are kicked apart. 'A clean environment. The law and order,' she continued in the tight voice, like she's speaking through clenched teeth. 'Did you know people can even go out for an evening and leave their front door unlocked?'

'Yes,' you cry out, suddenly afraid. Hating yourself, you then say, 'You do a brilliant job. I can see that.'

'So when an undesirable calls it a lie, it frustrates me.' A broad hand is placed at the base of your spine. You twist your head on to the side and peer behind to see what she is doing.

'No,' you mutter. 'Please no. Not again. It's too big.'

From around her waist, she unbelts a long black appendage that looks more like a Billy club than a sex aid. 'In fact,' she says, 'your kind of ingratitude makes me want to scream.' Bending her body over your back, she then hugs you with her thick arms. Is she going to simultaneously squeeze and sodomise you to death? You brace yourself for the crushing of your ribcage and the dreadful, ripping penetration. Against the skin of

98

your buttocks the object feels unnatural, cumbersome, big as a clenched fist, intrusive. But you don't dare to move or resist. You dampen those instincts. There was something in the way she bent you over the mattress that forewarned an equally swift but far more painful manoeuvre to make you submit – a finger bent back, a nerve squashed under vulnerable throat skin. So you just stand there and prepare yourself as best you can with shin bones pressed against the bunk frame, and hands wide apart but clenching the sheets.

'Now. Be warned. If you refuse to co-operate I can go right through you with this.' She nudges your anal bud with the club. 'But if you can steer yourself to seeing reason, to admitting your guilt in all matters, there will be no need to split you like a piece of soft fruit. In fact it can even get easier.' One of her hands reaches between your legs and holds your flaccid sex. The fingers are tightly clad in a leather glove. 'It could even be liberating. You know, to confess and get everything off your chest.'

'Yes,' you say in a trembling voice.

With an easy, slow, idle technique the hand massages your soft sex. She feels it grow in her hand. 'So can you see yourself co-operating?'

You nod. 'Yes. Yes.'

'I thought so. I could not believe anyone could be so stupid.'

'Just don't use that thing. Please.'

'This old boy?' Again, she pushes it against your anus. Hard enough to make you aware of its potential as a mining tool. You cry out for mercy.

'OK then. We have an understanding.'

Her hot breath, the weight of her bosom against your spine, the threat of being speared alive, the gentle hand between your legs makes your sex grow and grow until her fingers are forced apart and she says, 'Ooh. Ooh my.' And then, 'Mmm. That's good. Isn't that good? All

99

my boys like this. Even the big tough ones we sometimes get in here. They're never the same afterwards. They realise we only want the best for them. Want them to be happy in their work. Want them to be able to sit down and stand up while they pick up the shit from the streets. It's hard to work the litter patrol if you can't bend over.'

'Yes. Yes,' you say, and close your eyes with delight at the wonderful, effective, experienced hand at work on your manhood. She's done this before; has said as much. Likes her work. Likes the results. Is good at breaking down resistance. A big, curvaceous guardian who reprimands those big-talking runaways. Rubbing and softly squeezing you between her thumb and fingers, as if she's coaxing something to rise up the length and spray out the top, her hand speeds up. 'You'll confess to every charge. And you will show remorse when we turn the camera on.'

'Oh, yes. I mean yes. Yes, I'll do anything.' The leather of her glove becomes hot from friction. 'Definitely. Oh, that's good. Please don't stop.'

'Good. Now lick my fucking boots.' She releases your sex and seizes you by the nape of your neck. Pulling your face off the blanket, she inserts a booted foot before your face. 'Do it,' she says in a hissy voice. At once your tongue lathers the leather of her boot. Ankle, instep, heel, toe – your tongue wets her foot. Tasting shoe polish and something bitter like dusty floor wax, you close your eyes and forget all about resistance, about pride and shame. These women are too strong and clever; you could never beat them at anything. You tried to fool them and look at you now.

'On the floor. Lie on your back,' she says.

Clumsy in your ankle shackles and wrist cuffs, you obey, immediately moving into a prostrate position beside the bunk as she unstraps the implement from around her waist that so recently threatened to tear your insides apart. So there is mercy. You can only feel grateful to her for taking it off and will do anything to keep her calm.

'My feet are tired,' she says. 'They hurt in these boots. Been on my feet all day. And since you've shown me such a nice big tongue, I want you to soothe my feet. Find a use for that nasty little mouth of yours.' Over your face she unzips her boots and then places both chubby, fragrant feet on your face. It's hard to breathe with them pressing so hard against the bones of your brows and cheeks and nose and jaw, so you gasp mouthfuls of air as she rolls your head around the cement floor. 'Now that's good. You like it too. I can how pleased your little pee-pee is.' Three damp toes are pushed between your lips. So thankful for only a painless intrusion into your body, you suck and lick at her toes. You wash her soiled stockings with your mouth.

Pushing your debasement further and further, she then removes her feet from your face and zips the tight boots back up her legs before using you as a doormat. After wiping the gritty rubber soles of her boots on your stomach, she proceeds to walk up and down your body. Muscles tensing under her weight, you hold your breath as she nonchalantly steps from thigh to stomach to sternum to shoulder. But you don't complain; as she uses you as carpet, she also allows you the sweetener of an upskirt peek: a quick preview of the deep, shadowy, rustling secrets of her skirt. Offering the eternal cycle of corporate pain and seduction, exploiting every weakness, you marvel at their skill at mixing trauma and pain and humiliation with the promise of pleasures irresistible to the deprived and disempowered. Your eyes climb up the strong, broad legs in shiny nylon that stretch up to her pale inner thighs, whispering together over the ultimate prize that is finally unveiled when she steps off your body and stands above your face with her feet apart. Vast but carefully trimmed, you can even smell her sex. Then it comes closer.

Officer Smith rests her weight on her ankles and squats over your face. From her hot female insides, thick but clear ropes of her water fall and break across the bridge of your nose. And for a few seconds that feel like minutes watched on a clock, you are drenched, drowning, spluttering and swallowing as her bladder empties.

She then leaves you spitting in a steaming puddle and moves across to the door. She knocks the steel. Officer Dudley enters and closes the door behind her. The two women look at each other and smile.

'I'm glad the discussion went well,' the muscular Dudley says.

Officer Smith polishes her phallic strap-on device and then reattaches it to her belt. 'It did. I think I made progress. Really got through. He's eager to confess and I'm sure we'll never see him on the streets again. Have you anything to add, Officer Dudley?'

'Well. I'm curious about something. Have you noticed how it's always the losers from dogshit duty we get in here? The geeks in the white suits?'

'Now I've been thinking the same thing. The failures and the burn-outs are the biggest drain on security resources.' Clumsily, you rise to your feet and shake the excess brine from your face.

Jostling against you, the guards force you to fall back on the bed. You wince as your striped rump hits the mattress. Feeling giddy from the strength of their perfume and the sudden flood of the body's natural painkillers to your sore buttocks, you do not resist the younger officer as she unbuttons your suit. She raises one of her legs from the floor and pushes her shiny knee between your legs. Inside your soiled boiler suit, your erection maintains the true potential of its length and breadth. You swallow, both terrified and excited by the

102

presence of the tough, young guard's hands near your unwilting erection.

Your boiler suit is yanked open from your neck to crotch. Then Officer Dudley slips her leather-covered fingers inside the waistband of your briefs. She pulls them down below your tingling balls and then stares at your sex. 'See what I mean, Officer Smith? Just the same as it was during the search. No matter what you do to them, sooner or later we have to deal with this dirty thing.'

'You're not wrong there. Always the same,' her colleague says.

Red-faced from the total exposure, the powerlessness, and the fact that the thickened end of your sex is again hovering no more than a few inches from the fresh, red lips of Officer Dudley, you feel the skin of your entire torso goose. Her hard brown eyes stare into you. 'You know, some men actually run away from work to see their wives. But not many. Because the rest of you pathetic excuses for fugitives want to be caught. It's us girls in security you really want to see. You want to confess to us. And only us.'

'Damn right he did. He caused all that fuss tonight because he wanted a good going over. It's the sticks and the boots and the slapping they like.'

'No,' you blurt out.

'Well, if that's what he was after, then he shall bloody well get sticks and boots and slaps.' Dudley's face darkens with blood and she shows her teeth through a grimace. You feel a hand slip around your girth. The grip is firm. It begins to pump up and down the length of your shaft. 'I think there is something about us that makes them realise how weak they really are. How slow and stupid. Just big, dumb boys. They need direction. They need to be told what to do. Need a firm hand now and again. Oh, we understand all right.' Officer Dudley then raises her skirt to her slim, brown waist and straddles your groin. Eyes wide with shock, you stare at her muscle-cut thighs that stretch her nylons, and you gape at her naked sex perched a few inches above your straining phallus. From one of the smaller pouches on her belt she withdraws something made from steel chain. 'And we're always happy to oblige. It's what we're good at. It's why we're trusted. Given the responsibility. Isn't that right, Officer Smith?'

'It sure is. And it would be unprofessional to return him to the company without a bit of guidance. What would they think of us otherwise? We only send good boys back to do all that sweeping and polishing and washing and scrubbing and to pick up all that nasty litter. Boys who have seen the errors of their ways. Your superiors like to now that we're thorough. That you're in good hands down here. That the message will get through.' Your hands fist on the blankets as the first saw-tooth clamp is attached to your nipple. You then begin to pant as the second pair of surgical steel jaws are carefully attached to your chest.

'You bitch. You maniac. You –' But your mouth is struck hard, three times with the back of her leather hand. The blows leave you stunned. Fingers spread across your face and the palm of a small hand in a leather glove covers your nose. Officer Dudley then pushes your head deep into the mattress. With your feet on the floor, the remainder of your body is now stretched along the width of the bed. Assisting her partner, Officer Smith sits above your head, in a side-saddle position. She seizes your shoulders and presses them into the mattress. 'Don't worry. We've seen it all before. Many times,' she whispers, her face a grimace. 'You just stay put. Think on what I showed you earlier. What it felt like. So don't move until we're done or by God I'll make sure you leave here in a wheelchair. Understand?'

'Yes,' you say, but your voice is no more than a whisper between the pressing, squeezing fingers.

104

Between her legs, Officer Dudley inserts a hand and begins to rub herself. 'Did you think you were going to get this?' she says, with her fingertips busy on her mound. 'Is this what you ran away for? Mmm? A bit of pussy?' Her eyes are fixed on your suffering face and tortured nipples. The pretty, athletic sadist is enjoying your discomfort. Despite the profound smarting across your rump, the tang of urine in your mouth, the hot impression of the slaps across your cheeks and the humiliating exposure of your genitals in a prison cell, your erection not only survives but flourishes.

Holding your shaft at the base with one hand, so your sex is steady and upright, the small brunette rolls a pinky condom over your cock. Then she eases her muscular body down and over your sex. Her eyes roll back and she bites her bottom lip as you pass through her, from shiny head to base of shaft. Up and down, side to side the young officer then moves, taking her pleasure. Grinding you into the bed, taunting you with insults about the size of your sex and the pitiful nature of your life, you are engulfed and smothered and abused by her. Excited, she often tweaks the nipple clamps to make you shout out. A position you make no attempt to escape as the tight sex of Officer Dudley stretches and adjusts to a more comfortable fit over your meat. With her thighs you can feel her holding your hips still to keep your erect sex at a certain angle. In a steady, unchanging rhythm her hard body rises and falls. She breathes noisily through her perfect teeth.

Officer Smith begins to giggle like a much younger woman as she watches her colleague at work on you. Does your sex give them much pleasure? Or is it the nature of what they are doing that excites them so? You begin to gyrate your hips and to push your hard cock into the air, impatient for more friction from the tight but ever more slippery embrace of the tough guard's sex. Soon, her small and compact body is bouncing on and off your lap. She tries to talk; says something about you being a 'lively one' but she is unable to finish. She starts grunting instead as if she's punching or pumping dumbbells in the air. You realise this is an exercise for her. It's necessary and she likes to be aggressive, in control when she trains. It is a function; good for her body. And you are the equipment, nothing else. The thought makes you cry out. You come. Flooding upward in a scalding surge, you explode inside the small police officer. You have been used like a predictable, pre-programmed machine in a gymnasium. There is no affection or intimacy here; you are a stranger and she needs part of your body. She is detached, oblivious to how you feel, and yet she demands this workout from your body and is inspired by your supplication. The revelation thrills you. Gripping the nipple clamps with her fingers, her entire body shakes from her climax in your lap. You hear her call you a 'bastard' at least four times while she shudders on top of you.

After she has finished, there is a moment of inactivity when your exhausted body lies still and Officer Dudley's head is dipped over her chest. Smiling, she looks at you before punching you in the stomach. Coughing, you watch her climb off your softening sex. From over your head, Officer Smith removes the condom. 'Ooh. Look at all this,' she says.

Before they leave you in the dark, you watch them share the booty.

Career History: Part 9

Investment Opportunity

You cannot sleep. It's the anxiety of tomorrow and the sounds of the prison at night that keep you awake. In a cell two doors down, a man's voice cries out. First in rage: 'Bitches! Evil bitches!' Before it lowers to despair: 'How can this be happening? My wife is a good woman. Please, for the sake of my wife, I'll do anything. It was a simple mistake. Slipped my mind. It was only a bloody fax.' Reminded of some recently suffered injustice at the hands of the corporation and its minions, he then climbs out of bed and begins tearing at the bunk.

In response, you hear a single pair of boot heels clip down the cement corridor outside. This is followed by the clanging of steel as a reinforced door is unlocked. You hear the voice of a guard: the big matron who milked you over the bed as if you were some bovine creature in a pen. 'Now, this is not what I said, is it? Not what I asked for.' Her voice is tense, ready to rise and expand with fury. You know that tone of voice well.

'I have to get out. I can't stand it any more. Please. Please. Please,' the man cries. And through the stone walls you hear the whistle of a cane. Again and again it falls and ends in a muffled whump-sound as the thin, black stick finds its target. When the cane ceases to fall, there are new sounds of shuffling feet, the scrunch of bed springs and the occasional sob. The guard then

107

leaves a silent cell. Outside your door, her footsteps stop and the viewing panel is swished open. Lying absolutely still, facing the wall with your eyes closed, you pretend to sleep. All over your body, the welts seem to enlarge and rise off your skin in her presence; you imagine the marks on your flesh to be bright red in the dark and hot to the touch. The viewing panel is then closed and the sound of the guard's footsteps retreat from the passage.

A few minutes later, the occupant of the cell opposite you begins to talk. At first you think he is speaking to you or holding a conversation with someone inside his cell, but then you feel cold all over and are forced to swallow when you realise this is nothing more than a monologue of a mind unwound. 'You were never supposed to see it. My secret. They were all I had. Once I had a wife, but she went off with someone else. I got home from work as usual and things had changed. She had changed. So I took those beautiful things from your bin to remind me of a woman's smell, of her touch, her perfume. I had nothing else for comfort. You see, down in the barracks there are only men. There is nothing to remind us of what we once had. We were all starving. Dying for it. Oh, understand. Do you not know mercy? Any of you? How can women of such beauty be so cruel?

'Don't you see? That's why the fights broke out over my secret, my treasure. Everybody wanted to touch them and kiss them and smell them. It was full of you. I mean, you didn't want them any more. They were something you had snagged and just thrown away. Never gave them another thought. But for me they were special. I rescued them from the rubbish. I saw them as a gift, all curled up and silky in the waste paper. Like it was a pretty serpent who had made a nest. A beautiful thing that had been so close to your skin. They had been on your legs and feet. Your feet had been in those spiky shoes. The black ones that hypnotised me. I was bewitched by you. I worshipped you through this gift. Put my lips to it. At night, I could still smell you . . .'

You cover your ears. It's like some horrible reminder of what you will become. The anonymous prisoner's words create a vivid and detailed picture of your future. It seems more real than any other scenario you try to imagine. But some strange comfort can be drawn from the realisation that you are not the only individual who has been unable or refused to conform to the bizarre credo of this town. You recall science fiction stories about the paranoia and alienation of an individual in a once familiar situation, when everyone around him and everything once ordinary and familiar gradually changes to something sinister, though veiled by its apparent innocence and its illusion of the mundane. It has actually happened to you; the outsider trapped on the inside of an insane but perfectly successful system.

Outside in the corridor, you hear another set of footfalls. These are quiet. Immediately, you physically wince in sympathy for the mad figure opposite. The footsteps stop outside his cell and the observation slot is opened. 'Ssh,' a calming voice soothes. 'Here. Take these. They're for you.'

You hear the bare feet of the inmate pad across the cement floor of his cell. 'For me? My treasure returned?'

'New treasure,' the woman says. You recognise the voice of the captain. 'But you must be quiet. Can you be quiet?'

'Oh, I can smell them. Yes, mistress. Yes. You're an angel. I won't make a sound. I can smell the perfume. Thank you. Thank you. Thank you . . .' The inmate returns to his bunk, giggling like a child with whatever gift has been passed through the observation slot. The captain's footsteps make their way to your door. You hold your breath as the door is unlocked. Light from the corridor falls inside your cell; you feel it creep over the bedclothes. Then the door is shut, swiftly.

Unable to lie still with your back exposed to a potential threat, you sit up on your bunk. 'It wasn't me. I never made a sound,' you say to the presence in the dark.

'Be quiet,' she whispers. A torch is switched on. The beam blinds you. Behind the powerful light, you hear her voice. 'You are not alone,' she says. 'There are others who share your frustration. Your passion for revenge. They will contact you when you return to the corporation. You are needed for something important.'

It takes a while to fully comprehend what the captain is saying. And here of all places, in a chamber where so much torment and pleasure has been dispensed in the interest of control. It can't be. It must be a trap to test your loyalty. 'No,' you say. 'I don't believe it.'

'I'm sorry for what has happened. I did not dare interfere. Everything must carry on as usual. The suspicions of the other officers cannot be raised. Speak to no one of this meeting.' Her voice is sincere and she is tense, nervous, taking a risk. If what she says is genuine there are so many questions you want to ask. Hope dares to build again inside you. And the prospect of this new alliance, of an end to the isolation makes you tremble. You try to keep your voice calm. 'Who are they? How will I know?'

'There will only be one contact initially. More than one is not safe. Our communications are passed from one stranger to another. A network has been created. The word moves through each connection of the resistance and information is passed back down. Vital information that will damage the company.'

'But what do you want from me? What can I do?'

'Everyone has a role. Your will be a go-between. Someone will approach you and ask, "Can I put this somewhere?" They will be holding a cigarette. Once you take the cigarette, the connection is established. Others will follow. They will bring computer discs and CD

110

ROMs. Maybe printouts. You are to keep them all until a handover is arranged.'

'Where?' you ask in a thin voice. 'Where will I keep them? It's not safe. The barracks are searched.'

'Use you initiative. You got out tonight, didn't you?'

You fill with pride. Maybe tonight wasn't such a disaster. The resistance admire your ingenuity and courage. You have been singled out and selected. You have a purpose. What do you have to lose? 'OK,' you say. 'I'll do my bit. You can count on me.'

The captain breathes out with relief. 'Thank you. My instincts were correct. I was sure you would help. That I could rely on you. That you were brave. You know the risk I took in coming to you with this. I am your sponsor. I now rely on your discretion.'

You feel flattered; are unable to think of anything to say to this beautiful, uniformed ally.

'I don't have long now. So listen carefully. I will tell you how to stay safe. In Environment Services you are disempowered, you have no freedom, but you will move around the building on your cleaning duties. In the communal areas. Toilets, stairwells, carparks, the grounds. In time, tonight's infraction will be forgotten. They will always allow you one breakout attempt if you were married. But from now on, you will be humble, obedient, servile if necessary. Make them believe your will is broken. That they own you. It's the best possible cover and the only thing they will accept.'

'But . . . but what about my wife? I think she needs help. She's not herself.'

'Forget about her. She is not your wife any more. She's already registered as a divorcee.'

'They can do that?'

'They can do anything. She has already entered the suburban breeding programme. There is no going back for her. Unlike you, she had a choice. At least, she thought it was a choice. All that need concern you now

111

is your role in the resistance. Mention it to no one. Wait for your moment, then do your mission well.' She walks back towards the door and turns off the torch. 'Stay away from the water sprinklers and smoke sensors. They are the eyes and ears of our enemy.' Before she vanishes from the cell, she leaves you with her final remarks. 'Never underestimate the company. My safety is now your responsibility, as yours is mine.'

Company Profile 3

Selection Criteria

Magenta is the first to arrive at the meeting I scheduled in my office. And no matter how many times I have seen her in the past twelve-month period, in which she has run one of my two departments, I'm always struck by the same thing: her beauty. It never fails to disarm. Being six feet tall without shoes and even higher in heels, no doubt she is long accustomed to the attention her figure draws. But to be blessed with a strange beauty to complement these superhuman dimensions – this exaggeration of nobility she possesses through her Mediterranean looks, the long thin nose and those eyes of a startling width and impenetrable darkness – she does more than merely stand out, she stuns, instantly, both men and women. On meeting her for the first time, in that all-important moment when so many judgements are made, one is likely to pause, hesitate, clear the throat, become transfixed as if before a hypnotic and unworldly creature.

And much is expected of one with beauty. At once assumptions are made by the onlooker in the part of the mind that dreams. She is invested with magic – it is always presumed that she is special, better in all things. A man, particularly, casts his own spell and bewitches himself. And, from my observations, it appears that such beauty only becomes dangerous when the endowed is not only aware of their magnetism but has sufficient intelligence to manipulate those they attract. It is a power few can imagine. I sometimes wonder who Magenta's first victims were – teachers, babysitters, coaches or schoolboys perhaps? Because there have been many victims since she has worked for me. And was this incredible set of expectations also created when she was young? Because, like any goddess, part of Magenta is still a child at the centre of the world. She simply wants it all. She wants different things at different times; her appetite swiftly changes in accordance with her moods. Magenta has whims. Little patience is shown with the world when it occasionally refuses to bend to her will. And pouting, sulking and brooding fails to detract from her charms. In fact, her displeasure inspires the very opposite reaction. When Magenta is dissatisfied one's infatuation deepens, one promises anything, sacrifice one's own safety and will just to make that imperious princess smile again. And that would be the last mistake one could make, because Magenta is quickly dismissive of those who fall under her spell, while being even harder on those who refuse or cannot succumb. She can never be pleased and a suitor can never win. And this combination of beauty, ambition and a manipulative intelligence has made her cruel. In her department, I've watched her terrorise her subordinates until even I was forced to turn my face away from the sweating faces, the cries for help, the liquescent sound of a lash, the muffled screams. On several occasions I was tempted to intercede on the behalf of the victim, but always found myself drawing back and allowing her strategy to play itself out. Because she is not a mindless sadist; her flair for intimidation is specifically targeted and always produces results. It was even tactical the way she once drew blood on the office floor. Swiftly, she suppressed a rumour of dissent. There was also the matter of a naked male body, found trussed in masking tape inside a storage cupboard after a long weekend in the dark. Never again did one of her subordinates make a formal complaint. We mustn't forget the sweet girl from human resources, hog-tied in her own pantyhose and publicly displayed, who fell foul of Magenta's will when she refused to dock the wages of the entire department for missing an impossible deadline. But the time she spat into the eyes of a visiting executive, while cupping his fragile balls inside the cage of her long fingers, must be my favourite example of her policy. And, although diffusing the aftermath of the controversial incident stretched the very limits of my power, her action did convince a major competitor to move elsewhere. While in my service, she has proven herself to be ruthless, insensitive and maniacally driven by the certainty of her own brilliance. I have been a good teacher.

Sadie arrives next and precisely at the given time. Politely the two girls nod at each other. 'Hope I'm not late,' Sadie says, knowing full well she is punctual.

'Not at all, my dear,' I say. 'Magenta was here early. Do take a seat.' This makes Magenta look overly eager and she will interpret my comment to be a slight on her character: an accusation of anxiety, desperation or sycophancy. Magenta's full lips stiffen; she raises her long jaw then forces a smile. Not once does she look at Sadie, her rival.

Now Sadie, who commands the second department under my charge, beguiles mortals with more subtle strategies. Petite and blonde and svelte, her body knows no physical injustice either. But, unlike Magenta, she has the temperament of a saint to match the shape of an angel. One feels an urge to put her inside a small, ornamental cage made from thin gold bars, to keep and protect and adore her, to go home every evening and peer through the cage at her perfect hands and feet and face and bones, to own and to worship. She wins the

115

hearts of her employees with patience, understanding, compassion, sweetness, affection. Encouraging all, never forsaking tact or care, she has yet to raise her sweet voice in anger. A smile from Sadie inspires her subordinates to work harder; enthusiasm spreads through the office and attention to detail becomes obsessive. A sweet yawn can draw a group of eager faces to her desk, offering themselves to reduce her burden; the swift crossing of one slender knee across another will reduce men to the lovelorn condition of royal courtiers, stricken by the conflict between romantic love and baser urges. The exemplary performance of Sadie's department has matched the results of Magenta's team but through entirely different methods. And over the temporary wall that separates Sadie's domain from Magenta's realm, many times have I seen the drawn faces of the oppressed look across with envious eyes at their contented peers. There is something mythical about this divide; something reminiscent of Olympus and the underworld, of heaven and hell, an eternal balance.

They are my favourites. Of all the senior executives in my department no one else has ever filled me with so much pride. Efficient, fiercely loyal to me, talented, well-educated, refined, cultivated: who could choose between them? And my two girls, my darling girls, are now sitting before my desk to await the most important decision of their career. Their two departments are set to merge and I am permitted one executive to deputise over my territory. But which one will I choose? Someone is going to be upset this morning.

'Magenta. Sadie.' I look at each girl in turn and give nothing away. I have to pretend this is an opportunity for each of them to grasp a new challenge; that it will not make a detrimental, devastating difference to either one of their futures. But of course it will. Magenta would never allow herself to be overlooked and to take orders from the sweet blonde, the woman every member of Magenta's staff dearly wishes their own boss resembled. And Sadie could never survive in an environment of intimidation and fear that is the natural habitat of Magenta; she would immediately be seen as a threat and destroyed. Each knows that only one can remain in the department; behind those sweet smiles there is turmoil. And I must choose wisely; today I gain a new captain, but I lose a good lieutenant.

'We all know why we are here. This is an exciting opportunity for each of you.' They both nod as if grateful. I prolong the preliminaries, enjoying the tension and discomfort. I too was once in their present situation and all the time longed to be on the other side of the desk. Now I am. 'Of course only one of you can take the lead and be the executor for my will. A director, let's say, for my creative vision.' Sadie's smile broadens, perhaps to compensate for her nerves. Magenta's eyes narrow; she knows what I am doing and hates me for it. 'But the unsuccessful candidate can remain an invaluable partner for her senior colleague. Let's say, the right-hand woman in all things. An adviser, consultant, ally. That is, if there is a desire for such things.' Magenta's lips tighten in anger at the very notion: Sadie nods in agreement, but her usually graceful neck appears uncommonly stiff at the thought of managing Magenta's chaotic behaviour. 'My decision has not been an easy one. Originally, I chose well when I invited each of you to manage the two sections of my corporate responsibility. And, as a result, I have been blessed by the excellence of your leadership. And your work is applauded by those above me.' The girls nod in acknowledgement but the tension is becoming unbearable; one of Sadie's perfect eyelids has begun to spasm and Magenta's knuckles are white where her fingers squeeze the chair. 'Of course your approaches to staff management and office supervision differ.' Sadie breathes out, convinced her moral high-ground gives her the edge. Magenta pouts with defiance (I can almost hear her soft Brazilian accent saying, 'You wanted results, I gave them to you,' before she hurls a computer monitor through a plate-glass window). 'But each has been equally effective.' I smile and clasp my hands together. 'My darlings, my executive daughters, please appreciate my dilemma as I tell you the results of my long deliberations.'

'Of course. It must be so hard for you,' Sadie says, her voice a sing-song of sympathy.

Magenta says nothing; her eyes remain suspicious, challenging.

'Well, why don't I just get it over with.' I laugh in an inappropriate light-hearted way.

Both the girls stop breathing. Every sinew and nerve fibre in their bodies suddenly tightens.

'Taking charge of the sub-departmental merger, becoming my immediate subordinate in all things, enjoying all of the material and fringe benefits of the next executive level, I have decided to promote . . .' I pause and look deeply, sincerely into each of their eyes ' . . . Magenta, as my new deputy.'

Silence and then an exhale from the long Latin nose of my marvellous, dangerous Magenta. A gulp from inside the thin neck of angelic Sadie. The poor darling; all of the blood has drained from her usually healthy face. But she still finds enough of her sweet voice to say, 'Congratulations,' and to smile at her rival. But Magenta, her new superior, ignores her. 'Thank you, ma'am,' she says, looking at me – the only person who really matters to her now.

'The stipulations of a deputy director's position are effective immediately,' I say to Magenta. 'A contract will be forwarded to you via the internal post.' Then I turn my attention to the blanched face of Sadie. 'Sadie, please continue as normal until you receive a new directive from Magenta.' But I wonder whether she is

118

listening; she seems ready to cry, or to cry out that I must have made some kind of mistake, that I must be insane to inflict the satanic temperament of Magenta on even more innocent, working lives. But she wouldn't dare. Noble to the last, she says nothing. I feel for her, but how could I favour the harmony and magic of her management when it differs so much from my own style? Not once has she used the executive cane she has been thoroughly trained to wield. And she allows her staff too much room to discuss and suggest and cajole and breathe. Magenta is a younger, more energetic model of myself; she has already striped the skin of all her subordinates, both male and female. At night they dream of her and when they wake, they scream.

Now the girls have important business to attend to so I excuse them. Words need to be spoken. A new arrangement must be brokered. I have done my part. What was once equal is now unequal. This endless struggle to succeed and achieve in every office in our magnificent building, to rise one floor at a time until you reach the sky, to prosper while others fail, to be an accessory to injustice, has momentarily reached a decisive moment in the lives of these two bright and talented women. It is the way we do things here. Sadie cannot be simply moved to another senior position elsewhere, because then the victor will be denied a true victory and the taste of blood in her beautiful mouth. No, even the brilliant must fall for the successful rival to devour their spirit, to be empowered by their demise. No job is safe. But opportunities must appear to be endless for the ambitious.

Sadie clears her throat. 'Thank you, ma'am.' She will scurry to the executive bathroom; she needs time to think, to comprehend what has befallen her, to prepare her staff for Magenta's tyranny and the enforced change of allegiance that must follow for all of them. Then she must clear her desk and flee for her car. She has heard of the terrible fates of the fallen. By being perfect, by accounting for everything, she never suspected she could fail. Her beauty and grace and superior mind have brought her thus far and it was incomprehensible that these attributes could not take her right to the top. And now, stripped of power and influence, she must either beg for her survival or flee.

Magenta allows Sadie to leave my office. Then she stands and thanks me. We shake hands. Already, I see her thinking of her next move. For she must act swiftly; must deal with Sadie decisively before her sympathetic underlings can question my decision and bond further with their fallen leader. Head back, spine straight, Magenta leaves me in silence.

After the girls are gone I make myself comfortable in my leather chair. From my top drawer I retrieve my biggest sex aid. All of this intrigue and tension has excited me. Under my desk, I hike my skirt up to my hips. Opening my legs, I tease the inside of my thighs with the polished, black head of the latex organ. It makes tiny ripples in my stockings and my sex tingles in anticipation from the mere sight of it. Biting my fingers to stop myself from crying out with pleasure, I force the moist lips of my sex apart with the domed head. Reclining the chair, I stretch my long legs out. I kick my tight shoes off. Then I slip at least another three swollen inches of the vessel inside. It feels like a forearm and clenched fist has entered me. The discomfort is exquisite. Under the jacket of my suit, I reach with the long fingers of one hand to find my nipples. Through my thin blouse I can feel the little, hard clamps I applied to my flesh earlier. They are made from steel and bite my pink teats like little snakes. I give them a tweak and my eyes fill with salty water. Then I shove the rest of the baton inside my stretched birth passage so I am writhing in my chair.

Impaled and breathing slowly I gradually accustom myself to the intrusion. On the screen of my monitor, I then select the security option. In my sector, only I have access to the surveillance: the hidden cameras and microphones in every computer on every desk, and in every office or communal facility. No phone conversation, no electronic mail, no sigh of annoyance, no flicker of disobedience on a harassed face, no whisper in a store room or toilet cubicle is inaccessible to me. And now, with bitten nipples and a pierced sex, I intend to watch and enjoy this conflict of my own making.

'Oh, it's you. I was about to come and see you.' Sadie is forcing herself to remain calm, to maintain dignity, to not panic, to keep her mind clear when Magenta enters the executive female toilet and wedges the entrance shut by stuffing a clipboard under the door.

Magenta is smiling. 'This is as good a place as any. The walls of the offices are thin. And this is between us. The rest will know soon enough.'

The two girls begin to circle each other. Stiletto heels make little scraping noises on the tiles. Sadie inches towards the door, but Magenta stands firm. 'The door?' Sadie says. 'I'd prefer to keep it open.'

Magenta looks hurt. 'But people, they come in and out. And we must talk.'

'We have no secrets,' Sadie says, concerned by the absence of an escape route, but confused by Magenta's smile. 'And I can assure you that I will clear my desk and be off the premises by lunch. All I ask is that you let me say goodbye to my staff. We've come a long way together.'

'Of course, Sadie. Of course. And I want to thank you for training them so well. I look forward to working with them.' And it is here that Magenta's expression changes. Almost imperceptibly there is a widening of the mouth and the gradual extension of the fingers of one hand. Against the white marble floor you can see the dark blots of her crimson fingernails. Her other hand she keeps concealed behind her back.

Sadie is aware of Magenta's reaction but will not allow herself to be intimidated; she keeps her delicate chin up and her smile constant. 'You must appreciate this news has come as something of a shock to me.'

Magenta takes a step forward and Sadie backs away until her backside touches the wash basins; there are four basins below one long mirror. 'I sympathise,' Magenta says. 'But you are so calm. I admire your control. If it were I who had been treated in such a way, the whole company would have known by now that Magenta was an unhappy girl.' She laughs. 'But you, pretty Sadie, are always so serene. Maybe I could learn from you. Maybe not.' She takes another step forward until there is only a narrow space between them. Sadie is forced to look into those beautiful, unforgiving eyes.

Magenta tilts her head to one side. 'But all this talk of your leaving, it makes me so sad. Why must she go? I think to myself. The company still needs her. She could do anything, go anywhere. No?'

'You're too kind.'

Magenta giggles. 'They do not say that is one of my virtues.' She produces a parcel from behind her back that until now she has kept hidden. She passes the brightly wrapped package from one hand to another. 'But I have an idea, Sadie. To suit you and me. An arrangement.'

Sadie struggles to believe Magenta. You can tell she is confused by the way she swallows and makes a short, sweet laugh. But hope has also dared to enter the young woman's spirit. This is unexpected. Too much to believe. Dare she trust her old rival? 'Well, thank you. I don't know what to say. It's very generous of you. Of course I will consider any offer. My options are open.' Sadie laughs again; this time it sounds shrill.

Magenta reaches out and strokes Sadie's hair. 'Always so polite.' She looks at the ceiling as if seeking me, her sponsor. 'I love this girl. I could never let her go. I would miss her so much.' Sadie becomes uncomfortable with the hand against her hair. She moves away. Magenta looks hurt for a moment, then forces a smile. 'And I bring you this present.' Magenta holds out the beautifully packaged gift. The parcel is flat and square. The arrogance of the girl makes me smile; she knew in advance she would be chosen for the position and she has prepared for this moment with her fallen rival.

Sadie cannot contain her relief and feels guilty for her distrust. She shakes her head, smiling. 'For me? You really didn't have to. Oh.' She sniffs. 'I could cry.'

'A few tears is not so bad,' Magenta says, her voice purring. 'It is all part of change. Open it. It took me a long time to find something suitable. Something to help you, in your new job. The position I am offering you.'

Carefully, Sadie unties the bow and unfolds the wrapping paper. But then stares, dumbstruck, at the pink catering uniform in her hands. There is a little white cap too that complements the dress coat. She has seen these uniforms whenever she dines in the executive restaurant. Women wear them; sullen, shy women who refuse to meet her eyes across the lunch counter and seem surprised when she offers them a kind word, or asks them how they are feeling on that particular day.

Clearly in shock, Sadie is not aware that the wrapping paper has slipped from her hands and fallen to the floor. 'I . . . I don't understand,' she says, but her voice is no more than a ghost of its former sweet tones.

'Why, there is nothing to understand. It has all been arranged. You have no worries now. No need for a CV. No networking. And this way I can see you every day, and know you are close and still doing the good work for the company you love so much. Put it on. See if it fits you. You are so tiny and you start work tonight. There is little time for alterations.'

Sadie turns and drops the candy-pink uniform in a sink unit behind her. Facing Magenta again, she maintains a civil tone. 'I thank you for the opportunity, but I'm afraid I must decline.'

'Put the dress on.' Magenta is no longer smiling. Her face has paled and her forehead has smoothed. This face I have seen many times. And it's as if her eyes are seeing things with a new significance while those around her are blind to the truth. These jungle-cat eyes pierce and penetrate, they see and believe their own version of events and there is nothing anyone can do to stop this distortion.

Sadie does not meet Magenta's unmoving, unblinking stare, but looks past her towards the door as if to avert her eyes from something deeply unpleasant. 'I'm sure you have my best interests at heart, but you simply cannot expect me to work in the kitchens.'

'You are too good to serve your superiors? No?'

'I meant nothing detrimental about the occupation. But it is not for me. I am a investment executive. Until an hour ago, a corporate manager. Now, if you will excuse me, I would like to get on.' But as Sadie tries to pass Magenta, a long finger reaches between her breasts, finds her sternum and holds her still. Pressure applied through this digit pushes the petite blonde back against the washbasins. Mouth open in disbelief, Sadie looks down her body at the finger. Magenta removes her hand. 'I am not used to repeating myself. But you are upset, so I will overlook it this time. Now, put the dress on.'

Sadie glares at the haughty face before her. 'No. I will not.'

There is a pause when all the air and space of the bathroom seems to be sucked inward towards the pair of women who stand so close together. Then it is released outwards like a shock wave as Magenta slaps Sadie hard, four times, twice across each cheek. Her broad, tanned hands, swinging from left and right, carry sufficient force to upset Sadie's hair from its immaculate, almost bridal, arrangement at the back of her skull. Long strands of baby-blonde hair streak across her crimson face.

Magenta then controls herself sufficiently to speak, slowly and quietly, so even if she cannot be heard, her lips will be read. 'Put it on.'

The shattered glass of Sadie's perception repairs itself and she sees Magenta glaring down at her, the assailant's heavy breasts rising and falling with emotion under her silky blouse. 'No. Damn you. No,' she says through her little square teeth, now clenched into a snarl. 'I'd eat my own shit before I served you food.' And Sadie finishes with a long, silvery streak of spittle that passes from her pouting, pinkish mouth to splash on Magenta's left cheek.

Up in my office, this causes me to cover my own mouth with surprise. I never knew Sadie was capable of losing her temper, let alone swearing or spitting. But such an outburst has been a long time coming. I can see that. Even Magenta is stunned. But not for long. 'You speak with a dirty mouth. Because you are an ungrateful slut. A spoilt baby who does not like to lose.' Her hands shoot forward and clench on Sadie's disordered blonde locks. She then begins to wrench the smaller girl's head from side to side, as if trying to pull her head off and shake her body to pieces at the same time.

Forming the time-honoured hand-hold of female combatants, Sadie's slender arms then reach forward and seize handfuls of Magenta's glossy curls. With all her strength, Sadie tugs Magenta's head down, hard. To meet and destroy the broad Brazilian face, Sadie thrusts her knee upward. But her pencil skirt is too tight for such a move and all she succeeds in doing is exposing her undergarments. The split at the rear of her skirt becomes a ragged gash from knee to waist, causing the silk of her skirt and the satin of her slip to ride up her thighs, shimmery in flesh-tinted stockings.

125

Now with more freedom to move her legs, Sadie again tries to yank Magenta's face down to her little knee. Only this time the taller girl is ready. She screams as some of her hair rips, but manages to stop and then hold Sadie's leg by the thigh. Sheer nylon runs in both directions as Magenta's claws go through the thin fabric. Holding the thigh and then seizing Sadie's other leg, she bends her own legs into a squat and then lifts Sadie's diminutive body from the floor tiles before depositing her into a sink.

Stripping her jacket off, in preparation for combat, Magenta then steps clear of Sadie's kicking heels. She wears elegant, black sling-back shoes on her tiny feet, but the three-inch heels could go through a side of beef and Magenta is wise to stay clear of them. In the past they have often been a preferred weapon for her.

Struggling to free her tiny bottom from the marble basin, Sadie shrieks with exasperation and takes her eyes off Magenta for a second. It's all the Latin aggressor needs. Immediately, Magenta charges and gets between Sadie's legs to eliminate the threat of a spiked shoe. Once again Sadie's little hands sink into Magenta's tousled curls. The manoeuvre is allowed and while Sadie's hands are engaged in pulling and tearing, Magenta grits her teeth against the sting and rips Sadie's blouse apart from collar to waist.

'Bitch!' Sadie screams. But she is also unable to prevent Magenta from reaching down and knocking her shoes from her pretty toes. Sadie's heels clatter uselessly against the floor tiles. Unshod, she looks smaller than ever and her torn and shredded clothes seem to symbolise the tatters of her defences.

'I kill you, bitch! I kill you!' Magenta's scream of rage momentarily distorts the transmission of sound from the ceiling microphones. Sadie's hands are knocked aside. Strands of black hair drift from Sadie's pinkish finger-nails. Magenta's scarlet talons then sink down through soft blonde silk and lock at the scalp. Yanked out of the sink by her hair, Sadie is then wrestled to the tiled floor where she squirms on her back. She begins to squeal as the aggressor sits astride her stomach and traps her arms against her ribs with powerful thighs.

Magenta then takes a moment to catch her breath and to rake her tousled fringe from her eyes. 'You are a little slut. You are not a leader. No. You thought you could take me on. Thought you could hurt me? But you are a pussy. A *puta*. You are nothing now. No money. No power. Nothing. You think I don't know what you say about me?'

'I said nothing,' Sadie says.

'Bitch, liar, whore, traitor, I fuck you up!' Magenta back-hands Sadie's face twice. 'Now we see Miss Goody-Goody wiping tables and we all say, "She is not so smart." Eh? She gonna get down on her knees and scrub those floors, eh? Wash those dishes. Soon, you gonna look like an old woman. You gonna peel potatoes for ever. I see to it. And then everybody says, "Look at Sadie. This is what happens when you fuck with Magenta." It is brilliant. What do you say?'

'No. Please. I'll leave. Leave the town. I won't say a word. I promise. I'll do anything. Just let me go. You made your point. You won. You're the best. The strongest. It's you. Now just let me up.' Sadie speaks slowly. She is tired of struggling. Struggling against the grain of the company creed and against her own dark side. Now, all she wants is to crawl off somewhere where she can dwell on her foolishness.

'Never.' Magenta then leans down and kisses Sadie. And this time, to my inexhaustible surprise, Sadie allows the intimate contact. And she says nothing when those broad lips kiss across her cheeks and settle to nip at her throat. If I am not mistaken, Sadie's lips even part to release a sigh. When Magenta returns her mouth to the lips of her former combatant, Sadie responds to

127

that soft mouth with little licks and kisses of her own. Astonished, I watch this private moment, this unforeseen change in attitude, this awakening of desire in the vanquished.

'I hate myself,' Sadie says. 'I failed.'

Magenta nods in sympathetic agreement with her and then kisses her even more passionately.

'No, you don't understand,' Sadie says. 'I did things my own way. Resisted the discipline. Thought there could be another way. And I was wrong. I deluded myself.'

'You did,' Magenta whispers. 'And you missed out on so much. Such pleasures. As I am taking now. All of this was yours to exploit. Your people expected it. They wanted it.'

What Sadie, that adorable girl, then says brings a tear to my eye. Eyes glassy and staring into some distance most would be afraid to peer into, she leans forward and kisses Magenta on the tip of her magnificent nose and says, 'Make me hurt.'

Magenta laughs. She dips her face to Sadie and noisily kisses the blonde girl's mouth, forcing her tongue deep. Stroking Sadie's face, she then begins to whisper to her, 'Oh, my poor baby. My pretty girl. See why I cannot let you go? Why I need you. Need you to be my bitch. To take it in the sweet blonde ass from me, from Magenta.'

'Hurt me!' Sadie screams.

Magenta presses a hand over Sadie's mouth. 'Ssh. Hush, little baby. You have to be strong. You got to be a big girl, cos I am gonna hurt you. Teach you why Magenta is best. Then you gonna go and tell your staff that they work for me. Do as I say. Yes?'

Eye make-up running and lipstick smudged, blouse and skirt reduced to rags, stockings laddered, hair straggling around her clawed cheeks and neck, Sadie offers herself as a sacrifice. The fight has gone from her delicate body. Those little fists are no longer clenched and the strength has passed from those pretty legs and arms. She belongs to Magenta now and wants to be punished for her failing.

Muttering and laughing to herself, the Brazilian victor carefully removes the torn blouse, skirt and wrinkled slip from inert Sadie. Then she peels the girl's stockings down her legs before snapping them from her toes. With the hosiery, she ties the girl's ankles together, using a knot that would only yield to a blade. Removing her own spike heels, Magenta slips a long foot under Sadie's chin and tickles her throat as she rolls the first of her own stockings down to her ankle. They are black and seamed and stronger and appear altogether more suited to holding something still. Above Sadie's knees, Magenta makes a loop with her stocking, draws it tight and finishes it off with another formidable knot. Then she guides the compliant Sadie on to her stomach before removing her second stocking. With this nylon she binds the girl's slender wrists.

Stepping out of her panties, Magenta then pushes her skirt down to her knees. 'There will be a time for you to talk soon,' she says affectionately to the girl lying between her feet. 'But for now, I put these in your mouth.' Magenta stretches her panties between her long fingers in front of Sadie's eyes. 'I hope you like the taste.' Sadie's heavy breathing is immediately muffled by the transparent satin which is tied off at the base of her skull. 'Deep down, my angel, if you are honest with yourself, I know you have wanted to taste the pussy of a stronger woman for a long time. Trust me. I know what you want. So let Magenta take the pressure in this career while you taste pussy. It is for the best.'

Kneeling beside the girl who no longer offers any struggle, Magenta eases her on to her back. 'For the others I use a cane. Or I use the belt. Whatever. But for you, my friend, I want it to be more intimate. So I use my hand.' Raising Sadie's feet into the air, she exposes her naked buttocks. They are small and white, soft as lamb skin. Magenta nods knowingly, lost in some inner discourse as some fact is proven, another obstacle overcome, another desire sated.

And the blows are hard; you can tell by the sound and by the echo that spanks off the marble and steel of a corporate bathroom. You could count to two thousand between each blow as the broad hand rises and then drops suddenly. In an instant, all motion and energy is transferred from the hard, flat palm to the vulnerable cheeks which give a little shudder after every slap. Whimpers escape from behind the satin panties, now clenched between Sadie's teeth. Pink and then red, her buttocks colour. But the blows still rain in and it's as if Magenta is lost to the world; she stares out and somehow inwardly at the same time. Even when Sadie's tiny rump has bruised a dark crimson, the hand still keeps falling. The flesh must have gone numb because, soon, Sadie no longer cries.

No one speaks for a while after the punishment is finished. Magenta repairs her hair and make-up over by the sinks. Then she straightens her skirt and slips her naked feet back inside her shoes. After brushing the worst creases from her jacket, she withdraws a minia-ture straight-razor from the inside of her jacket. Bending over, she cuts the bindings from Sadie's ankles, knees and hands. But the girl continues to lie on the toilet floor. 'Finish me,' Sadie whispers.

Magenta smiles and then stands over Sadie's face before squatting down with her thighs apart. 'OK,' she says. 'Open your mouth and we can put an end to this part of your life. We can wash away your mistake.'

Sadie obeys.

'Close your eyes,' she instructs in a patient tone of voice.

Sadie obeys.

'Now I finish you.'

And there is no sound of protest from Sadie or any attempt to move her head when the thick, clear rope of her mistress's water cascades down and splashes off her pretty face.

Hair restyled but far from the usual perfection, the pink catering uniform snug on her slight figure, Sadie walks through her old department for the last time. As ever, she walks with grace and poise and with a neutral smile fixed on her pretty face, but things have changed for her. All of her staff can see that. In this place where no more than an hour earlier she was a leader, she comes to them dressed as a canteen assistant, as a slave; displaced, defeated, humiliated and parts of her body still briny with piss.

Men swallow and shake their heads; women hold hands over their open mouths in shock. Some begin to weep. And then, faces full of hate begin to look towards the door of my office; they know this is my doing. But behind that door, I smile as I push my toy harder and deeper inside my sex. They can do nothing. They will never protest again. And they should savour this moment because any reminiscing of the way things were, or discussion of their new leader, or even any mention of Sadie's name could result in any one of them sharing this same fate in the uniform of the services.

Towering behind Sadie, Magenta follows with her arms crossed. Immediately, she glares at anyone who has the audacity to look upon her with anything but respect.

Although they have tried to repair themselves, each woman bares the marks of a savage struggle. Sadie moves stiffly and scratches are visible on her neck. Occasionally, Magenta will reach up to her scalp and rub an irritation. The sight of these battle scars is too much for one woman who stands up to release a loud sob and then runs across the office to the nearest door.

'You!' Magenta cries out, her face trembling at the impudence. 'Return to your seat. Now!'

Dabbing her eyes, the woman teeters back into the office and is helped into a chair by two colleagues. One man stands up and offers Sadie a seat, but Magenta gets there first and kicks the chair away. Her fists are clenched also, but a punch is not necessary; the man quickly retakes his chair with a contrite expression on his face.

And Sadie's speech is short; in the bathroom she was told to be brief and even coached on what she was permitted to say to them. But not once does she break down; she keeps her chin up and bids her colleagues goodbye. Only when her staff applaud her, as she walks out to begin her first shift in the kitchens, does a long tear begin an inexorable roll down her face.

And then it was Magenta's turn to command their undivided attention.

I saw Sadie only once more after her dismissal. It was three months after her transfer. I'd just eaten a good steak and as I left the restaurant – situated on a lower floor that I rarely frequent – I heard a tremulous voice behind me. It said, 'Excuse me, ma'am.' And after I turned around, it took a moment to recognise the pretty but harassed face of the young serving girl who clutched a stack of soiled plates against her pink, uniformed chest. She had changed. She wore little make-up and stress lines had begun to show at the sides of her mouth and around her eyes. Work in the kitchens is hard for a young and pretty girl. 'It's me,' she said. 'Sadie.'

I nodded, but felt unable to smile. This intrusion annoyed me. Members of the services are not permitted to speak or interfere with the corporate staff unless absolutely necessary. 'Oh yes. What is it?' I kept my tone even.

'It's me. Sadie. Remember? I used to work for you. Was very good, you used to say.'

'Yes. Of course.' I then glanced around the tables. 'I hope they're treating you well here.'

Her smile vanished and the eager light died in her eyes. 'Treating me well? Well? Do you know what goes on in these places? Have you any idea?'

I frowned at her so she would know her tone was inappropriate and her subject distasteful.

'Why?' she said. 'Why did you let it happen?'

'It was not for me to interfere with the decision of one I appointed to a position of great responsibility.'

'But you knew she would do something like this. Come on, the joke is over. The lesson learned. I'm ready to come back.'

'You cannot come back. You know it. One can never underestimate Magenta,' I said with an undisguised pride. 'And if you have any decency, you may be pleased to know that she is doing very well. Very well indeed. Although she had to lose a few of your people. There were adjustment problems.'

'You won't get away with it,' she whispered, her face white with rage. 'You created a monster. One day she'll turn on you. I hope you know that.'

I snorted derisively. 'My dear, girl, when will you learn that there are urges that cannot be denied? And sometimes the innocent fall victim to these – how shall I put it? – these drives of ours. And power is only fully appreciated when it is exercised. Come now, you must have suspected that your type were an endangered species here. If not finally extinct.'

She could barely speak; her words came in tight little gasps. 'You are a witch. Inhuman.'

I smiled, but it was hard; by this stage I was clearly annoyed. 'And I think you are guilty of underestimating the delight of appreciating true punishment. The knowledge that the vanquished continue to suffer. Sometimes for ever.' And then I turned on my new Italian high heels and left the restaurant. She was lucky I never had a word with her supervisor.

Company Profile 4

Staff Recreation Facilities

And the cars arrive. They come to this place individually and if two should arrive at the same time they keep their distance from each other as their tyres slowly, smoothly ripple over the tarmac of the service road and then bump and crunch across the stony clay and the thin grasses that struggle on the surface of the wasteground. No more than four acres square and unlit by anything other the headlights of the dark cars, this unofficial carpark is situated on the perimeter of the county and waits to be developed as the corporation expands outwards from the giant glass obelisk at its heart. Like the keep of a castle in mediaeval times, the skyscraper is the centre of all things in this area: order, power, sustenance, fear. It reaches into the sky and its lights can be seen by planes for miles around as they bring their offerings and trade and barterings for peace to the private airport. From the top of the building everything below can be surveyed, as it stands ominously at the heart of this new city, and from anywhere on the ground it too can be seen. On any downtown street and from any suburban garden or driveway you only have to look up to admire the sky and it will catch and then draw your eye towards itself. From anywhere its message can be understood: all of this and all you own exist because I am here, I created everything, it all started with me, from here, way up high. I am responsible for protecting this domain and your future can only continue through me.

But if a person did not want to be seen, or if, for a while, they wanted to disappear from out of the mainstream and place themselves at the fringes of this society in a shadow the tower could not see, they would have to travel far out to the deserted parts while these dark places still last. And where the cars gather tonight there are no security patrols, no surveillance cameras and no facilities. There is little natural beauty either – few birds, little wildlife. Beyond the drainage trenches that hide in the neglected grass at the fringes of the carpark, defining its shape, only the flat, uneventful earth remains, exhausted by the old cattle farmers. Reaching towards the horizon, the bleached landscape gives the impression that outside the city there is nothing. So why would anyone need to venture to this place where the town runs out of road and where concrete and steel has yet to make its mark?

Parking as far apart from each other as possible, the cars line up and then soundlessly stop moving. The rear bumpers of these cars hug the boundaries of the area. Facing the centre of the wasteground, their headlights remain on and transform the clay and stones into an orange floodlit stage. But no one gets out of the cars to fill this space; the doors stay closed and the one-way glass of the windows stay shut as the powerful engines idle. A few sunroofs open but the cars and their occupants remain still. Perhaps they are here to watch the stars. Perhaps not. Perhaps they are waiting for something.

Inside each of the cars there is a single occupant. But as a group they have certain things in common. They are all female. They all own expensive cars. Most of them would be classified as mature; all have passed their thirtieth birthday, some have turned forty, and one or two are looking towards retirement. And a loose and informal dress code has also been followed. Like a form of ceremony, these senior members of the same tribe have adorned themselves in costumes reserved for these special midnight rendezvous. It is doubtful that such clothes would be tolerated or could be worn practically in their domestic or working situations. After they remove the overcoats that concealed them when they moved from the front door of their homes to their cars, earlier in the night, those women that wear skirts or dresses now hike them up to the tops of their thighs. With quick excited hands they smooth their stockings up their legs and adjust their garter fastenings if they require adjustment. Inside the tight blouses or skimpy dresses, no brassieres are worn. Cleavage is revealed. Perfume is sprayed on delicate throats, dabbed behind ears and misted down the front of their satiny shin-bones. Buttons and zippers are opened. Pretty eyes in heavy make-up peer into rear-view mirrors. Lipstick is relayered. Chairs are reclined. Mints are sucked. Watches are checked. Husbands and children are forgotten as the masks are slipped on.

One woman becomes a cat with whiskers; a pink nose and lynx ears sprout from her velvety headpiece. Another dons a simple and elegant sleeping mask to hide her eyes but dangerously display the rest of her face ('Oh, will I be recognised at work?'). Another, who has adorned her plump, naked body in chains, has written crude slogans across her belly and breasts with eyeliner pencil. Coated in a second skin of glossy plastic, there is also a woman who carefully unfolds her own tight rubber mask over her entire blonde head. Only the shiny material of this headpiece is plain and black, revealing nothing of her face but a set of painted eyes and thick lips. The latter perforation around the mouth creates a sex-dollish O-shape, ready to issue screams and invite sudden penetrations, but not necessarily in that order.

There is a bunny in an Alfa Romeo Spider too, a Jackie O in headscarf and sunglasses behind the wheel of an Audi, a schoolgirl in straw hat, a variety of Venetian masks and several veils attached to little hats perched in expensive hairstyles. Each woman conceals her ordinary self and displays a new individuality, adds the finishing touch to the role she is prepared to play amongst so many strangers, way out here, unprotected, in the dark.

In time, the headlights of a second stream of cars can be seen in the distance. Snaking down the service road from the highway, they travel in an orderly column, all together, no scouts, no stragglers. The way they approach this place gives the suggestion that they are arriving promptly at a specific destination for an appointment. They move more quickly than the first arrivals and bunch together like excited animals in a herd. Each closely follows the bumper and concealed number plate of the vehicle in front until they reach the entrance to the carpark that has been prepared for them. All lined up and waiting for admittance, it can be seen that there are at least four times as many cars in this column than there are already in the carpark.

Those waiting on the wasteground begin to flash their headlights, once, then twice more.

Gingerly, as if the vehicles themselves are self-conscious, the new arrivals edge into the light. Spreading out, they then park at a respectful distance between the waiting cars of the women. Nose-first, they come to a stop facing the grassy plains and quickly douse their lights.

For a while there is a communal pause. No one moves and nothing can be heard beside the water-cooled hum of a dozen performance engines at ease. But after one car door opens and then shuts, and a man stands alone beside his inert vehicle wearing a woollen ski-mask with holes for the eyes and mouth, other car doors begin to open also and then shut until a momentum and pattern

137

is established. Soon, over forty men with their heads covered in tight wool, or rubber, or leather with zippered mouths, are standing next to their driver-side doors. Without looking or speaking to each other, the men begin to stretch their legs or light cigarettes. Casually, they then walk to the nearest cars that still have their headlights switched on – the cars of the women. As yet, no one has dared to wander into the light at the centre or has made any drastic move. All the activity can be seen around the edges, and is slow, casual, relaxed. But the eyes glimpsed through the masks project tension and an excitement that is hard to contain.

And then the driver's windows of the women's cars slowly and soundlessly descend to reveal the occupant all lit up in white by the interior bulb as she waits, prepared and anxious. With the windows now open and the inner delights exposed, the men begin to crowd around the women's cars. The distribution of manpower is not even; some of the open windows are approached by pairs, another car commands half a dozen window shoppers, while most of the other vehicles initially get three or four onlookers. Then the men begin to quietly circulate until all of them are wandering between the cars to peep through every window at the women inside and their varying states of exposure. And it is now that the women speak to their audience.

'I'm looking for group sex,' the woman in the sleeping mask whispers to the faces that jostle outside her door. 'Hard, deep anal is my favourite. And I like cream.' Then she repeats the offer to the next group of men who cruise by. 'I'm looking for group sex . . .'

'Use this on me,' the woman in the latex cat-suit says, as she holds up a thin cane to the anonymous eyes that blink down at her. 'Over the boot of the car. Don't hold back. Really go for it. But just on my bottom. Then you can use me. There is a hole in the back of my catsuit.

Call me names too. And you can be rough.' Several men unzip and start to massage their hands along chubby lengths as she talks to them in her sweet, cultured voice.

The woman in the kitten mask puts her feet up on the dashboard so her spike heels are touching the inside of the windscreen on either side of the steering wheel. Between her long legs, coated in seamed nylons that reach right up to the shore of her platinum floss, she tickles the outside of her sex with a rubber penis. 'I like to be looked at,' she murmurs in an emotional voice. 'And I like my tits pinched too.' Immediately, a man in a colourful clown's mask reaches inside her car and begins to prod at her exposed breasts. Behind the red nose and under the violent spray of orange hair, his breathing is loud. With his other hand, he jerks at his sex.

One woman with curly, chocolate hair piling over the top of her china carnival mask, has moved to the wide back seat of her car. Wearing just a white garter belt, silver stockings and a high-heeled sandals, she has placed one foot on the parcel shelf and another on the rear of the driver's seat. Between her legs, her scarlet fingernails are busy making preparations. 'Just get in, fuck and leave. No talk,' she repeats over and over again, between her moans.

On the west side of the carpark, the driver door of a Mercedes saloon is wide open and a shapely white behind exposes itself like a ground-level moon. All the men can see is her back in the jacket of a silk designer suit and the pale leather soles of her high heels tucked underneath her body. 'You know where,' she says, in a trembling voice. 'You know where you want to go. Use the lubricant on the dash. As many as possible, please. Some of you might have been here last time. They'll remember I took sixteen in there. Let's beat the record tonight.'

Breaking free from the peripheral congress of cars and pedestrians, one woman eventually walks into the centre of the carpark. All the headlights shine upon her. Every pair of eyes follow her confident stride. She is dressed like a schoolgirl in white blouse and short skirt, complemented by high heels and black stockings. Wearing a harlequin's mask beneath a straw hat, she walks proudly, arrogantly, head back, hips swinging; a pioneer to stretch the boundaries of this already extreme situation. Coming to a standstill, right in the middle of defined area, she puts her hands on her hips and spreads her feet in a posture that issues a challenge and suggests expectation. But she is not alone for long. Five men peel away from the fringes of the wasteground and approach her from different directions. She has made her wishes known and they are reckless or brave enough to comply.

At first they form a circle around her and listen to her giggle and provoke. Then a man in a black ski mask approaches her and slips a hand between her legs. She responds immediately and begins to moan and gyrate her hips at the first contact from these strange, dry fingers in her most intimate place. Another man wearing a leather overcoat kneels behind her and caresses her legs before sliding his hands up inside her short skirt to feel her warm buttocks. Soon, four foreign hands help themselves to the buttons on her blouse and the breasts beneath. The last man stands back from the group and watches, his body stiff in concentration, one hand fondling the end of his erect penis.

Soon, her sex is being kissed and licked at. Bristly chins congregate between her legs. Their cheeks are rough on the soft skin of her inner thighs, while their tongues are ticklish and gentle against the lips of her sex. From behind, arms reach around her ribs and her breasts are mauled by long fingers. When she feels a tongue between her buttocks, circling her tasty ring, she shivers and lets out a whimper. The sound is interpreted as encouragement and she is soon bent over at the waist to receive a thick intrusion from behind. Chin up, voice defiant, she says, 'Come on, fuck me then. Fuck the slut. Fuck her.' Her mouth is soon filled too and her delight with this pacifier can be seen in the way her neck stretches towards the belly of its owner, and in how her lips and cheeks enthusiastically work at the skin and muscle. Becoming the tender meat on this bizarre spit-roast, both of her arms are then taken by the wrist and raised into the air. Between fingers and moist palm of these manicured hands, swollen objects are placed. Enthusiastically, she begins to stroke them while being thrust into from both ends.

Her surrender is a significant moment in the evening. Everyone else is encouraged to go so much further. Now, the other men begin to take the lead offered them. Face-down over the bonnet of her BMW, feet planted apart below the front bumper, hands held by men who stand beside the wing mirrors of her car, the woman in the latex cat-suit has her desires sated. Digging the spike heels of her patent boots further into the turf, she balances her body against the blows of the cane. Her knees cannot buckle and she cannot collapse because the front of her legs are squashed against the grille of her own car. Shiny in rubber, her tiny aerodynamic head whips from side to side and she softly grunts in response to each lash. The resounding crack, when seasoned wood meets the plastic stretched over a shapely bottom, echoes across the field. And the men take turns. Those that formerly kept her arms wide apart and her fisted hands steady, take up the cane and swap positions with the original punishers. And as they stroke her with the spiteful stick, she calls her confession into the night. 'I am bad. I am bad. I am jealous of my colleagues and neighbours and plot their downfall. It makes me happy to see careers in ruins and for dreams to end in disaster. I am spoilt and sulky and impossible to please. At every opportunity I will be rude and unpleasant to you. So you better get even now.' And indeed, after her quick speech, the cane does fall more swiftly and with greater force until she is unable to talk and shrieks out instead. And it is hard to decipher whether her cries are those of the pleasured or the tormented.

Windows become opaque with the steam of hard breathing and grinding bodies, the car of the woman in white and silver lingerie squeaks and shakes in its impromptu mooring. Lover after lover ducks his head and clambers on to the leatherette backseat where he then kneels between her raised ankles and inserts himself. Some of them are quick as they slam against her body. Others take their time and maintain an even pace as they stare down at the china mask and glossy curls arranged on the seat beneath them. And whenever she climaxes her sounds bring more suitors to her ever open door. 'Yes. harder. Fuck me. Fuck me. Fuck me.' And when these women climax while wearing such unusual outfits, in so many shameful positions and postures, the excitement and ardour of the men increases. It's as if this is what they really came to this forbidden place to see; some acknowledgement, some proof that the leaders and tyrants and wives in their corporate regime actually enjoy these momentary transfers of power, these surrenders to the oppressed rank and file. For a night no one needs to concern themselves with competitive thoughts of income and career potential because their status has been reduced and redefined to an anonymous and purely physical sense. The only criteria is to perform and satisfy.

Close to the Mercedes of the woman in white, a slim lady wearing a now ruffled evening gown of satin, with matching hat and veil, lives out her private reverie inside her husband's Mercedes. Front seats lowered, she has created a makeshift bed and allowed three young men to strap her hands and ankles down with the seat belts. Limbs stretched apart, her body forms a star-shape. All three of her lovers crowd inside the vehicle and take turns between her long thighs. While one heaves and grunts on top of her, the other two stroke her breasts and feed their erections between the bright red lips of her mouth. They seem content to spend the entire evening here, while other men pause as they pass the car to peer inside at the commotion and her quick-fire cries of passion. Her only stipulation is that her eager lovers remember to withdraw from her when the time comes and to ejaculate over her face and body. For some perverse reason, she wants to go home with her clothes stained and still moist. And after an hour her veil is wet and stuck to her face and her naked breasts are strung with loops and tendrils of the enthusiasm of the young men. Perhaps she was sent here by one that requires proof of her secret nature.

As the night progresses, though no one is aware of time passing, some women move from inside their cars to be positioned across them, or allow themselves to be taken into the open where a free-for-all commences under the beams of the headlights. It seems the most popular request is for group activity, but the motives vary: there is sometimes a desire to see the excitement and desperation in five different pairs of eyes, to test and feel the power of their own beauty and sexuality before uninhibited male lust, a need to be adored with the most extreme worship; or there is a desire to be used, to totally submit, or even be punished.

Out in the centre, a petite woman with silver-hair and discreet make-up lies on a tartan picnic blanket she has brought with her. Her hair, the fine bones of her face and her pleasant, well-spoken voice give the suggestion that this woman is an asset to her husband and company: responsible, orderly, precise, glamorous, kind, perhaps a devoted mother or efficient supervisor. But here, on this blanket, she craves to be someone else. 'Oh yes. And another one. Oooh, let's have them all,' she whispers in between her inoffensive, contagious giggles as three erect male organs are planted in her hands and sex. And it is only the thickest of the three muscular appendages that she clutches at greedily and then adores and worships between her dainty lips and small, feminine fingers. And she manipulates and arouses this cock so expertly, the man's climax is powerful. Heavy streams of his fluid dart inside her open mouth. She even raises her white head from the ground to get nearer the pumping muscle and to catch every drop of seed. Kneeling between her small legs, that are so attractively displayed in sheer black stockings to appeal to her lovers, a young man relentlessly thrusts inside her, making her small breasts quiver under the lacy negligee. When he sees her devour this ejaculation he suddenly loses control and increases the speed and vigour of his attentions. With a half-full mouth, she suddenly says, 'Oh, yes. Oh, I say. Yes,' before falling silent while her body judders for the few seconds her first peak lasts. 'Coming,' the younger lover says. 'Now. All of it. Inside you. Beautiful slut.' And his shoulders drop forward and his head dips as his loins empty themselves into this stranger twice his age. When he withdraws, she smiles and politely thanks him before requesting that he hand over his condom. And then, to the surprise and momentary shock of all, she empties the contents of the prophylactic into her mouth. Clamping the base between her lips and pinching the tiny bulb at the end of the rubber with one hand, she then slides the thumb and forefinger of her other hand down the length of the condom until its entire contents is safe between her cheeks. After a noisy swallow, she looks up at her boys, beaming, before asking them in an incongruous tone, more suited to the offer of a hot beverage, 'Now, who needs a pee-pee?' They are stunned, unsure how to react and not clear on what she is suggesting. 'Come on, then. Let's have it. On my face, if you please,' coaxes the fluid enthusiast. And as she massages her clit with a middle finger, she sits up and raises her face to the two men who stand over her. Closing her eyes, she then accepts the two thick, clear, spattery streams of their water directly over her kind face. As if drinking from a fountain, she occasionally opens her modest mouth to take in an amount which is duly swallowed.

Canes fall; spike heels spear the air; cars rock back and forth on their state-of-the-art suspension; women cry out in encouragement or ecstasy; men groan and men spit insults to those who demand verbal debasement; slender bodies writhe in the yellow beams of the headlamps; wrists are bound in canvas and nylon; the more voracious female appetites are fulfilled by at least a dozen lovers who pin them down and thrust deep: all over the carpark bodies move in erotic congress. Eventually, as so many become spent, people drift back to their cars and sit quietly, leaving only the insatiable few who want to continue all night, completely losing themselves in excess for hour after hour. One woman is overheard saying, 'We really do need more men at these gatherings,' as she steps back into her panties and walks away from three men who appear to be asleep on the ground beside her Range Rover. Another whispers, 'More. One more. Is anybody good for one more?' while she sways her red buttocks about in the air outside her driver's door. She has already been spanked by a dozen men and at least half that number have entered her anus and left a liquiescent calling card. 'All these are ruined,' says a woman with short highlighted hair as she holds up a pair of stained and laddered stockings, bedraggled panties and a dress that had been torn down from her shoulders. 'And I really don't care.' Another with a spiky, creative hair cut and large breasts dabs at her sex with her panties while she talks to herself: 'It's still coming out. How much is there?'

But most of the women are not so chatty. They slink back to their vehicles from where they have been lying on the ground, holding high-heeled shoes, forever straightening their masks, giving the impression that they are individuals of some importance and standing. And then the gathering begins to break up. The cars crawl back up the service road to the highway. Perhaps only now the drivers are surprised at themselves for what they have done on this unreal night.

Only a few stalwarts remain for hours after the main crowd has left: two sweat-soaked women, and seven men with enough stamina to continue. But when the sun rises, the carpark has become empty wasteground again.

Career History: Part 10

Multi-skilling

'Can I put this somewhere?' The girl's voice comes from behind you in a corridor on the eightieth floor. Smoking a cigarette quickly, she is standing with one hand tucked under the opposing elbow and anxiously chews at her bottom lip when you turn to face her. Finding it hard to look you in the eye, she peers over her shoulder at the empty corridor, as if suspicious someone has followed her, soft-footed, from the office she snuck out of. You've seen this look before, many times since your return to the compound and the start of your new role as a member of the resistance.

'Sure,' you say, and use her state of mental distraction to discreetly admire her slender body in the charcoal-coloured suit. Under the body-hugging T-shirt she wears beneath her jacket, her breasts are heavy and firm. And she has great legs too; long and elegantly muscular, like a dancer's legs, enhanced in the tight mid-thigh skirt and sheer, minky stockings that emit a subtle sheen under the electric lights. You cannot help yourself. You have to look. You sleep in a barrack with over a hundred men and, beside these quick and usually silent liaisons, your only interaction with women occurs when the matronly supervisors issue orders and take the register below. But, every day, as you move around the fringes of the corporate world you see thousands of well-presented, attractive women like this one; you empty their ashtrays, clean the toilets, pick up their litter and empty their waste bins while being starved and desperate for real contact with them. It is rare if a business woman even looks at you, let alone speaks to you. Invisible to them in a service uniform, because you are of no consequence to their work or personal advancement, you scurry, unobserved, in the background, pushing the utility trolley issued to you by Environment Services each morning after the assignments are given out. And this is why you are ideal for this role assigned to you by the resistance. Now you realise this; the police captain was right. Most of the people who have approached you have been wary or incredulous that a simple cleaner could be an agent, their first contact on the road to anarchy and an overthrow of the mighty company. You can't blame them; they have all been programmed by the corporation to become obsessed with the surface of things, like status and beauty.

'Not here,' you say to the nervous woman with the cigarette. You nod towards the water sprinkler peeping between the white ceiling tiles above your head. 'Follow me to the ashtray and I will extinguish your smoking materials, miss.'

When she looks up at the sprinkler and its little blinking red light, she becomes even more agitated.

'It's OK. It's not far,' you say, smiling to reassure her. 'Down here a bit.' She nods in agreement and follows you further down the corridor to where you park your cleaning buggy. 'What do I do with this?' she says, after slipping a computer disk out of the inside of her jacket; you see a flash of a cream silk lining and a bosom hammocked in lycra.

'Just drop it in here?' you say, and raise one of the flaps of the large rubber pockets that are strapped to the side of the buggy. Wasting no time, she drops it inside

148

the pocket and then steps back. Breathing out with relief that the evidence is out of her hands, she nods at you, but is not able to return your smile. Betraying her department and aiding the resistance will result in the most dire consequences for her if caught. You sympathise, but are more experienced in these matters. After all, you have fallen right into the pit, escaped, been recaptured and now continue to resist the company. For the first time in years you are proud of yourself and actually feel a greater sense of significance than you ever did as a member of the company executive. 'It's OK. Relax,' you whisper. 'You're not alone. There are so many on your side. So many with you.'

This seems to encourage her. 'So when . . . when does it happen?' she asks before lowering her voice to a barely audible whisper. 'You know, the day of action? We were told it was imminent. And that was a month ago. What's going on then? Have you any idea what they'll do to me if they know I gave you that fucking disk? Do you have any idea what's on it?'

Sage-like, calm, you nod with understanding and smile to reassure. 'We will know soon enough. But we need more information first. More intelligence.' But you actually have no idea when or if these risks you all take will amount to anything. And no one has told you anything about this 'day of action'. It is something people keep mentioning when you collect their disks and CD ROMs in corridors, on fire escapes and in lavatories, but no one from the actual resistance has even made contact with you since your return from the security forces. Your role has merely been one of collection. You have taken stolen files – the disks and occasional print-out – to the basement and hid them in a rubber bucket that used to contain toxic chemicals. So perhaps all this talk of a day of action is an incentive to get the disgruntled workers to turn traitor, to provide a purpose and a goal in their target-obsessed habitat. But another agent had better approach you soon to collect the stash; the container is nearly full and so much damaging material in one place is making you nervous. In addition, not one of the executives who have approached you so far has made it clear how they knew you were the agent of the resistance to approach with stolen files. The thought of a photograph of your face circulating this building fills you with dread, but you doubt the resistance would be so foolish. Perhaps a description has gone out, or perhaps those committed to rebellion are forewarned of where you will be in the building or on the grounds on a particular day. Your timetable is issued each day by Environment Services, so someone must be passing your rota out to other agents in the field. It seems plausible, but you have no real idea who is actually on your side until one of these strangers approaches with the password. It is exciting and the thought of revenge just thrills you, but you desperately want to know more about the resistance network.

The young woman who has given you the disk turns to walk away, back to her office. 'Oh, miss,' you call out. 'You forgot your cigarette lighter.' She turns and looks at you, puzzled. You wink and push your buggy to where she stands. 'Who told you where to find me?'

She is confused. It's as if you have asked a preposterous question. 'Well, from my colleague. He came to you yesterday,' she says in a tense voice. And he may have; there were five drop-offs the previous day in the carpark.

'OK,' you say, smiling. 'But how did he know I was the one to approach?'

'You don't know?' she asks, frowning.

'Er . . . not exactly.'

She shrugs. 'Don't ask me. I don't want to get involved that much. This is a one-off. A favour. It's all I can do.' She anxiously eyes the side of your buggy as if she has changed her mind.

You smile. 'And we appreciate your contribution. It's going to be a great help. Really. We mean that,' you say, although you have no clear idea on whose behalf you are speaking. 'I was just curious which agent put you on to me. That's all. Forget about it. It doesn't really matter.'

Wary, she looks at you for a moment and then hurries off, back the way she came. You feel guilty for putting her on the spot like that, but the feeling is soon pushed aside by the sight of her shapely hips and bottom and by her strong calf muscles in the shimmery hose as she teeters away down the corridor. You want a woman like that for yourself. But whatever your status in the corporation has been, these girls have been out of reach. Your only prior connection with them has been during those incidents when you have angered them and you have been punished. The vaguest reminder of the police officers and your demotion constantly makes you afraid but also giddy and warm all over in a pleasant way. The touch of the most maniacal of these corporate bitches will always haunt you. Of this you are certain.

You move down the corridor to the next silver bullet-shaped device that doubles as an ashtray and rubbish bin. Filling the deep stomach of your cleaning buggy with its butts, sandwich wrappers and used tissues, you then move on to the next bathroom. Despite all you have been through, you still see things at the corporation that surprise you. But these glimpses you catch through windows, on stairs and inside bathrooms, offer more and more evidence of how the corporation functions: the way it controls through terror and intimidation; the vengeful but unorthodox methods it employs to bully, re-educate or destroy; the promises, failures and success stories that circulate to keep everyone in line and focused on personal success; this never-ending but constantly mutating play of cruelty and seduction and greed. Those of you in the resistance

151

will have to be strong. How can anybody risk their necks when so many creative methods of correction and public humiliation exist? And who can resist the will of one's superiors when such quick and illicit pleasures can suddenly be offered or demanded?

And it is inside these gleaming steel and marble bathrooms of the corporate building where so much business is done and where so much illicit congress is conducted. There have been times when you were on toilet duty and terrible things have happened right before your eyes as you were bent over a sink, scouring and rubbing, or huddled inside a cubicle disinfecting a bowl with rubber gloves on your hands. Only a week ago you saw a tall brunette, some kind of Latin American woman, destroying a smaller blonde colleague. She was tearing her hair and clothes, scratching her, slapping her, dragging her to the gleaming tiles that you had just mopped, then she spanked the sweet blonde before squatting over her, like a woman caught short and who has to seek relief at a roadside or behind a tree, before urinating on the pretty upturned nose and platinum-blonde hair of the fallen angel. It is a true testament to your lack of substance, your complete disempowerment, your invisibility, that educated, successful women can do such things in your presence.

As you begin to mop out the toilet stalls of the ladies' bathroom on the eightieth floor, you think of the chubby, naked man you also saw being dragged around the tiles by his tie the previous morning. Red in the face, cringing, clumsy on his hands and knees, he begged his boss to forgive some oversight he'd made prior to a meeting. And his excuses – his claims of stress, of overwork, of balancing six tasks at the same time, of her caprices, her confusing and shifting order of priority – went unanswered, were ignored, by the middle-aged woman in the black suit and sling-back shoes. She dragged him stumbling to the sinks and tried to drown him in a bowl. Rubbed soap in his mouth and eyes with her manicured, crimson nails. Then forced the hapless, sputtering, choking victim to strip naked so she could laugh at his manhood before striping his buttocks with the cane that extended from her umbrella. Fearing demotion, disgrace and exile from the salaried, and the luxury suburbs they inhabit, the chubby man then offered no resistance to her desire for tongue-cleaned shoes, or her request to have her arse kissed and refreshed by the very same tongue that had so recently tasted her leather and hot toes.

And there are many like her who hunt in this part of the building. The higher you go, the more extreme they become. If you heard the sound of gunfire in an office cubicle or toilet stall you would not be surprised. With highlighted, textured hair and designer suits, they move swiftly through the corridors of power, on dangerously high-heeled shoes, in search of the weak and incompetent, to roar like lions before devastating them with a cane or leather belt. It seems there are times when the female executives are unable to withstand the pressure of responsibility any longer and so suffer these episodes; become unpredictable; break down with radical losses of control; become capable of violent, screaming fits; lash out at the most convenient or culpable member of their team. You wonder how many men and women fall beneath their trampling boots and spiking heels each week. But for every episode of fury and correctional punishment observed, you have seen the same women transform themselves into paragons of submissive femininity when dealing with a superior.

And yet such ruthlessness, such order, such discipline only serves to make the company stronger. Most of the time it seems ludicrous that any kind of resistance to the corporate will could even make a dent of difference.

Career History: Part 11

Networking

'You are the one.' Her cold blue eyes have fixed on you and there is nothing in her expression to put you at ease. She is beautiful, frosty, dangerous. Hair black and tied so tightly on the back of her head you expect her fringe to rip free of the smooth forehead at any moment. On tipped stiletto heels that crack like gunshots across the tiles, her statuesque body strides across the bathroom. Instinctively, you back into a corner. Panic and fear froths into your mouth like vomit. 'Me? What?' you say, but she still keeps coming until she has invaded your space, until her breath is hot and minty against your lips and the glare from her iceberg eyes stills the blood in your veins. Then a wave of perfume clouds your senses; stuns you with its scents of power and confidence and makes you light-headed. She is so tall, older than you and devastatingly glamorous. There is something larger than life about her, a quality reminiscent of the convincing drag queen, as there is about every exceptionally tall and well-heeled woman. 'Yes. It is you. Must be,' she says, looking you up and down as you stand still in your white boiler suit, ready to flinch into the foetal position. Her eyes mock. A playful smile moves her beautiful mouth. 'Don't look so frightened. I don't bite.' She pretends to nip at you with her perfect teeth. Instinctively, you flinch. Hands on hips, head cocked to one side, she laughs. 'My, my, they have done a number on you, haven't they?'

'Who?' you whisper.

'Oh, come on. I know all about you. The escape. Your incarceration. And what happened to your wife. It's incredible. Outrageous. I'm amazed you even got involved with this lot. Thought you'd have had enough by now, old boy.'

You swallow. 'Which lot? I don't follow.'

She laughs and places a hand over her mouth. 'Aren't you good at this? Is that real sweat? Oh, yes, sorry, I forgot. Do you have somewhere I can put this? No, that's not right. Can I put this somewhere?'

Bent over, hands on knees, you breathe out with relief. But you feel angry at her for being so flippant. You straighten up. 'That wasn't funny.'

She continues to laugh at your terrified reaction. Placing her long cold fingers on your cheek, she says, 'I am sorry. Really. Now let's be serious. I have something for you. It comes from the hundreds.' She's referring to the final ten floors of the building where only the directors have access. Some of them even live up there. Allegedly, they have their own gym, swimming pool, helipad and restaurants too. Once you make it to the final ten it is virtually impossible to be demoted. And this woman is one of the company's top executives. In the top one hundred and ready to betray. You find this fact astonishing. 'I've come a long way to find you, young man,' she adds. 'Ten bloody floors in these heels. And they're not for walking, dear. For the boardroom or bedroom only.' She laughs again but, despite her change of tone, her entire body still issues an iciness. Although long and slender, her arms and legs look hard, overtoned. You suspect her pale skin is freezing too and that something blue and synthetic pumps through her arteries instead of blood. And how is it possible that a perfume can smell so thoroughly of power? The sense of what she must have done to achieve such a high position in the corporation is in itself overwhelming. 'Here,' she says, and then puts one foot between your legs before hiking her skirt up to the top of her thigh.

You stop blinking and gape at her leg. One of the most powerful women in the entire city is exposing her long thighs to you. She wears sheer black stockings and beneath the top she has tucked a CD ROM. Plucking it from behind her garter strap, she offers it to you. Still transfixed by the sight of her leg and the dramatic contrast of her ghostly white skin above the black nylon, you hesitate in taking the disk. She laughs again and tucks the disk under your chin. She raises your face until you are staring into her eyes again. The disk smells of her leg, her intimate scent. 'At me. At me, if you please.' She raises an eyebrow and you apologise. 'I understand,' she says. 'I know you don't get much down there.' Seductively, she half-closes her eyes. 'Is it true you all sleep in bunkbeds like little schoolboys?'

You nod, because you cannot think of anything suitable to say to this woman you want to impress and be liked by, despite your fear. Regardless of all they have done to you, you still can't help yourself.

'Oh, how sweet. How adorable!' she shrieks. 'I should pop down and tuck the young ones in, eh?'

Nervously, you look up at the lights and fire sprinklers.

Frowning, she says, 'What is it?' Following your eyes to the ceiling, comprehension then dawns and she smiles. 'Oh, I see. You're worried about the microphones. Don't worry, they only respond to certain words, like –' she mouths the word 'bomb' at you and then winks. 'Believe me. I know.' She lets her skirt drop back down her slippery leg. 'Now put that somewhere safe. You won't get anything that good again,' she says, nodding at the disk. 'And I wouldn't walk around with that sticking out either,' she adds, peering at your erection, before throwing her head back and laughing in a lewd manner. 'Someone might want to take advantage of you.' You think she is probably mad, but so sexy and powerful too that you would risk anything for the briefest involvement.

You dare to smile and to allow your wide, lecherous eyes to admire her body. You swallow. 'Are there others?'

'Others? Like me? There's no one like me, sweetheart. They broke the mould and all that. Would never dare to make two, you know.'

She'll tell you exactly what she wants and nothing more, will play with you, flirt with you, reject at will, hold all the cards. You wonder about what kind of man could possibly hold her attention and keep her interest for more than a few minutes.

'You're beautiful,' you blurt out, blushing.

Sincerely, perhaps, for a fleeting moment, she smiles as if flattered. 'Oh darling, how sweet.' Brushing your cheek with a painted fingernail, she says, 'But should rebellion be mixed with pleasure, eh? Bit risky, I would say. Although that's the fun. Could you imagine if someone walked in and saw me fucking a cleaner?' She laughs, only stopping when she sees the anguish on your face for being reminded of your position. 'But it happens all the time, darling. I mean, who are you going to tell? You men in white are the safest bet. No blackmail, no commitment issues, no gossip. After all, you were created to serve.' Leaning forward, she kisses you: soft, hard, soft again, sucks your cheeks hollow and eats at your tongue, then soft again before she breaks away and smiles. 'I could eat you alive.'

You move forward to kiss her. A fingernail placed on your sternum holds you still. She winks. 'Would you like to collect your reward right here?'

'Reward?'

'For being such a brave soldier. It would be sexy, wouldn't it?'

'Oh, yeah.'

'Quick, then.' Seizing your hand, she then drags you into the toilet cubicle you have just cleaned. With her foot she slams the toilet seat and then sits down. Pulling your groin before her face, her long fingers go to work and unzip the front of your suit. 'Mmm,' she hums through her long nose. 'You are eager. Been a while, I bet.'

Before you have time to answer, to explain, you realise answers and explanations are unnecessary. She is taking you because she wishes to. Inside the wide mouth your erection passes. Her nose thins and she looks up at you with dreamy, adoring eyes as her mouth savours the rigid muscle and velvety skin. In any other situation you would be convinced that a woman who looked at you in such a way would have been in love with you. Cool fingertips touch and stroke your length. You moan and stare down at her legs. Reading your mind she hikes her skirt up to her stocking tops without removing your sex from her mouth.

Fingers spread wide on your stomach, she then pushes her head forward and takes most of your length deep inside her mouth. Slowly withdrawing her purple lips down your stem, she looks at you again and winks. 'Taste nice, sweetie. But what can you do with it?' She stands up and turns around. Pushing back at you with her buttocks, she creates some space over the toilet and spreads her legs. Sinking to your knees, you take a moment to admire her thighs, the pinkish lips of her sex just visible through her sheer panties, and the shapely globes of her buttocks beneath your roaming hands.

'Now. Do me now. Like a toilet tart. Now.' Her voice is insistent; the situation has made her aggressive. 'Take me.'

Peeling her panties down her thighs so they stretch wide between her knees, you slip your hand on to her sex and gently rub at her lips. Inserting two fingers to the first knuckle, you hear her whisper, 'God, yes,' at the first evidence of penetration. She slaps a hand against the ceramic cistern and dips her head. 'Go on. Bareback. I want it bareback from the help.'

Dizzy from arousal, you remove your hand and then nudge your sex between her legs. But the angle is wrong; she's too tall. 'Take your heels off,' you mutter. 'You're so damn tall.'

She giggles and steps out of her shoes.

'That's it,' you say, while fisting your sex into the soft, slick flesh that soon sucks the rest of your length in. How could you have imagined that such a tough, fast-talking, dominant woman would possess such a deep, moist and welcoming receptacle? 'Oh, that's good. I'd forgotten how good it feels.'

She laughs again. 'I hadn't. I couldn't do without this.' Looking over her shoulder she gives you a wicked smile.

'Don't,' you say. 'You'll make me come. I want this to last.'

Pressing her buttocks back against your stomach, she takes all of you inside. 'Come inside me. Push it right in before you come. Don't spill anything.'

Pushing your sex in and out of her, gradually increasing the pace, you say, 'You like cream?'

'Lots of it.' Her voice is more breathless than yours. Against the white ceramic lid of the cistern her fingers have become claws.

'Where do you get it?'

'Wherever I can find it.'

'Much of it?'

'Oh, more than you can imagine. I once took nine men inside a toilet stall. They all had me one after the other. Is that the kind of thing you wanted to hear?'

'Oh, yes.' You have to pause in your thrusting and clench the muscles in your sex. Much more of this dialogue and you know it will be all over for you. And you want this to last. 'If you so much as move, I'll come. It's too much.'

She giggles and begins to rub at her clit with one hand while you are impaled inside her. 'That was in a bar. I was drunk. But my record at work is four. Last Christmas. I kept finding this sticky stuff in my panties, three days later.'

Seizing her hips, you begin to plunge and thrust at her, harder than before, suddenly unable to pace yourself.

'That's it. Fuck me hard with your naked cock. Your beautiful naked cock.'

'I will. I will. I will.'

Her breath gets shorter; she tilts her head back and begins to make a hard chesty sound. 'Make me come. I'm going to come. Make me come.'

'Yes. Yes.'

'Put something in my ass,' she then whispers. 'Stuff something in there. Hard.'

Driving yourself inside her until her face is squashed and gulping for air against the wall, you quickly unclip a plastic brush from your utility belt. Under the arm of your boiler suit you wipe the handle clean of dust. 'Ready,' you pant. 'Ready for something thick and hard in your ass.'

She begins to climax and starts thrusting her buttocks back towards your body. Slapping the palm of your hand against her tailbone, you then place the tip of the brush handle against the puckered ring of this extraordinary woman's anus. 'Now,' you say, and apply pressure to the implement.

'Oh, that's so big,' she whines. 'What is it?'

'You don't want to know. It just gets bigger and bigger.'

Closing her eyes in ecstasy, she dips her head and begins to whimper as inch after plastic inch is fed inside her rectum. When the entire handle is finally secure

160

between her buttocks, you raise her on to her tiptoes and then pump her from the side, avoiding the brush.

Looking down at this statuesque and powerful woman you have plugged in the arse and sex, as she climaxes again from the squalid and perverse use you have found for her in a toilet stall, you feel yourself unable to hold your own powerful conclusion at bay any longer. 'Inside you. Coming. Coming inside you.'

'Oh yes. Oh yes,' she shouts, no longer concerned about discretion, the company, her status.

'All of it. Every last drop is inside you.'

'Oh. Oh. Don't pull out. Please. Leave it inside.' Her voice has softened and become affectionate. It surprises you as you stand still and feel your sex gradually soften inside her. So she will never know what thick and uncompromising tool had been applied to provide her with a double penetration, you ease the brush handle from her anus and reattach it to your belt.

Zipping yourself away, you watch her take a seat on the toilet. She mops her mouth and face with tissue and then smiles at you. 'Mmm. I needed that. It'll keep me going until the afternoon. Thanks ever so much.'

You shake your head in disbelief and watch her roll her stockings down her legs. Pinching them off her toes, she stuffs them, still warm, in the chest-pocket of your suit. 'Take these. You can trade them for snout, down in the dungeon,' she says, laughing. 'I expect you to get a good return.' Steadying herself by putting that cold, long-fingered hand on your shoulder, she slips her shoes back on and then straightens her skirt. 'Better get back upstairs before you start pouring out of me. There is so much of it, you naughty boy. What do they feed you downstairs?' Then she bends forward to kiss your forehead before squeezing past you and leaving the cubicle.

'Can I see you again?' you ask, as she walks towards the bathroom door.

Pausing at the door of the bathroom, she looks back at you and pouts a kissy face in your direction. 'Who knows?' she says with a wink and leaves you alone in the smell of disinfectant and her power. In your mouth you can still taste fresh lipstick.

Career History: Part 12

Personal Effects

'Stand by your beds!' The overhead lights snap on in the barracks. Then, up on the walls, the alarms begin to ring. The command is repeated: 'Stand by your beds!'

Driven from sleep by the voices, the shrill siren, the commotion of men sitting up or falling out of their bunks combined with the staccato of boot heels racing down the central aisle, you rise from a dream and stifle a scream. Your waking mind is convinced that they have found your stash of disks and documents in the basement stores, that the supervisors are coming for you and only you.

'Come on! Out of bed. This is an inspection,' says Cora, the youngest of the three supervisors and the strictest disciplinarian. Already, her face is flushed and the tight mouth warns that no tardiness will be tolerated. You have seen her break canes across the backs of grown men and wrestle muscular assailants to the ground with a bone-crunching effectiveness. Immediately, you are on your feet. Dizzy, you look around and see other men rolling out of beds, rubbing their eyes or automatically declaring their innocence. 'Not me, ma'am!' 'I didn't do it.' Or, 'Please. Please. Please,' from one who has recently experienced the fullest vigour of their discipline and doubts his buttocks can take any more.

Between the beds, you see the three supervisors go to work with the backs of their hands at any man who has been tardy in leaving his bunk. The women wear white uniforms and full make-up. Their knee-length boots always shine because of the inexhaustible list of men eager to polish. Extendible canes are sometimes broken out, but generally these women responsible for Environment Services do not experience much trouble from any of their boys. They are used to a high level of respect and obedience. Only the new entrants ever dare to disobey, and they soon regret it. The supervisors remind you of those female teachers who taught you at school, who were in possession of an indefinable quality that issued fear and commanded respect, while others were hapless to control a classroom.

'I want everybody standing at the foot of their beds. Now!' cries the chief, a woman called Margaret. Her hair is white and for a woman with such broad hips she moves down the aisle with a surprising pace and alacrity. Her two assistants are younger and slimmer than the supervisor. But less weight also seems to represent less patience than the leader. You would rather deal with Margaret than Mary and Cora.

The men gather at the bottom of their bunks while the two junior supervisors move from bed to bed. Nobody has had time to dress and you all stand in the white pants and vests that you sleep in. Sheets and mattresses are tossed by Cora and Mary. The one drawer in the little bedside cabinets, that is permitted to each worker, is then turned upside down and emptied before the toe of a boot sifts through the contents. Checking under the beds with torches for stashes of contraband, the women then move on to the next set of bunks.

'Oh no. Fuck. Fuck. Fuck. No. No,' you mutter to yourself. Even though you stashed the contraband for the rebellion collected yesterday on your rounds in the

164

usual hiding place, you kept the stockings given to you by the manager in the bathroom. They are tucked inside your pillowcase. To make matters worse, as if this is some omen of your fate, three bunks down, a brassiere is discovered under the mattress of a man who used to command a respected position in overseas investments. 'And this belongs to who?' Cora bellows at the two men who stand beside the bunk. 'Which stinking little pervert is sniffing this out? Eh?' Titters and giggles spread down the length of the dormitory.

'Silence!' commands Margaret, the chief supervisor, from where she now stands in the middle of the central aisle on a chair. Usually, you enjoy discreet peeks at her shapely backside and inside the discreet slit at the back of her white dress-coat, but the thought of the hosiery in your pillowcase makes you feel sick instead. This is no time for such pleasures. In fact, it was a perverse, secretive urge that landed you in this dilemma. If discovered, the underwear will be held up for all to see before you are disciplined; you will never live down the shame.

Gripped by the ear, the investment merchant who has confessed to ownership of the brassiere is hauled into the central aisle of the dormitory. Red in the face, naked, stripped of all dignity, Cora pushes him to the ground. He is then ordered to remain naked and face-down on the concrete floor. She was spoiling for a fight after being made to rise so early and is eager to deal with this miscreant personally. You swallow as Mary continues the search on your side of the aisle.

Up on the chair, when Margaret begins to survey the men on the other side of the dormitory, you duck down and creep across to your pillow to retrieve the stockings. Jerky and making sudden darting movements, you lack full control of your hands. They fumble with the pillowcase. You are terrified. Mary is now only two bunks away and has just found one of Margaret's

165

discarded slips hidden inside a man's towel. The culprit is ordered to strip and lie face-down on the floor like the man caught with the brassiere. Digging your hands inside the pillowcase, you feel the silky material of the stash and whip it out. Straightening your back, you are just about to stuff the article down the back of your own underwear when a hand seizes your wrist.

Spun around, you now stare into the ferocious face of Margaret. 'Did you think I couldn't see you from up there? I see everything. Now let's have it. Come on.'

Gulping to remove the sudden constriction in your throat, so you can explain why you have hidden women's underwear inside your pillowcase, you gingerly hold the nylons out in front of your body. You hear a sharp intake of breath from your neighbours when they see what you have. Margaret snatches them from your fingers and holds them up to the light.

'Ma'am, please. I can explain. They were given to me.'

'Shut up,' she says, in a quiet but curt tone as she surveys the craftsmanship. 'Now these are lovely. Very pretty indeed. And I wonder where a toilet cleaner could get his hands on such a prize. I wonder who the rightful owner is. We shall have to find out now, won't we?'

'Yes, ma'am,' you say.

She looks at you with a stern expression. 'You know the drill.'

You slip out of your underwear and then drop to the freezing concrete floor.

When the search in the remainder of the dormitory is complete, the rest of the men are marshalled down to the showers. You and the other two unfortunates are led to the staffroom. You walk behind Margaret. In front of her, you can see the chap who was caught in possession of the slip. Judging by his self-conscious walk, you know he has an erection and is trying to conceal it with both hands. He should think of something to make it wilt; the supervisors don't like to see such things. 'Grubby,' they call it. Or 'mucky'. Mary is especially hard on men who are unable to keep their sex flaccid at all times. Rumour has it she was once a high-ranking executive, demoted to the department for an indiscretion with a junior. And now she is the enemy of anything associated with sex. But it could just be another story, or wishful thinking on behalf of her many admirers in the barracks.

Alone, you follow Margaret into her office and force yourself not to stare at her bottom – through the fabric of her bleached and starched uniform her garter straps are visible in the form of small indentations. And you keep your eyes averted from her shiny boots too. Wearing these boots, she once pressed your face into the floor. It was after you were returned to the department by the police following your escape. She didn't beat you – perhaps because she could see the many welts already marking your body – but just had a quiet, threatening word with you while the sole of her boot squashed the back of your head. Above everything else, Margaret wants to do a good job, and workers who escape make her look bad. But you suspect she felt sorry for you after your capture; the boot on your head was just for show, because Cora and Mary were watching. They both think their boss is too soft on the 'boys'. And, as far as you are aware, Margaret has never interfered with her wards during the night. Once you even overheard Margaret telling her subordinates that, 'These poor wretches have lost everything. At least let them preserve a little dignity.' You are glad it was Margaret who caught you.

'Stand there,' she says, pointing to a spot before her desk. Then she closes the door and locks it. She draws the blinds and turns the light on before sitting behind her desk. She puts her glasses on in order to write a report. Spectacles suit her; they make her look distinguished. 'Now I must say that I am surprised that you would take such a risk, considering the trouble we've had from you in the past.'

Contrite, you bow your head and cringe inside at the implications of what you have done, of what she must think of you for hoarding women's underthings like a depraved adolescent. You want to defend yourself, but can think of nothing to say. As you stand there in silence looking at your feet, you can feel her eyes assessing you as she considers what should be done with a repeat offender.

'I am surprised, yes. But I also admire you,' she says, keeping her voice soft.

You look up, thinking you misheard what she just said. Is this some kind of cruel joke?

Looking you in the eye, she nods her handsome head. 'I know it must be hard to suddenly lose a marriage and job. And to then spend a night in the cells also, after realising the horrible truth about your wife. Many never recover from such an experience. We are forced to send them to the sanatorium where they live out their days in restraints.'

'Dear God, no. Not that. This was a stupid mistake' – you point at the stockings she has laid out on her desk – 'but I was lonely. I'm flesh and blood. Weak.'

She holds her hand up to silence you. 'I understand the men's affection for this kind of thing. I have worked in this department for ten years. Believe me, I have seen it all. Every kind of infraction you can imagine. And even our heroes, our crusaders, have moments of weakness. I know. It's all right. I know.'

'Sorry?' you say, confused. Did she just call you a hero?

Gravely, she nods her head. 'We're sorry we had to set you up like this.'

'Set up?'

'Yes. The woman who gave you these is our leader. She organised the resistance from the start. You being

168

caught with her stockings is a coded message for me. It means it's time for the first handover. It will also deflect the suspicion of my colleagues when I detain you in here. A nice touch,' she adds sarcastically, and holds up the hosiery. 'Just like her,' she mutters to herself. 'And she will give the signal for the day of action. It is nearly time.'

Dumbstruck, you ask, 'You are one of us?'

Margaret nods. 'Yes. Agents and sympathisers have infiltrated all of the lower departments. And, increasingly, the higher floors also. It is I who inform my contacts of your whereabouts in the building. They then mention your location to those they know want to join or help us. You have quite a reputation. Your discretion and stealth is much admired.'

'Me? No.'

'Afraid so. You see, the last two who gathered intelligence for us went missing. They were never seen again.'

'Never?'

She nods. 'You have taken a great risk. Now, where is the material you have gathered?'

You tell her about the toxic waste bin in the storeroom and she informs you that she will collect it shortly. There will be a handover tonight at the main gates. Outside help will then smuggle the incriminating evidence out of the city to the powerful friends of the resistance who work in a rival company. Shortly, they will go public with all you have gathered. A takeover is envisaged after plummeting stock.

'Good,' you say. 'About time. People are getting nervous. Someone is bound to get found out sooner or later. And I have so much. I'm terrified Cora or Mary might find it.'

She nods. 'Don't worry. It'll be safe with me for the time being.' She checks the watch on a chain that hangs over her left breast. 'We'd better hurry.' She looks at you, her face grave. 'I'm afraid I will have to punish you. It's unfortunate, but necessary. The others will expect it. If they think you have got off lightly, there will be reprisals. I'm sorry.'

'It's OK. Really. Fine,' you mumble and feel a warmth between your legs. 'But . . . may I ask a question?'

'Make it quick.'

'How did you come to be here? Down here?'

She smiles. 'A long story. I was once a member of the original executive that founded the corporation.'

'No.'

She nods. 'Our early success created an inevitable power struggle. The more ruthless elements took control of the company. I was ousted. And in the style of the new management it was important for me to fall a long way while always being visible.'

You shrug. 'I'm sorry.'

She smiles. 'Now please bend over my desk. Bite a pencil if you wish. I promise to make it quick.'

You follow her orders. Hands spread out on the wood of her desk top, you watch her unlock a cupboard in the corner of the office. She takes a moment to select an instrument.

Approaching you, she looks embarrassed. She clears her throat. 'I believe some of the men prefer their correction while I'm undressed. Or partially dressed. I'm certainly no model, but I believe it makes the punishment easier to endure.'

You nod. 'Yes. Yes. Please. I think you're lovely.'

Her face blank, she unbuttons her dress coat with one hand and then removes it from her body like a gown. Seeing how you devour her body with your eyes, she is forced to smile, even blushes a little. Wearing a large bra, made from sheer, white silk, matching French knickers, flesh stockings and polished knee boots, she takes up position beside you. 'Let's get it over with. Ready?' she asks.

170

'Yes. Yes, thank you,' you say, looking at the dark triangle of her fur beneath the gusset of her panties.

And, like a true professional and an effective agent in the field, she leaves nothing to chance. Even if you were inspected by Cora and Mary a day later, they would still see the marks of their supervisor's cane on your buttocks. You cry out; partly for effect in case prying ears are listening at the door, and partly because the thin piece of wood stings more than any other you have felt since the demotion. Tears fill your eyes and you perform a little dance in your bare feet. The pain is so profound, you cannot keep still. But she seems to know when to pause – at the moment you are about to scream or lurch away.

Shortly after the first flurry of blows is complete, a wonderful warmth floods to your rump. And just a glimpse over your shoulder at the powerful body of the woman who wields this cane inspires stimulation of another kind. Your sex juts out from between your thighs. Every nerve ending along its length demands the touch of soft fingers and painted nails. It seems to be reaching for her.

After she completes the next ten strokes across the fleshier region of your shoulders, Margaret places the cane on the desk beside your clawing fingers. 'Sorry, darling,' she whispers in your ear. 'Now let me help you. It's OK. Our heroes should be rewarded.' She leans over your back and reaches underneath your stomach. Plump fingers encircle your shaft. 'Our leader requested that I personally perform the honour.' Her skilled hand moves up and down the muscle, the taut sinews and the soft coating of skin on your sex. And for a while you wonder how often this experienced, matronly hand has been at work on the erect indiscretions of her wards. Whispering sweetly, she coaxes you until the maximum length, girth and firmness of your poor, overstrained organ is achieved.

'Turn around, my sweet,' she says when you are pumped and primed to her satisfaction.

You turn about to face her and rest your body against the front of her desk, placing your hands between the wooden edge and the inflamed flesh of your buttocks. Slipping to her knees, Margaret smiles up at you as she settles between your thighs. Cupping and tickling your balls with one hand, she strokes your anus with the index finger of the other hand. Slowly, her handsome face descends into your lap and her thick lips envelop your sex. Moaning through her nose, she slides her mouth right down your length and then back to the tip of your foreskin, leaving stains of burgundy lipstick behind.

Biting a finger, you suppress the desire to cry out with pleasure. This mouth is exquisite and her gently lined face looks more appealing than ever as it works to relieve and pleasure you. Soon, she has swallowed your entire length and scooped your balls inside her mouth too. You must be reaching right down her throat; your sex seems to be occupying the whole of her head.

Easing her mouth back to the head of your shaft, she then teases the swollen, purple head with tiny licks and kisses and sucking techniques, until you are sure you will explode. 'Ma'am,' you mutter. 'Oh, ma'am. I'm afraid I might . . .'

'Mmm,' she murmurs, quickly rubbing your shaft through her right hand. 'Now, that's all right. You do just what you want, my dear.' Her mouth covers your sex again.

Looking her in the eye, you place your hands on the smooth white hair above her ears and begin to make tiny thrusts between her jaws. Closing her eyes, she breathes heavily through her nose. You look down at her pendulous breasts in the transparent hammock of white silk, and then at her thick but shapely thighs in the fleshy stockings and you feel the inevitable, hot

172

eruption scorch through your length and vigorously pump from the end.

'Oh, my,' she murmurs, pulling her overflowing mouth off your sex to allow the rest to splash over her lips and chin, before angling the hose downward so your seed squirts on to and between her warm breasts. 'So much of it. We'll have to deal with this more regularly.' She then places her mouth back over your still erect sex and cleans it of sap.

Company Profile 5

Unscheduled Meeting

The directors of the corporation wait until all ten thousand members of staff arrive at work. Rubbing their hands, they watch the cars park on the acres of asphalt, in the shadow of the skyscraper, just like they do on any working day. Only this day is going to be special.

Grinning with satisfaction, they watch the security footage, piped from the hidden cameras, as the work-force rise through the building in the elevators and up the stairwells, before walking to their offices and sitting behind their desks. And only when the building is full do the directors turn from the windows and smile at the head of company security, who waits patiently in the directors' lounge. Nodding in acknowledgement, she then makes a phone call and issues a simple instruction: 'Lock down.'

Within minutes of this phone call, over one hundred uniformed and plain-clothes security officers lock the gates to the carparks and every entrance to the ground floor of the building.

Career History: Part 13

Emergency Procedure

You are cleaning urinals on the fortieth floor when you first become aware that something unusual is happening in the building: a sudden announcement is made on the company intercom. It is a woman's voice; young and feminine and well-spoken. Usually these announcements make you think of fresh lipstick on a pretty mouth, but this one makes you suddenly feel cold and then uncomfortably hot inside your white suit: 'Would all members of staff please return to their departments immediately. Remain at your desks until further notice. There is no call for alarm. This is a drill designed to protect the company against security leaks. Thank you for your co-operation.' The message is repeated four times.

Almost as soon as the fourth message concludes, a man bursts through the door of the bathroom: 'You! It was you! You set me up, you bastard.' Red in the face, shirt and tie dishevelled, he staggers towards you and points at your face with a shaky hand. You recognise the man: he gave you a small box of computer disks two weeks ago while you were scraping chewing gum off the tarmac of the executive carpark. Back then he was nervous and would only speak in whispers, but you knew he was an important man because of where his car was parked.

Lost for words you raise your hands in the posture of surrender and back away from him until your buttocks rest against the sink units. Reading the confusion in your expression, he pauses in his approach. Like those enduring a great and sudden attack of anxiety, his train of thought quickly changes. 'They're coming for me. I've got to get out. Your suit. Give it to me. I need it.' But before he can get his chubby fingers on the zipper of your white uniform, the bathroom door is thrust open for a second time. Two women enter. You have never seen them before. They are dressed in plain black suits and ties with their dark hair slicked back. Although their jackets and knee-length skirts are smart and formal, there is something sinister about the leather gloves, aviator sunglasses and tight boots they wear.

While one young woman holds the door shut, the other approaches the terrified man who has stopped scrabbling at your zipper. 'Mr Austen, you were asked to co-operate. Now come quietly. We don't want any fuss. These questions are only routine. In no way do they implicate you.'

'Stay away from me. I know why you're here. I demand to see whoever is in charge of this witch-hunt. Now!'

The two women exchange glances. The one at the door then nods to her partner.

As the frantic Mr Austen backs away towards a cubicle, he shouts, 'Stay away. You have been warned.'

Without another word the woman closest to him removes a pistol from her leather shoulder holster, points it at the retreating executive and discharges the weapon at close range. There is no bang from the gun; more of a hiss, like gas escaping through a hole. This is immediately followed by a shriek of pain from Mr Austen who then falls into an open toilet stall with one hand clutched at his side.

Shocked, you remain still and are unable to tear your eyes away from the preposterous scene that is played out before your eyes. Sheathing her sidearm in the shoulder holster, the chic security agent shakes her head as if she has been forced to do something trifling but avoidable. Then she takes a plastic hand-tie from out of her pocket and approaches the figure sprawled around the porcelain bowl of the gleaming toilet. Eyes open but vague, Mr Austen begins to jabber and mutter as if speaking in his sleep: 'I just wanted to make things fair. That's why I downloaded . . . downloaded the files. To help people, you understand. I'm a loyal employee . . . Ask anyone . . .'

Stepping around his legs, the female security officer secures his hands in the white plastic loop and then drags him out of the stall by his feet until he is lying still in the middle of the bathroom. He must have lost consciousness because he has stopped muttering. His body is then tagged with a sticker. Without even acknowledging your presence, the women leave the bathroom so you are alone with the unconscious form of Mr Austen.

Gingerly, you approach the body. This Mr Austen looks like he is sleeping. Sticking through his white cotton shirt you can see a small red dart. It struck him between the ribs. Kneeling down, you read the sticker attached to his forehead. There is no text on the paper, but a familiar line drawing instead. It features a stick figure dropping a single piece of waste paper into a wire basket.

Career History: Part 14

Fire Escape

Out in the corridor the announcement continues to drone its polite instructions in a reassuring tone. If this truly is a witch hunt for members of the resistance under the guise of a security drill, you can only anticipate the worst for yourself. Astonished that you are still at large when Mr Austen was hunted down and shot within minutes of arriving at work, you hover in the doorway of the bathroom and try to think of an escape plan.

Now the cool and conditioned company air is full of the electronic voice again that speaks of a security leak. Can this be the day of action? Or is this the day before the day of action? Have the corporation found out? You refuse to accept this.

To your right, three figures turn a corner and come into view in the corridor to which your bathroom is attached. Two women, dressed much the same as the agents who dispatched Mr Austen, hold the elbows of a pretty blonde executive woman and march her swiftly down the corridor towards the nearest elevator. 'Please,' the woman says. 'Please. I can explain. Please. This is outrageous.' Dressed in a chic pinstripe suit and high heels it seems improbable that this is the kind of woman who would resist the company and upset security. Lately, it's a thought you have entertained many times as power-dressed men and women have handed you confidential material.

Stepping back inside the entrance to the bathroom, you watch the three women pass. What you then see of the captive's face stimulates your recall: she was the lunch-time jogger, wearing a red baseball cap, who dropped a list of computer passwords at your feet while you raked leaves in the grounds near the incinerator.

And only when the elevator doors open does she finally attempt a struggle. But one of her arms is immediately pulled up her back and she is deftly struck at the back of the knees by the toe of a boot. She collapses forward and a shoe dislodges from one of her feet. Then, she is effortlessly dragged inside the steel elevator. The doors close and her cries are sealed.

In the empty corridor, a single, patent court shoe rests on its side. If you were not so afraid, you would probably seize this item and take it down to the barracks where such artefacts are highly prized as a currency amongst the men. But there are more pressing concerns facing you. This can be no coincidence; two of your contacts have been seized by force. The company must know of the resistance; its plans and collaborators. This alleged drill is definitely a cover for a witch-hunt and round-up of every suspect.

But how did they find out? Were you observed or did someone betray the cause? You don't know, may never know, but one thing is for sure: soon they will come for you – the middle-man, go-between, prize fool. It now seems ludicrous that any of you even dared to stand up to this company.

Time to save yourself. Head bowed, a protection mask across your mouth, you push your buggy into the corridor and head for the nearest stairwell. In the confusion, you may have an opportunity to slip out of the building and then out of the grounds. If not, you are finished. Thinking of what your supervisor, Margaret, said about the sanatorium and how the inmates are kept in restraints, you abandon the cleaners' buggy by the first fire exit you can find and then duck into the stairwell.

You have an urge to just hand yourself over to the guards, to get it over with and end the suspense. And it's hard to breathe with your heart thumping like this. Already it feels like you are wearing a strait-jacket around your chest.

Company Profile 6

Teamwork

There is chatter in the office. People are nervous but excited by the announcement. It offers a break in the monotony of stress and self-interest that constitutes life in this vast building. But is this really a drill? Everyone is suspicious. No one really trusts the person who sits next to them every day, let alone what they hear on the company intercom. Rumours spread in this company the way diseases whip through developing countries. Back-stabbing is more common than in the ancient Roman senate. No job is safe; no one is irreplaceable.

Behind their desks, where they are instructed to remain, every person in this office takes a moment to replay in their minds all of the things they have done that might cause displeasure to the company: the short cuts they have taken with correct working practice, the infringements of the many rules, the odd break with protocol, a hastily made and loose comment to a stranger in a restaurant or in an elevator, the day one wore an inappropriate tie, or stammered through a meeting, or forgot to greet a manager with the customary enthusiasm and grace, the unreported bumper scrape in the carpark, a pen that went home in a shirt pocket and is still on the kitchen counter. Who are they looking for?

The chatter stops when the four female security agents enter the office. Dressed in simple but elegant suits, their emotions hidden behind dark glasses, hands protected by supple leather gloves that leave no marks, boots polished and ready to stamp corporate authority on any resistance, the women approach the glass cubicle at the end of the administrative area. This is where the department manager works. The agents enter the tiny office and close the door behind them. Through the blinds of the manager's office the staff outside can see that words are being exchanged between their manager and the agents, but they can hear nothing. No one breathes in the office but there is the sound of someone swallowing. The manager then seems to agree with something the agents have said. She stands up behind her desk. Through the blinds, she then points at two desks in the office outside. Then she turns her back on her staff and sits down behind her desk again.

Immediately, there is a commotion from the two desks the manager just pointed at. 'Why are you all looking at me?' one man asks. The electric lights flash off the lenses of his spectacles and the beads of sweat on his forehead. 'Stop staring. Cut it out,' he says. But an uneasy silence has already descended to surround his desk like a moat. This is followed by a subtle withdrawal from the area he occupies by those who sit nearest him. Chairs scrape and creak. People turn in their seats to glare. And all the man in glasses can focus on are the many faces turned towards him – some accusing, some disbelieving, many disappointed. And behind this terrible wall of faces, he can see two women in dark suits approaching his desk. Lifting his chin with defiance, he folds his arms across his chest and makes a decision not to be moved.

'Please come with us, Mr Reynolds. There are some questions we would like to ask you,' the taller agent says.

He searches for her eyes behind the opaque lenses of her sunglasses and says, 'No. I will not. I demand to see my lawyer.'

In another part of the office, a woman in a black suit suddenly stands up behind her desk. Lower lip trembling and eyes already filling with tears, her colleagues can see her struggling to control herself; to turn this sudden flood of emotion back with her reason. But passion wins the inner struggle and she suddenly makes a dash for the door of the office. In the wake of her hasty charge for freedom, a chair falls on its side, a phone crashes to the floor and a container of stationery empties its bowels across the carpet tiles.

Cut off by the other two security officers before she can reach the door, she stops running, spins about on the spot and peers at her colleagues for support. As if she is contagious, the desks around the place where she stands suddenly clear of their occupants. 'Stephen,' she says, imploring a colleague with her eyes. 'Please.' She sniffs and wipes at an eye. Stephen shakes his head and backs away. The two tense security agents inch closer to her.

'Ms Smith, we want you to think about what you are doing and where you are. Don't make a scene. Don't make it worse.'

'Fuck you!' Ms Smith screams as she lurches at them. Slapping at the first agent with both hands, who calmly steps back to avoid the blows, Ms Smith is quickly seized from behind and pulled back by the second agent. The woman she struck at then rushes forward and slaps Ms Smith hard across the face, twice, to subdue her. But Ms Smith only laughs like a hysteric. Her body goes limp too so the guard behind is forced to support her weight and drag her across the floor towards the door. Then Ms Smith suddenly stiffens her legs and arms, spits an obscenity at her opponents and grates her high heel down the shin of the guard who holds her arms behind her back. The grip on her forearms loosens and she breaks free to leap on the agent who faces her. Their lithe bodies instantly crash together, smash against a desk and then fall to the floor, wrapped about each other. Breathing hard and tearing at each other's hair, they roll and scuffle on the carpet tiles. Skirts rise and sheer stockings ladder. Glimpses of panty are flashed and pretty mouths open to swear and grunt. Office workers now jostle around the mêlée, their faces flushed with excitement. They are safe and relieved; today the corporate security came for someone else. An opportunity is presented to release their own pressures.

Their colleague, Ms Smith, puts up a heroic struggle. She slaps and kicks herself free of the agent's stranglehold and leaps into the air brandishing an extendible cane she has managed to unhook from inside the jacket of the fallen agent. With the weapon, she slashes at the second guard who now suffers a limp. This agent immediately staggers away from the berserk Ms Smith and mutters into the microphone hidden inside her collar. Speaking in code, she calls for reinforcements.

Hair in disarray, cheeks red, scratch marks like gills on her pale throat, the desperate Ms Smith suddenly smiles with satisfaction at the realisation that she has won the first stand-off with the smartly dressed representatives of this tyranny. But before she can turn and race for the door, something occurs that she could never have foreseen.

'You bitch!' 'Traitor.' 'Knew you were a little liar.' 'Fooled no one.' 'Slut!' A group of enraged female co-workers surround her, their painted claws extended and their perfect white teeth revealed behind glossy lips. 'Thought she was better than us.' 'Teacher's pet.' 'Slut.' 'Slag.' 'Bitch.' Faces painted like news readers but now transformed into witchy grimaces, her colleagues draw closer to the suddenly bewildered office girl. They know this is the last chance they will get to exact a revenge on the girl they never liked; the prettiest, the smartest and, until recently, most valued junior member of the team. It's not enough that she will be carted off and interrogated, forced to work in the corporate equivalent of the salt mines, or never seen again. Not enough.

Bitch fight.

'Bitch fight! Bitch fight! Bitch fight!' the men start to chant, much to the bemusement of the agents Ms Smith successfully fought off – the two women who now stand to the side of the new mêlée to catch their breath, straighten their skirts and rub their bruises.

'No!' Ms Smith screams at her co-workers. 'You arse-lickers! You sheep! It'll be you next time!' She raises the cane and threatens the women who circle her. Three of them have kicked off their shoes, ready for combat. And the oldest woman of the team has unzipped her constricting pencil skirt and allowed it to fall to her ankles. Immediately, she assumes a Thai boxing stance. Roaring with delight, the men jostle forward to see her seamed stockings and see-through French panties.

The pursued girl recognises none of these people she has worked alongside for years; in only a few minutes they have changed from the polite and efficient colleagues she knew to the point of familiarity, over-familiarity and then loathing. But now they want her blood. The women close on her.

Four pairs of feet kick, four pairs of hands slap and tear, four slender bodies that have never allowed themselves to be an ounce overweight, throw their slender dimensions upon the prey. Like predator cats their fangs and claws sink into silk and the flesh beneath. Then they try to pull the quarry to the ground where they can complete the kill.

With a shriek, Ms Smith strikes out twice with the stolen cane. Lining one shoulder and clipping another ear, she manages only to fuel the fury of her hunters before the cane is ripped from her hand. Their numbers are too great. This is her last stand; her last moment of liberty. Down to the conservative grey carpet tiles she goes. Falling on her back, she issues a final, defiant scream before the angry felines are upon her.

Rip: the blouse is opened. Innards are exposed: a pale tummy and her little breasts in a white brassiere. Tear: down to her ankles the skirt and slip are forced. Then her pink thong is whipped over her thighs, knees and feet before being tossed to the male hyenas who cheer around the fray. Snapping free of her suspender clips, her flesh-tint stockings are then shredded from her legs by cruel fingernails that flash like rubies tossed into the air. Discarded remnants of her clothing are quickly snatched up by the jeering, shouting male members of staff and spirited away to become trophies.

The tribe has turned on the outsider, the misfit. Bad voodoo, black magic: the scapegoat is harshly dealt with before her banishment from the community for ever. Wrists held by her captors, blonde head forced face-down, slim buttocks pulled into the air, legs trapped under knees and pressing hands, Ms Smith is prepared for ritual sacrifice. The older woman who removed her clingy skirt in order to move more freely in the fight, assumes the role of high priestess. Raising the cane like a staff, she commands a cheer from the crowd. They are hungry for blood. The cane then slices through the air with a hiss and splats against the naked backside of Ms Smith. She squeals, but her cries are drowned out by the applause, the jeers, the demands for more. Then the crowd counts aloud as the cane falls again and again: two, three, four, five . . .

Head covered in the jacket of his suit, Mr Reynolds, the second traitor, suffers a sudden change of heart. Led by the other two security agents, this sweating man in glasses now scurries around the fringes of the office and heads for the door. Resistance is for fools. These women in boots are for his own safety. He even urges them to hurry while his colleagues and friends are busy with Ms Smith: 'Fuck the lawyer, let's roll. Get me the fuck out of here,' he mutters from under his protective cowl.

Inside the glass office that belongs to the manager, the white blinds are drawn.

Company Profile 7

Redundancy

Up on the seventy-eighth floor of the building, there is a man sitting alone in his office. He turns the photo of his wife face-down on the desk top. He does not want her to see what is about to happen to him and he does not want to see a reminder of that which is now his past. It is best he forget about his wife, the house and their dog. After what he tried to do to the company, he knows he will be permitted to keep nothing. Not even his hair.

Loosening his tie and removing his jacket, he wonders where he will be sent. Thinking of the bald men in the white boiler suits who mow grass, collect litter and tend the flower beds, he opens the top drawer of his desk and removes a flask. Silver inlaid with gold; the flask bears the inscription of the country club's golf team to which he previously belonged and once captained. Will he ever have an opportunity to play golf again?

Sipping straight from the flask, he leans back in his chair and waits. Waits for the door to open. They should be here soon.

Five years of his life were spent in the junior executive of the merger's department before he was given this office. He will have lost it in less than a year.

Perhaps he should be frightened. But he feels an unnatural calm. Even relief. His leading role in the attempted coup has come to nothing, but at least the rash of nightmares leading to the bouts of insomnia, the loss of appetite and the episodes of sudden terror whenever a phone rang late at night, or another manager called his name aloud in a deserted corridor, are over. And there is no point in running either; they know exactly where he is. They came for his two dour-faced accomplices two minutes ago and it is his turn next. Leave the bigger fish until last. From somewhere in the ceiling, or a light, or harmless fixture, he knows he is being watched, and has always been watched. Despite the secrecy of the resistance network, the company still found out about their plans. Perhaps they always knew. And the corporate security teams moved swiftly this morning. Those suspected of dissent must have been watched from the moment they closed their front doors before the working day began. Maybe even before breakfast, while they shaved or applied make-up. And fleeing or begging will just make matters worse; if that is at all possible.

Swivelling around in his chair, he stares out of the window at the surrounding grounds and parkland. It is a beautiful day. The strong sunlight pours into the trees and grasses and redefines the landscape into a myriad of bright greens and yellows. A good day to be outside. In the distance, he sees the orderly matrix of the suburbs and town centre. Perhaps it was folly to believe this place could have been wrested from the hands of the directors; that it could have continued to be safe and orderly and civilised, only with real freedoms for the population too. Because there is no real freedom here. Hasn't been since the early days. People have forgotten what freedom is. Perhaps they prefer the current system.

Behind his chair, he hears the door click open. After taking a deep breath, he smiles to himself and turns around.

'Morning, Max,' Mrs Crocker says. She must have come downstairs especially for this unscheduled meeting. And today she is wearing her finest: a black Dior two-piece suit, a transparent camisole peeking between the lapels of her jacket, seamed black hose and her highest heels. As symbolic as a judge's cowl, she only ever wears these shoes when it is time to cancel or demote a member of staff. He has seen the patent sling-backs before, many times.

Standing up and meeting the glare from her dark green eyes, he says, 'Morning, ma'am.'

Before Mrs Crocker closes the door to his office behind her, Max spies the two women from internal security leaning on his secretary's desk. They too are dressed for a certain kind of business: black knee-length boots, black suits and ties, sunglasses, gloves. They were dressed like this when they removed his predecessor from a company barbecue eight months earlier. And Jan, his secretary, is no longer at her post.

With the door shut, Mrs Crocker teeters across to his desk and places her briefcase next to his reading lamp. The attaché case is made from leather and opened by a zipper at the side. Max has never seen this case before, but he has been told about what she keeps inside it. Involuntarily, a shiver runs up his spine and makes his right cheek and eyelid twitch.

'I don't suppose I have to waste my breath by telling you how bitterly disappointed I am in you,' Mrs Crocker says.

'Guess not,' Max says, with a smile. 'Sorry.'

'Oh, you're not sorry. You don't even know what to be sorry for. Not yet.' She smells good and her cosmetics emphasise her thickish lips and cold eyes. 'Tut, tut, tut,' she adds shaking her head. 'Three of you. Three of you turned against me. It looks bad, Max. Bad for the department.'

'The department will be fine,' he says, confident. 'But when this is all over, it might look bad for you, ma'am. You hand-picked us. "I always get the best boys and the

189

best from my boys," you were always fond of saying.'
Mrs Crocker shoots a glance full of undisguised loathing across the desk at Max. Perhaps he should stop baiting her. But he can't. His feelings are too strong; especially after what she tried to do to his wife during the spring. 'In future, you should hire women, ma'am. I know you don't get along with them. Always have trouble with the young ones. The pretty ones. The clever ones.' He raises his eyebrows. 'Too much competition? Who knows. But I do know one thing, business cannot be run like a fashion parade, or a singles bar where you're the only woman invited –'

'Enough,' she says; her face trembling. 'There is no punishment sufficient for what you have done. And believe me they will be creative. You'll be amazed, Max, at what is coming your way. The company doesn't like your sort. Never has. The next few months are going to be very hard for you.' Max feels compelled to lower his eyes from her beautiful but nonetheless evil face, but he refuses to be stared down. 'You won't even recognise yourself after they're done. But let me tell you something, Max. Even given all that, it's still not enough for me.' She taps a red fingernail against the desk top.

Max laughs. 'That's because you're an egotistical, conceited and vengeful woman. Rude, unpleasant and impossible to please. A company girl. A modern, independent woman of means.' He laughs some more. 'It's no big surprise that you feel this way. But what does amaze me is that you find my treachery hard to comprehend.' But before Max can finish, she unzips her leather case and opens the cover. Mrs Crocker has heard enough. Silent and pale, she begins to place one item after another on the shiny wood of the desk top, right under Max's nose. Silver cuffs on a short chain; ankle braces of steel; a rubber hood with built in choker-gag; an extendible cane with a platinum handle: all beautifully crafted and hideous in their perfection.

Calmly, Max removes his tie. He winks at his boss, her face now white with emotion, with belligerence and anticipation. Then he unbuttons his shirt and cuffs. After removing the shirt, he unclips the bracelet of his Rolex. Greedily, Mrs Crocker eyes his lean and well-developed torso, the flat stomach and groomed chest. Max points to his belt and raises his eyebrows, questioningly.

'All of it. Underwear too,' she says quickly. Although her chin is raised and her lips are tight through an attempt to retain her dignity and authority, her eyes expose her real feelings: the familiar overachiever's expression of self-importance and defiance – what you need to survive in this place. Still smiling, Max unbelts his trousers and lets them fall to his feet. Slowly, knowing she has called in a favour with security to spend some time alone with him before he is taken away, Max removes his shoes and socks.

She cannot remove her glare from his crotch in the tight, white designer underwear. She is unable to speak for excitement. With one hand she gropes inside her attaché case and removes a small portable camera.

Max steps out of his briefs. His genitals are finally exposed to the company. He must be the last man in the department who has not been forced to reveal himself to the mighty Mrs Crocker. 'Despite every attempt to the contrary you never did get to see this, did you?' Max asks her.

She rests her weight against the desk. A lock of hair falls across her eyes, that seem to have darkened with hot blood. 'You're making things worse, Max.'

Max knows the drill: he either goes along with her wishes now, or she whistles for the girls outside who will willingly assist his boss in getting exactly what she wants. Compliance will make things easier, but he will not be silenced. What has he got to lose? She'll be hard with him anyway. 'Come on, Mrs Crocker, the time for

191

pretence is over. Admit it. I'm history. So we can talk about these difficult matters. It can be liberating. Remember the drunken passes you made on the company outings? Three, at the last count. The Christmas gifts must have set you back at least four thousand in cash too. I loved the new driver, but you really shouldn't have. I mean, I was a married man. But you knew that. Wouldn't let that stand in your way though. What with those anonymous letters to my wife. And the phone calls at night. I knew it was you. And now, finally, after all that, you get to see it. So tell me, do you like it?' Max cradles his scrotum and flaccid cock on the palm of his hand.

Leaning on both hands, she bows her head between her shoulders. Her knuckles are white and her thin shoulders tremble. 'Bastard.'

'Here it is, Mrs Crocker. Come closer, take a look.'

Despite her rage at how he has dared to speak at her, and despite her humiliation at being confronted with this evidence of her attempts at seducing her favourite employee, she slowly raises her head and stares at what lies, thick and heavy in Max's hand. Her lips part, her forehead becomes smooth and her eyes refuse to blink for several seconds.

'Hope it doesn't disappoint,' Max adds, smiling.

Her neck stiffens as she raises the Polaroid camera. Each feature of her face freezes – the lips curl, the eyes lid, the nostrils flare – as she takes aim. There is a flash from the bulb followed by a buzzing sound as the photo begins to process. Then she places the camera back inside her case and drags one hand across the desktop so her painted claws rake the surface.

Max swallows; he has never seen her so angry, so taunted, so tempted before. She tries to laugh at him but it comes out as a cackle. She tries to smile but only succeeds in looking evil. Steadily losing her reserve, she clenches her fists, then gasps before stuffing one hand inside the jacket of her suit. As she twists and pinches a nipple, her eyes roll backwards and she whispers the word, 'Bastard,' at the ceiling. 'You bastard. You bastard. You bastard.' Then her other hand begins to work on the second nipple until tears flood her big eyes.

'You won't see me again, Mrs Crocker. We always did have a special relationship. I think you'll miss me. So you better make the most of it. Bitch.'

'Fuck you,' she hissy-whispers.

Max moves around to the front of his desk. Bending over he stands with his ankles apart. 'Goddamn it. Just do it.'

There is a high-pitched whining sound from behind him that does not sound human. Then he hears her high heels scrabbling on the floor behind his taut buttocks, but does not dare to look. Max keeps his eyes shut. Cold fingers touch his face. Stroke his cheeks. One long fingernail slips between his lips and hooks in his cheek. Painfully, his mouth is pulled wide apart. Then the finger disappears. More of the whinnying devil laughter occurs before the rubber hood is pulled over his head and snapped under his chin. Rough prods with her middle finger stuff the rubber pacifier deep inside his mouth. Up behind his back he bends his arms and cuffs his wrist with gleaming, freezing silver. He takes a sudden breath. Between his feet she strings the length of chain and clamps his ankles into a hobble posture. Now he is an incapacitated rubber-headed baby boy, and the woman in high heels is going to reduce him, peel away every layer, destroy what he thought he was. This is the end of his old life.

Panting for breath, his skin tingling with anticipation for whatever scorching sensation she may choose to inflict against his body, he silently curses the resistance for failing, for falling into a trap, for gratefully taking just enough rope from the company in order to hang itself. But he wants this. Can't deny it. Always gets what he wants: the girl, the job, the cash, the house, the car. And now Max wants to hurt. Max wants to feel failure. Max has never allowed himself to fail, but the company was just too damn strong for his will and skill. He suddenly hates himself. He has been beaten by the likes of the vain Mrs Crocker – spiteful, sadistic, petty, pretty Crocker. She has won. This is not rubber he tastes in his mouth; it is his own shitty, sweaty failure. Max wants to acknowledge that deep down he always knew he was never good enough. For the first time in his life Max wants to give in.

'You're not that clever, Max,' his captor says. 'If you were you would have known what was good for you. I knew. I had plans for you. Plans for us. We had a connection, sweetheart. But you chose to wipe your fucking shoes on me. Eh? Spit in my face. Eh? And now . . .' breathless with excitement, she can barely talk '. . . I'm gonna fuck you over.'

Cutting dead-centre across his buttocks, the first strike makes his head do a big roller-coaster swoop without moving, and his knees nearly give way. Grabbed by the scruff of his neck, Max is repositioned on the desktop. One hand on his lower spine to keep him still, Mrs Crocker then goes mad with her cane.

White light, white heat. Streak lightning up the spinal column to the wipe-out of conscious thought. Death of ego through an unrelenting corporal, caning firestorm. The temperature and split-nerve-ending sting of his discomfort bleaches his arms and legs of strength. The final mutter of his survival instinct tries to make him crawl over the desk and away from the woman with napalm at her fingertips. No chance. Face down, body flattened by shock waves from his candy-striped buttock, he is too weak, too full of self-pity and self-loathing to attempt escape. Successive strikes of the bony, whipping cane continue to paint fresh welts from his thighs to the back of his knees. Screaming with all the power in his lungs, he expects the hood to burst like

194

the peel of ripe fruit from off his head. It does not. Instead he makes the noise of an overheated motor turning oil to piss-steam. But still the cane falls. Above his wriggling body, something wet spatters against the ceiling tiles and hisses on the light fittings.

Head lolling like a galley slave hunched over an oar, he peers through the teary slits on his rubber hood at the svelte, diminutive shape of his mistress behind him. Her face has gone all red and her hair has spiked across her teary face as she masters the precocious child. He's never seen her so excited or heard her laugh so hard. The jacket to her suit is open too. Under her sheer camisole tiny biting clamps of steel are now stuck like leeches to her brown nipples. Through this electricity of pain they both feel, in this short circuit of their collective sanity, she wants them to be more intimate. Both of them have to be in pain. It is the only fitting situation for their desire and hatred of each other. It makes them closer. Like lovers.

He knew the punishment for crossing her would be severe. And when he first accepted favours from this demented, black widow, spider-queen – the promotions, the trappings, the office – he knew it was expected of him to be her partner in business and bed. Part of his resistance to her was a repressed perversity; he can see it now through the rubble of his former self. He often dreamed of what it would be like to disappoint such a woman. Fantasised about her small feet in the highest heels and her manicured fingers unzipping the briefcase that had become the stuff of legend in his department. And before the moment of orgasm when he made love to his wife, Max always took a moment to think of Mrs Crocker stripped to her expensive knickers and going at him like the devil on horseback. While hating her and his time in her service, he always wanted to be bad and to be caught. His role in the resistance was a denial of his true desire; his craving for her demoniac touch.

Now the pressure was off: the struggle to resist her will and the daily cliffhanger of staying one step ahead of the competition, dressed in Armani, but braying for her favours outside his office door. Time to exist in the present. His future and his past were currently being erased by every stroke of this demon's cane. The merest thought of what he was losing and what might happen to his wife could crush his sanity like a grape under a car tyre at any time. Don't think. Keep the pain on the surface of your punished skin. There would be time enough for such thoughts when he was bound like Prometheus on the mountain and taunted by the chorus of Porsche drivers who once lost to him at golf.

The small bloodless hand is finally removed from the base of his spine. Mrs Crocker steps back and wipes her blade with a scented tissue. Shortening its despicable length she then resheaths the weapon and straps it back inside her case. Slowly, Max sinks to the floor and lies on his stomach. He is silent and still. Mrs Crocker sits on the desk above his body. The thin heels of her shoes dangle over his striped back. She repairs her lipstick and then looks into a compact to wipe away her eyeliner where it has smudged. With a snap, she closes the compact. After patting her hair flat, she bends down to where Max lies on the floor. 'Max, I know you can hear me.' Smelling salts are wafted over the nasal perforations of his mask. He chokes and splutters; he is conscious. She smiles. 'Who's the bitch now?' she says sweetly, and then kisses the top of his rubber head.

With each stiletto heel planted on either side of his face, Mrs Crocker looks down at the naked and chained body with pride. 'Like in all good tragedies there is a closing speech. And this is mine. Soon they will take you away, Max. When you are gone, you will cease to exist up here. All your hard work and ambition will mean nothing. You go to the worst place of all. The worst kind of hell for people like us, Max. You go to a manual job with no prospects. You smell shit and you pick up litter, Max. But, occasionally, while I'm ordering dinner in the best restaurant in town, or sipping champagne by my pool, I may wonder what ever became of you. Your wife will too. At least for a while. The company is good at helping people get on with their lives.' She laughs long and hard – a black-lipped desert scavenger roaring from inside a reddish ribcage.

Inside the tight rubber hood, Max smiles like a clown who has been sucking back the crazy gas. Even when she kicks at his ribs with the pointy tips of her high heels, he keeps on smiling. With a disappointed sigh, perhaps because she broke him so easily, she kneels down beside him and unlocks the cuffs from his wrists and the hobbles from his ankles. But Max's hands stay in the same position, as if he does not even realise that the steel has been taken away. Max just keeps on smiling.

Mrs Crocker steps over his body and reaches across the desk for the speaker phone. She wants to call in the girls to drag this piece of garbage away, out of her sight for good. So much time has been wasted on this one. But as she reaches for the phone, she never sees the tall hooded figure rise from the dead behind her. When her scarlet nail is an inch away from depressing the green button to open the communication channel, the figure in the hood suddenly clutches her around the waist and lifts her into the air.

'What? Huh?' But before she can gather her wits and scream for help, the hooded man swiftly waltzes her body around the desk to the other side of the office. Planting her feet back on the floor, he then stoops over, picks up a discarded silk tie from the floor and then gags her painted mouth. 'No!' she quietly screams into the material. Snatching up the discarded steel cuffs from the desk, that were previously cutting red lines into his own wrists, he then forces Mrs Crocker's arms behind her

197

back. The biceps and pectoral muscles she often stroked through his Italian shirts, at the vaguest opportunity for physical contact with her subordinate, suddenly stand out on his body as he wrestles her hands into position to apply the steel.

Clunk, click, shnick – the cuffs close. These two beautiful white hands with the shiny scarlet nails could probably manage to hold a tennis ball now, but are rendered useless for just about any other purpose. Gently, her upper body is bent over the desk. Carefully, the padded mouse-mat is slipped under her cheek for comfort; it's going to be a turbulent ride. And, at last, Max removes his hood.

Pinching the hem of her skirt, he then raises it up her thighs, pulls it clear of her stocking tops and wriggles it over her thighs and narrow hips until it is ruffled around her tiny waist. Nodding with satisfaction, he surveys her legs in the seamed stockings and punishment shoes. Everything is especially shimmery and glassy on her lower half now the sun is pouring through the windows behind them to bathe her legs in solar warmth.

Curiously, there is no struggle from Mrs Crocker. Wide-eyed, she turns her head on the desk to watch what he is doing. Raising the transparent fabric of her black panties from the cleft of her buttock cheeks, Max then tears a slit in them. As the torn panties then settle back on her skin she can feel the warm air as it comes in through the fresh rend. The draught makes her feel particularly vulnerable back there. Under her clothes, her skin gooses. She sighs, closes her big eyes, then clenches her teeth on the gag. When she opens her eyes, the light of reason has gone from them. Instead, they shine with lust.

Strong brown fingers sink into the flesh of her hips. 'Been so worried lately, I've not been able to get aroused. When that happens to a man, he gets a backlog. A build-up. I must be potent by now. Guess it's time to let it all go, ma'am. What do you say? Hmm? You about ready for this?' There is a groan from her and a gnawing at the tie between her teeth. 'Sure you are,' Max says. 'Never knew a pussy could get so wet. Look at this –' He holds two shining fingers under her petite nose. 'Soaking. It's even running down the inside of your thighs. Guess we're both ready.' Max sucks his fingers clean. Using one hand, he then nudges the outer lips of her sex with his engorged phallus. There is a long and insistent moaning sound from Mrs Crocker. 'Reckon this stuff is so potent, it might even get you in a little trouble, ma'am. Might mellow you out.' Another muffled moan from the gag. 'I know,' Max says, in a reassuring tone of voice. 'Not long now. Sorry for being such a tease for so long, but things were different before. Couldn't let myself go. Now I can. Now I can show you who was in charge all along. I know you had the power on paper, but with this thick piece of muscle between my legs, we both knew who –' But before Max can say another word, Mrs Crocker thrusts her body backward so hard, she impales herself on his erect member, right down to the root. There is a strangled yelp from behind the tie as his thickness descends through her. This is followed by her heavy, desperate breathing.

Max groans and clenches the muscles in his sex to reinforce its rigidity. 'This is what you wanted all along. And not getting it made you mad, made you mean as a snake.' Max then withdraws from her glossy pink insides before thrusting deep and hard.

'Bastard.' Her voice is muffled but he understands what she thinks of him: she loathes him for making her so vulnerable with desire. She has craved and dreamt of this penetration. It was always her will to break him and to master him thoroughly only so she could then engineer a brief transference of power in which he would be permitted to hold her down, handle her and have his brutish way. She did the same thing to his colleagues.

'Yes. Harder. Yes. Bastard. Harder.' She would keep all the power until it suited her to submit. And no other woman could be allowed to interfere with such a bond. Not even a wife. 'You bastard. Oh. Oh. Oh. Bas–'

Max thrusts hard again. Using all the muscles in his back and thighs, he smashes his sex inside her. Holding her little shoulders, he yanks her back to meet his pummelling, to force his sex even deeper inside his nemesis. 'This is what it came to. What it had to come to,' he says, while panting from the exertion. Through the rend in her panties he can now see his wet shaft rifling in and out of her softness. It increases his desire when he sees the connection, at how they are joined in this most base method like two animals in a forest or field, mating in a frenzy for the survival of the species. It is a terrible, sinful, irresponsible thing he does with a woman for whom conflict is a way of life. But, for some inexplicable reason, Max cannot ever remember being so excited.

She begins to utter a chesty, choking sound and her body stiffens. Legs shaking and fingers pointy, she begins to climax, hard. In tatters, his tie slips from between her smudged lips; Mrs Crocker has chewed right through it.

'This is what you wanted. My cock. Am I right?' he presses her.

She refuses to answer the question. 'Fuck the slut. Fuck her,' she says, instead, wanting to be taken even harder.

Max clenches his fingers in the hair at the back of her scalp and lifts her head from the mouse-mat. 'Tell me. This is what you craved?'

'Yes,' she croaks at him. Clenching her teeth, she speaks with difficulty. 'You could have taken me at any time. Any time. I was ready for you every day.'

'And I was yours. Weak for you.'

'No!'

'Yes! So remember my cock when you're sitting alone in the best restaurant in town.'

'Bastard.'

'I'm coming. In your mouth. Drink it. I want you to suck it back.' Max pulls out of her sex and takes a step back from the desk over which she is sprawled and grasping. 'Now,' he commands.

Swivelling around and then falling to her knees, Mrs Crocker seizes the thick and oily shaft between her employee's legs. Using her lips she pulls and tugs at the pulsing muscle, swallowing the thick strawberry head at the same time. Unable to tear his eyes away from the sight of Mrs Crocker's greedy face, hurriedly gulping at what pours and pumps from his sex, frantically milking his shaft, Max groans and pushes himself deeper inside her mouth. 'At last. At last, you have it,' he whispers. 'Finally, I put it inside you.' And she remains on her knees with her thickish lips strangling his sex until every last drop has been taken inside her body.

Leaning back against the drawers of his desk, legs apart, one high-heeled shoe missing, make-up smudged, Mrs Crocker then watches him with eyes both adoring and slovenly while she cleans her lips with her tongue. 'Go to hell, you evil bastard,' she whispers.

'I'll see you there,' he says, smiling. 'If you're lucky.'

Sitting still and silent, she watches him dress. Only when he stands up and begins to walk across his office for the last time, does she move. 'Max!' In her torn panties and snagged stockings, with the silver clamps still biting her nipples beneath the camisole, Mrs Crocker crawls after him, across the floor. 'Max. Don't go. Max. Stay. Please. I can pull strings. I can do anything here. Let me help you.' But Max closes the door behind him.

When he appears outside his office, the two security agents leaning on his secretary's desk stand up, their toned bodies immediately tense, instinctively expecting confrontation. Wincing from the discomfort under his suit, from the deep welts Mrs Crocker has imprinted on his flesh as a branding, agonising sign of her devotion, Max raises his hands in surrender; he is drained and there is no more fight inside him. Bowing his head, he lets the women tie his hands together behind his back with a plastic loop before leading him to the nearest elevator.

Career History: Part 15

Gazing from a Window

Taking three steps at a time and falling twice, you hurl yourself down the emergency stairs, towards the ground floor. But from a window in the stairwell something outside the building, down on the grass, catches your eye. You can see the beginning of an assembly in the company grounds at the foot of this skyscraper. Below on the lush, hand-reared grass, little white objects begin to collect. From up here they look like seagulls who have landed on the earth to peck at worms. Only these objects are not scattered about. They are lined up in rows and columns to form one giant square. And none of them are moving. But other small figures, though these are black in colour, walk between the orderly lines of the motionless white shapes.

After descending another dozen floors, the activity on the ground becomes clearer. And what you see fills you with horror. Naked people are kneeling on the lawn by the foundations of this mighty tower. Behind their bare backs, open to the sun's yellow warmth, their hands are tied with thin nylon loops. Heads bowed as if in prayer, reverence or shame, none of them speak or move; they just remain still and calm, breathing in and out, as if in reflection, or dejection, looking inward. Their shaven heads point towards the divine edifice of glass, concrete and steel.

You stop running and walk down the next ten flights of stairs. Breathing heavily and constantly wiping the sweat from your face, you are unable to tear your eyes from the spectacle below. Now you can see that a black apparatus has also been fixed to the freshly shorn scalps of the naked people. Rubber straps circle the back of their skulls and then, like a horse's bridle, the straps pass over the ears and across the cheeks to finally enter the mouths. There, between teeth and pressing down on the tongue, you know the straps join a rubber ball and prevent the jaws from closing and, it would seem, the mouth from speaking. Around every pair of eyes, a black ribbon or scarf has also been tied.

Some of the kneeling women have painted toe- and fingernails in different colours – you can see this from the eighth floor. Body sizes differ too but, gradually, the more you stare at this orderly arrangement of kneeling nudes, the more similar they all become to each other. Individuals don't so much vanish as become absorbed into the arrangement and uniformity of the general state of undress and hairlessness. They would have to talk to you, or at least look you in the eye, before individuals could be separated from the mass and be recognised in their own right. But that cannot happen because of the gags and blindfolds.

Beside this square of kneeling men and women, a large pyre is being prepared. Slim attractive women who wear sunglasses, leather boots and gloves and black two-piece suits, are methodically throwing articles of clothing, shoes and the occasional wallet on to this triangular bundle. None of the women in black talk to each other, or smile, or seem particularly interested in their surroundings. They only pause in their work – the constant patrolling between the rows of shaven, kneeling people, or the building of the pyre – when others, dressed like them, appear from out of the front entrance of the building, usually in pairs. Between these new arrivals in dark suits and glasses, a naked man or woman is held by the arm and led to the square. They too are blindfolded, wear the black rubber gags on their heads, and their scalps also have the pinkish-grey tint of the freshly shorn.

Steadily, before your eyes, the human square grows in size. New rows are being added all the time. You estimate that over two hundred people are currently on their knees with no hair and a rubber ball between their teeth. Treasury boxes filled with personal effects and black rubber bags full of clothing and shoes are also transported from the building and added to the rising pyre.

Security must be moving up through the building, floor by floor, to round up the traitors who they then process before transporting to the lawn. Soon, down there, you know there will be a place for you too.

Company Profile 8

Staff Announcement

'Colleagues, we thank you for your time and for your patience today. We appreciate you are all eager to get back to work. And soon you may return to your desks and carry on with the excellent work that has made this company a market leader and an example to all.' Standing on the small portable dais that resembles the little stages that politicians use when speaking to the press, a man talks into a microphone and addresses an enormous gathering of people. He wears sunglasses and a dark suit. Hair slicked back from his forehead, he never stops smiling at the entire workforce of the building who are gathered around him. Ten thousand men and women, dressed in the formal attire of business, have been evacuated from the skyscraper and assembled into loose departmental groups. A register was taken by each supervisor. Now, they all stand silent around the dais.

Directly before the podium, a large square of the company grounds has been cordoned off with plastic tape attached to thin iron poles, sunk into the turf. Inside the paddock, the naked, gagged and blindfolded people kneel, as if bowing down before the suited workforce. The number of the captives has swollen to 532.

The man on the dais smiles. 'I have been asked by the directors of our company to make this short address.

We know you are all smart people. You wouldn't be working here if you weren't' – there is a rumble of mirth – 'and you may have guessed by the events of this morning that this is an unusual day for the company. An unusual situation we all find ourselves in. And, as is our way, we have proved ourselves flexible enough to overcome this obstacle, so that our purpose, our focus, our very mission can continue as efficiently as ever.' He pauses and drinks from a glass of water. 'Gathered before you are a number of individuals who used to work for the same company as you. People you may once have recognised and treated as friends and colleagues. People trusted and relied upon to play their respective roles in our continuing prosperity and growth.' He pauses and swallows. Then shakes his head in disbelief. 'But they had other ideas. They weren't as smart as the rest of us.' Again he pauses; his voice has developed an edge of emotion; it begins to break. With fond eyes he gazes at the giant glass obelisk that rises into the blue stratosphere. Tilting his head right back he squints at the place where the summit disappears into a thin veil of drifting cloud. Then he turns to survey his entire audience once again. 'I know we all find this hard to believe. To comprehend, considering the company portfolio, our strength in every market we apply ourselves, our track record, our beautiful town and our way of life here. But these few' – he waves his hands over the heads of the naked, kneeling people in the paddock – 'tried to destroy it all.' There is a communal sigh, the shaking of heads, mutters of disgust from the crowd.

The speaker holds his hands up, palms out, to command silence. 'I know. I know.' Again he looks at the sky. 'And what is worse than the theft of privileged information – this security leak we plugged in ample time, I might add – what hurts us all so much more than the physical act of betrayal, is the fact that they broke their vows. Promises we take very seriously here. Oaths that all of us made when we agreed to work for this great organisation. Declarations of secrecy and of loyalty that all of you have managed to honour.'

'Hear, hear,' members of the crowd shout.

'Today, after a long investigation, I can reveal to you that it was their intention to sell us out to a major competitor and to destroy our advantage in the market-place.'

His final words are almost drowned out by the crowd. The office workers have become restless, confused, angry. Scores of voices cry out, baffled that such treachery could even exist. Dozens cry out for justice. Thousands more shout, 'Hear, hear.'

The spokesman continues at a time when there is a pause in the communal outrage. 'So why have we gone public with this? Why have we asked you to gather out here on the grass? You know why. Because we share. We share opportunity, growth and prosperity with you all. And so we intend to share the burden of our disappointment and outrage. We want you to see the individuals who let the team down.'

Applause begins in a trickle at the front of the audience where the senior managers stand. Everyone at the front then turns to make sure those behind are also clapping their hands. And so on. And so on.

Spattering outward in clumps, the applause soon gains momentum until there is a thunder at the foot of the building. And even after the applause fades, a restless, noisy electricity remains amongst the office workers. People want to do more than just clap. Feet are moving, shoulders are jostling, throats are being cleared, discussions have begun. The crowd pushes forward, closer and closer to the enclosure. Everyone wants to see the monsters; the freaks who were capable of such atrocity and ingratitude.

From the podium the speaker hurries his final re-marks. 'There will be ample opportunity for you to get a closer look at them. They're not going anywhere special. I can assure you of that. So, if you wish, have a quiet word with them. Pick out those who worked closest to you. Or a stranger. Does it really matter? They were all driven by the same ambition: your downfall. The choice is yours.' There is more applause and much excited laughter. 'Our security staff who executed an efficient and wholly successful sting operation this morning, will provide the relevant ordinance at the far corner of the pen for those of you who prefer a more direct approach.' The spokesman points towards the long portable rack on wheels that has been set up beside the paddock. Hundreds of black canes hang from the steel pegs. 'Fortunately we outnumber them. But unfortunately this means you are only permitted to make one corrective stroke each. Refreshments will then be served on the mezzanine before the lunch interval. Thank you again for your time.' The man steps down from the dais and is spirited away by a dozen security agents. They escort him to a small electric car. Waving his hands at the cheering people he is driven to an entrance at the rear of the building.

Thousands of people then form a giant, snaking cue that leads towards the armoury of canes.

Career History: Part 16

Tying up Loose Ends

From the stairwell of the third floor you sit and watch the spectacle. Horrified at first, then numbed by the mass punishment ritual, and finally exhausted by the sight of the constant rise and fall of the canes amongst the kneeling rows of the naked captives, you finally just sit alone in quiet despair. Guilty at having somehow evaded the initial purge and correction, you know you belong down there on the grass. It is you who should be stripped bare and kneeling with the rubber plug between your jaws. You should be flinching and then biting down against the sting as each cane falls. Because you took the files, the floppy disks, the mini disks, the CD ROMs, the printouts, the passwords from all those pairs of trembling hands and stored them in a utility cupboard for the resistance.

And now, every single person you came into contact with is hunched over on the grass as their buttocks are lined with a company cane. Faces down and blindfolded, they must be able to hear the spike heels and leather soles of the Italian brogues of their former colleagues as they stride between the rows, crushing the grass flat, getting closer and flexing their shoulders before delivering a blow. Who will be next? Maybe the prisoners can also hear the excited chatter of the men and women who pass between the columns in search of a familiar face; down there on the lawn, old scores are being settled. And maybe the fallen can hear the impact of wood on the fleshy backside of the traitor in front of them or at their side.

The old compulsion for surrender and subjection rises inside you like the urge of an addict. Tired of being an outsider, of sneaking around alone, part of you wishes you too had been forced to take your place at the foot of this false god of steel, glass and concrete. To be ruthlessly sacrificed in its honour; your pain and muffled yelps a tribute to its continuing strength and to all the long-legged women who traverse its corridors hungry for power. At least then you would have had closure; the mystery concerning your fate would have been over.

You did try to leave the building but every door on the ground floor was locked save for the main entrance where security maintain a constant presence. Denied access to the grounds, you then fled into the barracks where your colleagues lay helpless and subdued in their bunks, awaiting their next instruction from the wardens. Then you ran into the utility room where you had stashed the intelligence gathered for the resistance. Of course, finding the toxic waste container empty was no surprise. Someone had been there before you. Maybe Margaret, maybe someone else. For all you know, Margaret is down there on the grass right now, shivering and preparing herself for the next whizzing sound before sharp wood indents her matronly flesh. Then you returned to the stairwell, to watch and wait.

When the reinforced firedoor to the stairwell finally opens behind you, you breathe out with relief. The condition of limbo is over. It was only a matter of time before they come for you and the delay is giving you too much time to think. Two pairs of high heels clatter on the tiles of the landing. You turn your head and look towards the sound.

'My turn?' you say, grinning. But the security agents in black do not return the smile. Tall and straight in

211

their tight boots and pencil skirts, they merely look down at you. They look so alike they could be twins.

'Stand up.'

You obey.

'Follow us, please.'

You follow them through the door and back into the corridor. It is empty. The whole building now has an atmosphere of vacancy. 'Won't take you long to get me ready. My hair was cut yesterday,' you say and run one hand over your shaven skull. Neither woman responds to your facetious tone. They march to an elevator and depress a button to summon this carriage to your execution.

'So how did you find out?' you ask. Again, there is no answer. When the door to the elevator opens, the women stand aside to let you enter first. When the doors close, one of the agents selects a floor.

'We could have taken the stairs. It was only three flights down,' you say, while eyeing the long legs of the female security officers. It might be your last chance to look at such incredible women. Out of habit, you wonder if they are wearing pantyhose or stockings, and if their underwear is identical; is it part of a uniform, or are these cold, impassive women allowed to choose their own undergarments? Are they even capable of choice or have they become part of the company will?

The elevator seems to be taking its time and you glance at the steel panel to see which floor you are passing. Twenty-nine lights up as the elevator ascends. 'What?' you say aloud. The elevator is rising and not descending to the ground floor as you expected. 'Where are we going? The party is downstairs. Will one of you please answer me?'

The agents exchange glances. One of them says, 'You will be briefed shortly,' and then turns her head back around to face the door. This you never expected. As far as you know, security control is on the lower floors, as

212

are the interview rooms. Most correctional procedures are carried out close to the ground, so why are you now passing the fiftieth floor? Screwing up your eyes, you scrutinise the panel of the elevator and look for the destination of this lift. The only other floor lit up in red corresponds to the one-hundredth floor. Which cannot be right. No one has access to the higher levels of the building beside the directors. But this elevator has been programmed to rise to the very top. You begin to sweat.

Career History: Part 17

Chairmen of the Board

With no idea of why you have been brought here while your comrades bite rubber down below, you are ushered out of the elevator by the two security agents who have escorted you this far. But after steering you by the elbow to the door, neither woman follows you into the reception of the one-hundredth floor. You turn to await their next instruction and see the doors sliding shut across their cold but beautiful faces.

'Good afternoon, sir.' Immediately your eyes are drawn to the pretty blonde girl in the dark suit who sits behind the black stone desk in reception.

You point a finger at your own chest. 'Me?' Then you look around for someone nearby in a suit, entitled to this form of address.

As the receptionist smiles, her pinky lips part to reveal a set of dazzling white teeth. The smile is warm, sincere. 'We've been expecting you,' she says. 'I'll let them know you've arrived. Please take a seat while you wait.'

Around her, the rest of the foyer resembles the lobby of an exclusive hotel. Minimalist in design with a black marble floor and simple executive furniture, the space is elegant and you can't help feeling immediately soothed inside it. Gingerly you lower yourself into a leather chair and mop the perspiration from your face with your sleeve. You feel disorientated by confusion. No force was used, or shackles and cuffs employed to bring you here and now this girl is smiling like she's pleased to see you. She presses a button on her desk and then speaks into her headpiece. 'Ma'am, he's here.'

'Who am I meeting?' you ask.

The girl doesn't answer. Smiling, she dips her head towards a glowing computer screen. Frowning with concentration she begins to type. To the left of the desk a glass door opens and another woman enters. She too is smiling at you. Immediately, her appearance and her pretty face disarms you. Unable to stop yourself, you look her up and down. The discreet ceiling lights catch the patent leather of her sling-back shoes. Long and lean, her legs shine in black stockings to the knee. Shapely thighs are then hugged by her pinstripe pencil skirt. Her tiny waist and firm breasts are pronounced by a tight white blouse that peaks through her jacket with the shoulder pads. Shiny black hair with a straight fringe is piled up on top of her head. One or two strands have fallen loose from the arrangement at the back to tickle her pale neck. Wearing strong make-up and glasses, and unbothered by your stare, she says, 'Good afternoon, sir. My name is Ms Berry. I am the private secretary to the board of directors.' You shake the cool, delicate hand that is offered. 'The directors will see you right away. Please follow me.'

The directors to see you? Bemused, you follow the woman across reception and through the glass door through which she arrived. Once more, after a brief period of independence, you sense a loss of control over your existence. It's as if you are a part of something much bigger that manipulates your every action and thought. Unable to think of anything to say, and doubting whether you will be told anything specific even if you ask a question, you follow the woman in silence, with most of your attention offset by her buttocks and strong calves. As she walks her thighs rub together and produce a pleasant hissing sound.

The cool, conditioned air smells of fresh vanilla. All the floors up here seem to be made from marble too and the interior design is simple, chic and looks expensive like the reception. It makes you feel self-conscious in the boiler suit and flip-flops you wear.

After you reach the end of the short annex corridor and approach another glass door, the situation and atmosphere changes on the one-hundredth floor. At first the sounds are muffled; emitted nearby but dampened by walls and the thick door. You can hear the pulse of loud bassy music and feel it through your feet too. The air changes also; becomes warmer and somehow bustles with anticipation.

And it is when you pass through the second set of doors, that your guide opens with a swipe-card, you see that a large celebration has already begun. With the rebellion crushed and every traitor currently having their buttocks licked by wood down on the grass, it seems the owners of the corporation have much to be pleased about. But nothing could have prepared you for what you next see and hear.

The noise briefly stuns you. Loud music pumps from ceiling speakers to fill every space with a continuous, pounding rhythm. Raucous male laughter, the sounds of female squeals and shouts of excitement pour from every open office door and compete with the music in the corridor. Disorientated, hesitant, wary, you stop walking. Your escort turns and smiles, indicating that you should follow her.

Moving more slowly, you begin to pass the first offices housed in this section of the building. Some of the doors are closed. You cannot restrain yourself from peering inside those that are open. These rooms are large. Most of them have the space for an enormous desk, a couch, an impressive drinks cabinet, an exercise machine and sometimes an artificial golf green without looking cluttered. Some of them are empty but the occupants of those that aren't appear to be unconcerned by the scrutiny of passers-by. Seduced ever forward by the hypnotic sway of your guide's bottom, most of what you now see comes in a quick series of glimpses and flashes, making it difficult for you to process the information. But everything you see will stay etched on your memory for a long time.

In the first office there is a tall blonde woman dressed like a schoolgirl in a pleated mini-skirt, shirt and tie. Bent over the oak desk with her skirt raised, she allows an older man to strike her buttocks with a bamboo cane. Wearing a dark gown over his smart suit, the silver-haired punisher delivers his strokes with an easy, regular method without breaking a sweat. Red in the face, moaning and rubbing her thighs together, it's hard to tell if the woman is in discomfort or a state of arousal, while the master's face remains dour and stern, as if this procedure is necessary and that it is important the correct technique is employed.

Two doors along, you hear the quick, breathless voices of two lovers before you actually see them writhing on the red velvet couch. Peering around the door, you see a pair of long legs, sheathed in dark stockings, raised in the air so the points of the woman's stilettos spike towards the ceiling. Between her tanned thighs, a trouserless man thrusts his bare cock inside her sex. Hands gripping the armrest under her head, and with one socked foot planted on the floor, he stabilises his position on the pliant couch in order to work on her soft body with as much vigour as he is able. 'Dirty boy. Oh, you dirty boy. You dirty, dirty boy,' she calls out, taunting him to continue his uncompromising handling of her. Across the shoulders of his blue shirt, her crimson fingernails claw and scratch as if she is terrified he might try to escape before she has further proof of what a dirty boy he is.

'Some of the directors have retired from the main celebration early,' your guide says, and then follows this exclamation with a girlish giggle. 'They prefer to make their own entertainment.'

'They are directors?' you mumble.

The woman nods and smiles. 'Besides a small contingent of support staff, recruited especially for the top two floors, everybody you see up here is a director. A very important man or woman. So don't be fooled.'

'What are they doing?' you ask, and immediately feel stupid. 'I mean . . .'

The woman laughs. If you look at her wonderful red mouth and perfect teeth any longer, you may suffer a paralysing infatuation. 'These are the perks of power,' she says and then turns around.

On the floor of the next office you see a man positioned on his hands and knees. Other than the rubber hood and studded leather harness he wears around his chest and groin, he is naked. Cradled between his hands is a preposterously high-heeled shoe of patent leather. Gently, like a kitten licking its paw, his tongue darts out of the mouthpiece of the mask and bathes the sole and toe of the pointed shoe. Between his thighs, his violent-red sex is erect and pointing at the wearer of the extreme shoe. Dressed in an unfeasibly tight black dress, made from shiny rubber, with her waist cinched into an impossibly tiny circumference, a woman lounges on the couch with one leg stretched towards the man on his knees. She sips at a Martini and casually inspects the back of one hand. Over the shiny gloves, clinging to her flesh from fingertips to biceps, she wears an elaborate diamond ring. It is the jewellery she idly gazes upon. Back-combed and teased into a fountain of bright red hair, her wig and dark sunglasses suggests to you that she is not concealing her identity, but changing it. 'Enough,' she says sharply. 'And this is not straight like I asked.' She points at the crooked seam of her stocking, behind her knee. The hooded man immediately attends to the task with careful fingers.

218

Ms Berry strokes your elbow and whispers in your ear, 'She directs our mineral and petroleum interests. And he is a venture capital genius.'

You nod and try to look impressed.

It seems the directors have selected specific outfits with a fetish theme for the party. You see few in the formal attire of business or dressed casually.

Between green vinyl screens of the type you would expect to see in a hospital, you next observe the prostrate form of a naked man receiving some kind of medical treatment on his desk. In a mixture of both shock and concern, you pause and stare into the room. Attached to his face is a clear plastic mask through which the patient inhales gas or oxygen. Teetering around the bed in white stilettos, two Asian nurses work quickly to prepare equipment for the impending operation. Surgical implements – cruel clamps, tweezers, vices, needles – are steamed and washed in stainless steel trays and glass sterilisation vats. Above the white masks the women wear over their mouths, their large eyes, smothered by heavy eye-shadow and thick eye-liner, concentrate on tasks they perform. Beside them, the patient continues to lie still with his eyes closed. As the nurses pass to and fro you also glimpse some kind of clear plastic apparatus attached to the man's genitals. It looks like a vacuum chamber with a white hose-pipe fixed to the top. You cannot see where the other end of the tube leads. One of the nurses spots you standing in the doorway. Immediately, she minces over. You stare, mouth open with wonder and desire at the tight plastic uniform and her small legs shimmering in white hose. 'Are you the doctor? I was told to expect a woman and you don't look like a woman,' she asks you.

You shake your head.

Placing her hands on her hips, she sighs with exasperation. 'There can be no visitors,' she says, and slams the door in your face.

Dumbstruck, you turn to look at your guide, who continues to smile at you. 'The head of overseas development is a hard-working man,' she offers by way of explanation. 'It is essential for his health and the health of the company that he receives only the very best private treatment.' Swivelling on her heels, your guide continues along the corridor leaving you unsure as to whether she was being serious. Shaking your head, you follow the raven-haired beauty to the end of the corridor and pause only once more to listen to the sound of a woman screaming on the other side of a closed door. The temptation to open the door and peer inside is equalled by your aversion to seeing whatever implement is presently being employed to make these sounds of wet leather being slapped across a smooth stone.

But whatever you glimpsed in the first collection of offices was little more than an appetiser for the scene currently being conducted in the large conference room that Ms Berry now guides you through.

Several of the men turn and greet your guide with a nod, smile, or a brief word, but none of them look at you. They continue to drink and eat from the impressive, colourful platters of finger food on the vast table, or to watch the woman in the leather harness, suspended from the ceiling on thin silver chains. Ankles and wrists cuffed to the steel support struts, so her legs are wide open and her arms secured above her head, she sits in a leather swing, waist-high to the man who currently thrusts himself between her legs. Moaning after every lunge through her sex, the blonde woman rolls her head in a circle, seemingly unaware of the large crowd that watches, or the small group of men who quietly undress and wait to take their turn between her stocking-clad thighs. Seated behind her, three women in similar leather basques that are buckled tight up their pale backs, sip champagne and talk amongst themselves. Occasionally they look up with mild interest at the woman in the bondage hammock.

'I thought there was a limit. Three each. And this one makes five,' a woman with a Cleopatra hair-style says to her neighbour.

'Oh, leave her alone,' her older, but handsome colleague with the white hair adds. 'It's her first time. And the last two were ever so quick. What's more, the men like her. They've been trying to persuade her to have a go for months.'

'Doubt it will be her last ride either,' the third woman adds as she brushes crumbs from her knee, using the pads of her fingertips so her long black nails don't ladder her grey, seamed nylons. 'She's a natural. I knew it all along. I said so.'

'Are you coming?' your guide asks. She reaches out and gently takes your hand. 'There will plenty of time to see everything. I expect this party will last for a few days. You have to learn to pace yourself.' Incredulous at her blasé attitude, you look from your guide to the woman swaying in the harness. Her lover begins to pump her quicker, groaning and muttering as he approaches climax. After a great cheer from the other men, and a polite round of applause from the three women on the chairs, the muscles on his back strain to a rock-like cut before relaxing and disappearing under his skin as his sex floods her womb. Breathing hard and smiling, he steps back from the harness and places one hand on the table for support.

'Oh, more, more, more!' the woman in the swing cries out, to the delight of the men.

'No. No. No!' the three women say.

Before you leave the conference room you look up at the giant video screen on the far wall. Detailed close-ups of the rebellion's fate, spliced with cut-aways of the entire spectacle, filmed from above, are being piped through to the directors' orgy. But few of the directors seem to be watching the naked, blindfolded and gagged woman, who is the current victim of this electronic scrutiny, as she raises her buttocks to allow a stranger his turn with a cane.

Something about the public nature of the directors' party, and these visions from the corporal punishment currently being applied to hundreds of backsides on the ground below, horrifies and intimidates you. But, the sights, sounds and the impact of everything against your overworked senses also arouses you to the extent that you now have to walk with one hand over the tumescence of your groin, now visible through the material of your suit. You make a connection between these events and a similar scene observed in your own living room when your wife was welcomed and initiated into the corporate community. Back then, you could not prevent yourself from being seduced by the overt nature of such deviance while your better instincts begged you to flee. You are losing control again. Failing to resist.

From the conference room, you enter another wide communal corridor. Amongst the fountains and tropical plants in this plaza, you are forced to watch further evidence of the depraved recreational activities of this immensely powerful elite in their secret world. Pulled by the hand, you now stumble after your guide. Head whipping from left to right, your mind overloads with the stimulant from so many glimpses and whispers of perversion: large breasts being noisily sucked through the holes in a leather brassiere; a woman in dagger-heeled shoes walking up and down the back of a man mummified in plastic who breathes through a tube the size of an ordinary pencil; 'My ass. My ass. I want all of it in my ass,' a youngish blonde woman says, while her fingers whiten on the back of a chair that has been positioned in the mouth of a dark office. Finally, against a wall, between two South American creepers, you are transfixed by the sight of a couple having sex while standing up. Legs wrapped around her lover's waist, a dark-skinned woman with waist-length locks of curly hair is pushed up and down the wall as her younger partner grunts and heaves between her thighs. Over her sex, a messy hole has been ripped into her sheer pantyhose. It seems the coupling is desperate, perhaps longed for and previously denied. Deep reserves of strength seem to have been found and then used by this man to lift her entire weight from the floor and to subsequently support it, while he pounds at her womb. And she is wordless; her eyes have the dreamy vacancy of the lost or medicated.

'Mmm,' your guide whispers in your ear. 'Doesn't it just . . . I dunno . . . make you so hot?'

Baffled and so aroused, you suddenly want to seize your guide and take her. You turn to face her and immediately try to fall into a kiss. But with a wicked smile, she turns her face away and pulls you around the naked man in the rubber hood you have nearly trodden on. Looking down, you watch this hooded figure's slow progress across the polished stone floor. Sweating, he struggles to pull the weight of the small black chariot he is bridled into, and the leather-clad woman who sits in the tiny seat of the carriage, smoking a cigarette. As you pass, she pulls up on the reins of her steed and taps your leg with her crop. Behind the cat mask you can see a pair of clever but spiteful eyes. 'Oh, so you made it up. About time,' she says. 'We must catch up soon to discuss the proposition. I'll make reservations.' She then lashes the rump of her steed who yelps and lurches down the corridor.

You look at your guide for clarification. This woman in the chariot seems to think she knows you and speaks with a brazen familiarity. As you pass through a group of drunken women, dressed in tight rubber and thigh-length boots, Ms Berry winks at you. 'Oh yes, you're quite a popular man up here. Flavour of the month, you could say. A lot of people will want to meet you soon.'

'Why? What the fuck is going on? Who was that?'

'Oh, she's the head of Human Resources. And the man in the harness controls all of our money in Eastern Europe. But there will be time for introductions later. Now, come on. We can't keep them waiting. We'll take a short cut through the restaurant.'

Silver tiers of sandwiches and cakes rise above pyramids of caviar on crushed ice. Forests of champagne bottles fight for space with broad trays of canapés, olives and oysters on the giant table. There is enough food and drink here to sustain an army for days. It seems the directors will need much sustenance to prolong their orgy; a cycle of anticipation, arousal, intense sensual peaks and recovery, repeated for days and nights until every whim, no matter how perverse, is sated in this seat of their power.

Scantily clad women wander around the table and pick at the delicacies. Naked men lounge on soft leather couches, drinking and laughing, occasionally pausing to admire a shapely body that passes their resting place. At the head of the table, you see a woman on all fours wearing a blindfold. She has severe cheekbones and a beauty spot and sucks a man who stands before her face. Kneeling behind her, another man grinds himself between her buttocks.

Four tall women in tiny leather maid outfits teeter amongst the guests and serve drinks from elegant silver trays. All of them struggle to balance on the extreme Cuban heels they wear. Seamed black stockings coat their long athletic legs and lead one's eyes up to the pale and firm buttocks that protrude from under the white trim of their mini-dresses. They speak in broken English to the guests and you suspect they are Russian. Perhaps hand-picked and flown to the building, especially for this celebration.

On the video screen in here, you see more footage of the punishment ritual below. Like a close-up from a

224

televised sporting event, the camera has focused on a woman in a pinstriped suit who is screaming at one of the male captives as he kneels in the grass. She seems to know who he is. With one high-heeled foot pressed against the back of his head, she rubs his face into the earth. After every outburst, she lashes his raw backside with her cane. Then, as the camera pans back, you see a panorama of the spectacle: hundreds of suited members of the company faithful stalking amongst the fleshy rows and berating the captives with sharp tongues and even sharper sticks. And at the borders of the punishment paddock, the indifferent female security agents continue their patrol.

Stepping around a middle-aged woman – who wears only see-through panties, hold-up stockings and high heels as she rides the crotch of a younger man while clawing his hairless chest with her crimson nails – you approach the last third of the banqueting area and find yourself unwilling to linger too far behind Ms Berry.

'A friend of yours?' Ms Berry then says.

'Sorry?' you say, but as you follow the direction in which her laughing eyes look, you are quickly shocked into silence.

At the head of the table, partially obscured by two women in high-heeled boots who enthusiastically pleasure a naked, white-haired man, you see something that slows the blood in your veins. Belted into an upright metal gurney – the sort of thing once used to strap down the inmates of asylums – is the tall and rangy body of a woman. When you look up at the gagged head, you recognise the face of the female director who seduced you inside a toilet cubicle: the intimidating giantess who hid a CD ROM of privileged information inside her stocking top. 'No,' you say, shaking your head. Her piercing eyes meet and then wither your stare. Cold and dispassionate, her face betrays none of the concern or discomfort she surely must be suffering. Not only is her beautiful mouth stoppered with a rubber ball, her nipples are clamped beneath criss-crossing restraints of leather, and both her vagina and anus are plugged with thick, smooth and tapering steel devices that are attached to an inversion of a chastity belt, fashioned from silver chains and a waist bracelet.

'Go on. Get closer,' Ms Berry says excitedly. And for the first time, you find her tone sinister. 'She is unique. The first director to ever turn traitor. Go on. She can't hurt you now. She's powerless. She's ours.'

'What will happen to her?' you ask and then swallow, refusing to get any closer to the extraordinary body of the captured director.

Eyes half-closed with pleasure, Ms Berry takes a deep breath. 'After being displayed, her punishment will be legendary.'

'Let's go,' you say, and turn your face away from this bound spectacle of the fallen goddess who tried to share power with mere mortals like yourself.

From the restaurant, you follow Ms Berry through a network of corridors, from which more of the private offices are attached. You then pass a large gymnasium and a swimming pool, where a nude couple enjoy vigorous sex on an inflatable raft. Eventually, the silent and exquisitely perfumed Ms Berry leads you up a small staircase to an elevator door made from steel. She gains access by punching a security code into a little keypad. In this lift you rise another floor and disembark into a small, unmanned lobby. 'This part of the building houses the presidential suites and the Chairman's boardroom. I will escort you to the boardroom and then you are on your own. When you have made your decision I will be waiting outside.'

'Decision?' you say. 'What decision?'

'Choose wisely,' she says with a reassuring smile.

Suddenly intimidated by the realisation that you are now standing in the territory of the owners of this entire corporation, this tyranny that brutalises all who serve in it, you feel faint and sick with nerves. 'I can't. Just send me down there where I belong.' You point at the floor.

Ms Berry smiles in sympathy. 'Now, it can't be all that bad, can it? I mean look at this.' She slides one finger up the protuberance in your boiler suit. 'These are very important people, so you need to relax. You won't be at your best if you're all hot and bothered. I think I can help. Stress-relief is my speciality.' She sinks to her knees before your groin and promptly unzips your suit. Pulling your erection out from your shorts, she murmurs appreciatively, 'Mmm,' before slipping the swollen head of your sex between her lips. Gently beating your shaft with her tongue, but at the same time squeezing you tightly with her lips, Ms Berry works on you as if it is she who is desperate for relief after observing the directors' orgy. Keeping her big eyes open behind the lenses of her glasses, she holds your stare. Tickling you behind the scrotum with her lacquered nails, you begin to shiver and moan with pleasure.

'That's good. So good. Oh, yes.' And it is: you won't last long.

Using one of her pale and cool hands she then massages your shaft while licking and kissing the tip of your phallus. It is now you decide to give her no warning, damn it. Suddenly pumping yourself through her fingers and inside her mouth, you feel both energised but dizzy as you approach your climax. Already you can imagine your thick cream spilling over her red lips, before running down her sweet chin and falling into her powdered cleavage.

'Come on. Come on,' she whispers, and stares at you with an intensity that seems psychotic.

'Yes,' you say, and cannot prevent this cascade of images that suddenly flash through your mind: two people rutting on a red velvet couch, Asian nurses in white high-heeled shoes, a woman thrust up and down the wall by a man who lunges his sex through her torn pantyhose, a mature schoolgirl rubbing her thighs together as she is caned, the plugged sex and anus of a beautiful director who faces an unimaginable corrective punishment. It's too much stimulation. The depraved world of the executive elite has thoroughly polluted your soul; it controls your mind and body.

Between your legs, Ms Berry pushes more of her mouth on to your sex as you come. Jabbing her head back and forward, she caresses your phallus with her wet mouth that you fill with one long spurt of cream after another. It just keeps coming. Scalding through your sex and splashing on to her pinky gums and against the slick inner walls of her cheeks. Then you can hear her gulping at your seed while squeezing your penis like a tube she wants to completely empty inside her greedy mouth.

Dazed by the intensity of your climax, you lean against the wall and feel like weeping from both despair and ecstasy. Ms Berry regains her composure and presses a tissue against her lips. 'Delicious,' she whispers. You help her to her feet and then try to kiss her. She avoids your mouth but lets you peck her cheek. 'Now come on. They're waiting. And you will have to take a lot in so I hope that cleared your head a little.'

Without another word she walks out of the lobby and into a corridor that is more reminiscent of a university reading room than an international corporation. A silent and warm place. Original oil paintings hang on the red walls papered with silk. You recognise a Picasso, two Bacons, a Hooper and a Matisse. The occasional door you pass is made from heavy wood. Glass cases positioned on stone columns display an eclectic collection of antiquity: stone tablets from the classical age; ceramics from central America; a broken marble face; a delicately carved wooden hand. The air is tinged with the scents of the distinguished: varnish, wax, brass, china, old books and that indefinable flavour that issues from anywhere that contains the immensely wealthy. You could be in the offices of an old and successful law firm, or the surgery of a world famous analyst; it's like you have stepped back in history to a place of old values and old money. And Ms Berry in her pencil skirt, seamed nylons and fifties haircut seems profoundly in harmony with this place. Before you even meet the directors of the directors, you have an instinctive sense of who and what they really are. You realise at once that this is an environment procured and developed to make certain people comfortable; an atmosphere generated to make old money feel at home. So, down below, what is the struggle for if the real money and power stays within the confines of the old ruling class? Is all that ambition and the obsession with advancement necessary if such an implacable corniced ceiling is still in place to protect the old order and subjugate the new? Is everything below a tortuous but futile struggle in the pursuit of an illusion?

'This is the directors' boardroom.' She stands before a heavy double door with ornate brass handles. Her confident smile now teases and mocks the man who wears a mechanic's suit and rubber peasant shoes; a man grateful for blow-jobs in corridors. 'At the bottom of the table you will find a place has been prepared for you.'

On either side of the door is a wooden display case, similar to the glass-fronted cabinets used in museums for exhibiting bones and fossils. Inside the cases, antique canes, leather straps, members of the tawse family and faded dunce's caps hang from small brass hooks. You turn your pale face from the display cases and look at the smiling Ms Berry. Not even a sign marking an unexploded mine could have filled you with so much trepidation.

'Remember,' she says. 'This is a privilege so few have known.' She then opens the double doors of the board room, but makes no attempt to follow you inside this dark place.

Only from the light from the television monitor that is fixed into the centre of the heavy table and angled towards you can you find your way to the leather armchair, pulled out and awaiting you. The blinds on the windows are drawn and none of the table lamps are switched on. A crystal pitcher of water and a single glass has been set at your place.

Standing beside the chair, you look back at Ms Berry for some kind of reassurance or instruction. But with a final smile, the beautiful young woman closes the doors and seals you inside.

Anticipating a moment when your existence may be fundamentally altered, yet again, you take a seat and pour yourself a glass of water. So preoccupied have you been with the directors' orgy and the delightful ministrations of Ms Berry, you have forgotten to hydrate. Gulping at the chilled spring water, it is as if you are in the cinema: the monitor screen is the only thing in the room that emits any light. Everything else at the far end of the chamber remains in a state of impenetrable darkness.

Your eyes are automatically drawn to the monitor. Straight away, you catch sight of someone who looks familiar. A woman in a black uniform who is standing near the camera's real interest – a group of three naked men, all aged in their forties, being flayed with canes by an excited group of young women wearing pastel suits: secretaries. When the camera retreats to a wider angle you get a better look at the solitary woman in uniform who first caught your eye. Zooming closer, as if willed by you, the camera then focuses on her arrogant though attractive face: chin raised, the smile playful but smug and the pretty eyes wide with both interest and satisfaction at what they see. And you have seen this expression before. It was during the night you escaped from the compound and went home to your wife. This is the face of the police captain who ended your flight from the suburbs.

'Bitch,' you mutter. The very woman who initiated you into the resistance was on the side of the company all along. But then your initial surprise fades. Desperate and gullible, you were an easy target for her, and would have trusted anyone back then who had a kind word for you, let alone a promise of re-empowerment. And how can you trust anyone that works for the corporation? Half the time you can't even trust yourself.

'We would agree with you. She has all the attributes of a bitch. Cold, incapable of compassion, pathologically selfish and very, very cruel. A model employee.' It is the voice of a woman that originates from the top half of the board room. 'She was quite disappointed to learn that you were not to join the others, down on the grass. She wanted to deal with you personally.' And then the voice breaks into a laugh that both frightens and angers you.

'But we wanted you for ourselves,' a second woman says from out of the darkness at the end of the table.

For a split second, you then think of opening the door, knocking Ms Berry aside and running. To where you don't know. But of one thing you are sure: whatever the security forces could devise to punish you – and their impromptu visit to your cell in the police station was very effective in reducing you to a condition of total subservience – it would be nothing compared to what the owners of these chilling voices could devise. In the dark, your mind is suddenly full of an image of the fallen director again, strapped into the steel gurney and exhibited in the restaurant, her sensual lips sucking a rubber ball.

'Yes,' a third female voice says. 'We wanted to meet you in person. We have never had that pleasure. And yet, it's as if we have known you all our lives. We have been with you for a long time.'

231

'Only I never knew it,' you say, in a tense voice, screwing up your eyes to peer into the dark.

'Precisely,' all three women say at the same time, before breaking into peels of unpleasant laughter.

'Who are you?' you ask the darkness.

The third and oldest of the disembodied voices answers your question. 'We are the chairmen of the board.'

Career History: Part 18

Minutes from the Chairmen's Meeting

You: Why me?

First Chairman: A good question to start.

Second Chairman: Can't think of a better one.

Third Chairman: You may or may not have realised this fact, but all our staff are selected long before their first interview.

First Chairman: We choose them before they see a job advertisement.

Second Chairman: They are ours before they realised they needed a new job.

Third Chairman: We have agents throughout the international business community. You too were chosen for a specific role.

First Chairman: We needed an individual who fitted a certain profile.

Second Chairman: A natural victim. A man who craved unfair treatment. Confirmation that he was an outsider and destined for persecution. Someone who craved debasement and submission. Self-pity is such an aphrodisiac.

Third Chairman: An unpredictable man who could not control himself around a certain kind of woman and a particular brand of stimulace. In short, a man who

233

would allow the theft of his wife and livelihood as long as his tormentors wore high heels.

First Chairman: A sensitive man who preferred to serve strong women. But a man who resented this essential weakness in his character. A man in conflict with himself who would strive to overthrow a regime in which he feels inferior.

You: No.

First Chairman: Yes.

Second Chairman: Without a doubt.

Third Chairman: You have proved yourself worthy of our selection procedure. You were seduced by the women of the corporation. You feared but also desired their discipline. At the same time the company made you feel inferior, low tech, left behind, an underachiever. Despite this, you still needed the approval of the smart girls in high heels. But it was inevitable that you would fail before them, be reduced to nothing and then seek revenge. Like a phoenix rising from the ashes. Something typical of many men we have here. And we contributed little for you to achieve your potential.

First Chairman: Just a little push here and there. But generally, it was a textbook exercise.

Second Chairman: Don't be disheartened. We are very pleased with you.

You: The rebellion was your idea. You did it for amusement. Watching the end of people's hopes and careers gave you pleasure. You are sadists.

First Chairman: Ah! Our second purge.

Second Chairman: The last one was ten years ago.

Third Chairman: A necessary and wholly effective device to weed out those who grow tired of the status quo, or disapprove of our methods, or become too ambitious even for our company. The communists did the same thing in China. We learn from our enemies.

234

First Chairman: And can we be faulted for being a little creative with our staff downsizing? Far superior than redundancy.

Second Chairman: And you played your part marvellously.

Third Chairman: It was our intention from the very start that you, a new recruit, an outcast and someone unfit for the coalface of commerce, would play a central role in the downfall of those who threaten our power. Every so often we need to consolidate our position. That was your job. So we took everything from you. Gave you no other choice but to join the resistance. News of your downfall and treatment at the hands of the company brought many sympathisers out of the woodwork.

First Chairman: Grubs.

You: You all seemed so fucking pleased with yourselves.

First Chairman: Oh, don't try and be angry. By now, I would have thought you would be tired of underdog role, the tragic and isolated hero of the rebellion. It must become boring after a while.

Second Chairman: And can you say that you have been miserable with us?

Third Chairman: Yes, has life been unbearable in our little town? Or have we provided you with an opportunity to achieve your potential, your most secret desire for this fall? This slump into submission?

First Chairman: To take your most illicit and perverse curiosities to their natural end?

Second Chairman: To rid yourself of responsibility and to escape the effort of trying to be something you are not?

Third Chairman: Do you now have a better understanding of yourself? Of who you really are? Of what you really desired? Have we not removed every obstacle so you could find a true liberation?

You: You trapped me. Coerced me. Manipulated me. You gave me no choice. I might have wanted something else. A good career. Could have been a good husband. Played golf.

First Chairman: Wrong. We made the choice you were afraid to make on your own.

Second Chairman: No one can be trusted to make the right choice for themselves. People spend to much time watching other people and feeling inferior. Coveting their neighbours and their neighbours' wives. But do they know what they really want? Stress? Pressure? Death of the imagination in return for a nice house?

Third Chairman: Not everyone can be successful. And success is pointless unless it makes others feel inferior. It is the highest praise. That's why the rich flaunt themselves.

Third Chairman: So what many people really desire is much, much simpler. But is buried under all the expectations forced upon them. So we make the choice for them. We let them serve. Service has its own rewards here. Honest manual work and sexual fulfilment. Our methods, customs and rules are unusual, but no one has ever resigned from the company.

You: Because they're afraid.

First Chairman: Isn't that a thrill in itself? To be punished here is to know intensity.

Second Chairman: Given the choice, would you really have left all this behind?

You: Yes!

First Chairman: And then spend the rest of your days dreaming of the corporation? Of what you lost. Would you ever have known such excitement again? You would have dreamt of canes. Or a pair of severe shoes glimpsed in a stairwell. The time you witnessed the adjustment of a suspender in a bathroom. Or the glimpse of a woman through a French window revealing her basest desires.

236

Third Chairman: Industry learnt many years ago that one cannot completely subordinate an individual's will and purpose to the machinery of a corporation with only the promise of advancement and material rewards. That path can satisfy only a part of man. His atavistic and more animal urges have to be catered for also. His wayward instincts can never be completely erased. Distractions will always be found for release, for a temporary escape. But harness and provide for that part of his nature through his working life? Make it part of the very structure and fabric of his career and his community, and you will have his devotion for life. He will be an addict. Our system is his drug. And here, there is no rehabilitation.

First Chairman: Take care of his darkest needs: sadism, masochism, voyeurism, exhibitionism.

Second Chairman: His fixations, fetishes, desires, needs.

Third Chairman: All of the things that are irresistible, dangerous, taboo. Repressed and outlawed in a civilised world but catered for here. Part of his everyday life. Everything in this company reminds him of his baser urges. And we make these desires a bedfellow to particular kinds of shame and punishment that is exhilarating. You have seen this for yourself. We trust ourselves to ultimately provide and control these sluices for excess. We create the original opportunities for depravity. We cultivate the deviance. Direct it. And when, through guilt and humiliation, they need to return to purity, hard work, discipline, honest endeavour, the company is only too willing to exploit these more profitable qualities again.

First Chairman: Sex and punishment are inseparable.

Second Chairman: No one could leave such an opportunity to fulfil their most secret needs. The system works.

Third Chairman: Our success speaks for itself.

(Long pause)

You: So what use am I now? Why was I brought here?

First Chairman: Ah! Of course. Your fate.

Second Chairman: After all you have done for us we would be reluctant to let you go.

Third Chairman: We wouldn't hear of it.

First Chairman: But you're no good to us in business.

Second Chairman: Couldn't trust you with the tea money.

Third Chairman: A hopeless case.

First Chairman: But there are other places for your . . . abilities and interests.

Second Chairman: Aha! Now he's interested. Look at his face.

Third Chairman: He looked at Ms Berry the same way.

First Chairman: When she was down on her knees.

Second Chairman: Such enthusiasm.

Third Chairman: He is the perfect candidate for what we have in mind. But for once we shall let him choose.

First Chairman: A car outside is waiting to take you to the airport. A private jet will fly you wherever you wish to go. If you take this option, our business with you is concluded.

Second Chairman: Unless you speak to anyone of your time with us. Then we will be forced to silence you. But, besides your continuing discretion, you will be a free man.

Third Chairman: Or, you can trust us to place you in a new and more stimulating role than those you have occupied previously, if not briefly, with us. You will sign a permanent contract to serve out your working life here.

You: What is it?

First Chairman: All we can tell you is that it will involve a great deal of responsibility.

Second Chairman: A special kind of assistance to a certain kind of woman who is accustomed to the very best service.

Third Chairman: But you have to trust us. So what will it be: the airport or the job?

(Long pause)

You: I'll stay.

First Chairman: I knew it!

Second Chairman: You have made the right choice. Congratulations.

Third Chairman: Return to the party. Enjoy yourself. The Head of Human Resources is waiting. She will take care of the details. Thank you for your time.

Second Chairman: We have enjoyed meeting you.

First Chairman: Ms Berry, will you come in, please?

(End of minutes.)

Career History: Part 19

Multi-skilling

You set it all out on the tray: macrobiotic drink; natural low-fat yoghurt; pot of coffee with skimmed goat's milk; bowl of fresh fruit. Inside the little glass vase you insert the stem of a yellow rose. Napkin straight. Cutlery polished. This is how she likes it. Then you look at the clock that is mounted on the kitchen wall. Thirty seconds to go. When the clock reads seven sharp, you straighten the vitamin capsules and then lift the tray from the marbled counter.

From the vast and gleaming kitchen, you venture up the stairs to the master bedroom. On the way up you peer about at the banisters, window sills and ornaments to make sure you cleaned them of every granule of dust the day before. There is so much to do here. Waking her up at the designated time, with the breakfast she picks at while propped up in bed, is the easiest part. But collecting her dry-cleaning, retrieving her purchases from the stores and delicatessens, preparing her evening meal – if she bothers to tell you she will be home for dinner – cooking, cleaning the house, firing off invitations and always being punctual with the car when she requires you to drive her, is proving to be a tense and complicated process. These days, it's best to rise early; in your one-room apartment over her garage, you tend to set your own alarm for 6 a.m. This morning, before

240

making her breakfast, you managed to wash and wax the car, deodorise the interior, stash the champagne bottles she left in the fireplace from last night in the recycling bags, and alphabetise her post on the little silver dish you take up with the food.

Outside her bedroom, you clear your throat. Then knock the door. 'Ma'am. Good morning. Time to get up.'

You hate this part because she hates this part.

On the other side of the door, you hear a long moan as she wakes.

Taking a deep breath, you knock again and then enter.

'No,' she mumbles. 'No. Can't be. What time is it? I've just fallen asleep.'

'Seven, ma'am.' It's dark in the room with the thick curtains closed. Gingerly, you cross the floor, testing the terrain with your toes before planting a foot on the wooden boards. Last week, you trod on a Versace sandal and fell with the breakfast tray. She woke up screaming. When she realised it was only you, she leapt out of bed and took a fly-swat to your back as you lay among the debris of wholewheat crackers and a slick of carrot juice. Yesterday was the first time she has spoken to you since the incident.

Guiding yourself by the electric light that falls into the bedroom from the hallway, you place the food tray on her night-stand beside the canopy bed. Then you open the curtains and the room fills with pale grey light. Among the thick white pillows you can see the top of her head and her curly brown hair spread over the silk sheets. Groaning, she raises her long pale fingers to the sleeping mask and removes it from her eyes. Her face is sullen. 'Oh, it's you. Might have known. You always disturb my best dreams. I was in the strong arms of a gorgeous man. And when I opened my eyes I saw you. Imagine my disappointment.'

241

By now, you should be used to this kind of greeting. But you still suffer a pang of anger. The worst thing of all is your inability to answer back.

'It wasn't a dream,' another sleepy voice says from under the sheets. It gives you a start. A man's head, tousled by sleep, appears on the pillow next to your employer. She starts to giggle and then they kiss. You had no idea one of her guests stayed over. A large group of noisy people came into the house with her after midnight to drink champagne, but you had been sent to bed after making them the sandwiches and opening the bottles. She had said she was sick of the sight of you and was tired of you always being under her feet. But you were grateful for the early night, knowing you had the limousine to clean first thing this morning before taking her to the airport.

But you shouldn't be surprised by the presence of this intruder: although she often doesn't come home until the next morning – regularly calling and ordering you to pick her up from a lover's flat – when she does sleep in her own bed she rarely sleeps alone.

Now, her guest has slid his body down the mattress and put his face between her legs. From under the bed linen that you will have to launder today, his two tanned feet stick out. His body is moving under the sheets. As if you are not in the room, she begins to roll her head around on the pillow and whisper, 'Nice. Nice. Oh, nice,' to him. Her face has screwed up as if she is going to cry.

Obediently, you pick up her clothes from where she dropped them the night before to tidy them away – for someone who hates seeing things left lying around the floor, she makes no effort to remedy the problem. But, you suppose, that is why she owns you.

While her lover eats between her legs under the sheets and you are forced to listen to her murmurs of encouragement – 'Oh, Tony. Oh, baby. Oh, Tony. Fuck me. Fuck me. Fuck me now' – you pause as you scoop a pair of see-through panties off the floor. Unable to resist the urge, you caress them between your finger and thumb. They are tangled up in the flesh-coloured garter belt and the stockings. Then you find the matching brassiere, draped over the black high heels with the ankle straps she was wearing the night before. Then, beside her backless dress, you see the three pinky condoms. They are all used and must have been dropped over the side of the bed early this morning. That makes ten you've found since Sunday and it's only Wednesday morning.

Peering up at the bed you can see that her lover, this Tony character, has moved her on to all fours. You watch him insert himself between her lean, pale buttocks.

Slut. Slut. Beautiful slut: you mouth the words to yourself and hold her soiled lingerie against the bulge in your trousers.

Against her backside, he begins to thump his groin. Making a whining sound, she bites the fingers of one hand. Holding the back of her head, he presses her face into the pillows. This she likes and immediately starts to talk dirty: 'Fuck me. Hold me down. Fuck me. Use me. Use me.'

As if innocently attending to your duties, you put her dress on a hanger, place her shoes in the correct cubicle in the walk-in wardrobe and then drop her lingerie into the laundry hamper she keeps beside her dressing table. Hand-wash only, you think, smiling to yourself. There are perks to this job. Surreptitiously, you then peek at the bed and watch your employer being pounded – head down, fingers clawing the sheets, little feet raking. Even the canopy frame is shaking and squeaking now. You often hear this sound when lying in your bed, alone, over the garage.

Bitch, you say to yourself. And on the other side of the bed, you make sure to wipe your feet on Tony's clothes. In the en-suite bathroom you then turn the shower on and set it at the desired temperature. From the airing cupboard, you retrieve two fluffy white towels and one of the overnight guests' robes before placing them within easy reach of the shower cubicle. Inside the bathroom you can hear her cries building to a crescendo – 'Bastard. Bastard. Fucking bastard' – and decide to go back and take a look. Peering from the bathroom door, you can see the bed reflected in the mirror on her dressing table, arranged on the other side of the room. You angled it in such a way as to be able to observe the bed from the bathroom.

Now she is on her back and he has placed her feet on his shoulders. Fingers indenting her long thighs, he begins to thrust harder and faster than before. Shaking about on the mattress like a rag doll, her pretty face red and mouth gaping, you can see the eyeliner, left on the night before, that has stained her cheeks. You shake your head and sigh. What is the point of buying her such expensive cleansing lotions – more costly per gram than gold – when she doesn't bother to wash her face before going to bed?

'Coming,' Tony says, and all the muscles on his back are showing through his brown skin.

'Oh, oh, oh. Baby. Make me pregnant. Give me a baby,' she cries out in response. Now she is reaching a climax too. She always says this at the crucial moment. Doesn't matter who she is sleeping with, she always finishes with the same verbal flurry. The other chauffeurs that you talk to outside the parties say it is a common orgasmic request amongst their employers.

From the bathroom, you cross the bedroom and close the door behind you. It slams.

The traffic is sparse today. The traffic is sparse every day. How you long for congestion on these smooth, wide roads. Driving relaxes you. But you get everywhere in this city too quickly – even when following the rigidly enforced speed limit.

Checking the rear-view mirror, you also check out madam. She's 'putting her face on', as she calls it. Never had time before you left home because she was too busy riding Tony in the shower. Pouting her thick lips, she runs a scarlet liner around them. Her mouth looks wet and red like glossy meat. You study her leather two-piece suit. The skirt has ridden right up to the top of her thighs so you can see a teeny triangle of black panty material, stocking tops and the milky inside of her thighs.

Between your legs you feel a familiar and unavoidable swelling – created by a combination of frustration, jealousy, devotion, desire, anger.

'I know what you're looking at. Pervert,' she says, without a trace of irritation in her tone.

You smile.

'I see you. Looking all the time. Don't think I don't notice. But don't push your luck, buster. This isn't for you. So just keep your eyes on the road. I'm not wearing my seat belt.'

'Yes, ma'am.'

'Now go through the list I left you, so I know you won't fuck things up when I'm away.'

You clear your throat. 'I have it all written down, ma'am.'

'Tell me!' Now she is annoyed. 'Why have you always got to back-chat me? You're so facetious. And that silent treatment doesn't fool me either. I know what you're thinking. Remember that. Nothing you think or do is safe from me. I've got my eye on you, sonny.'

Odd her calling you sonny when you are at least ten years her senior. 'I'll sanitise the pool first. The food order is ready, so I just have to pick it up. Then I'll call the agency for catering staff. I'll take the garden furniture out of storage and hang the lights in the garden.'

'And what else?'

'I'll prepare the dungeon. Clean the leather things and make sure the new rubber is laid down in the den.'

'Good. But there's one more thing I have to ask of you.'

'Yes,' you say with a sigh and then immediately hope she didn't detect the sarcastic inflection.

'Set up the camera equipment. I want you to film the party.'

You swallow. Now this is a new development. You check the rear-view mirror. She has put her make-up things away and is now smiling at you. Her legs are crossed at the thigh and she is pouting sexily.

'Really?' you say, but it comes out all high-pitched and squeaky. 'Really?' you repeat in a deeper voice.

'You're going to make a movie for me. A home movie. I want you to film us all. In the dungeon.'

'Of course.'

'See how good I am to you?'

'Yes, ma'am.'

'Now all that should keep you out of mischief when I'm away.'

You grin. Don't you believe it, ma'am.

'What's so funny?'

'Nothing, ma'am.'

She raises an eyebrow, but is excited by the business trip and cannot sustain her usual enmity towards you.

You take the next filter road signposted for the airport. On the back seat, your employer begins to fluff out her hair. 'What did you think of Tony?' she asks you nonchalantly.

This still surprises you. By increments, as your time in her employ has lengthened she has begun to ask your advice and trust you with personal information. But it's hard to get used to this role of confidant: most of the time she is either screaming at you, flogging you or ignoring you. But then she has also called you 'My little hubby,' twice on the phone when she has called in from the office to issue a request. Generally, though, like a spoilt child with many toys, she mostly takes you for granted.

You clear your throat. 'All right, I suppose.'

Grinning, she moves forward so her chin rests on the back of your seat. 'He's got a lovely cock.'

You remain silent but feel the inevitable twist and pinch in your gut.

'Great body. Real brainy. He's a broker. In arms and munitions. He might be the one.' She's referring to the father of her proposed child. 'But I'm not sure. He's perfect and all that, but . . . I dunno. He's so up himself. Might still go for IVF.'

'I really couldn't say,' you add.

She leans back in her seat with her eyes half-closed. 'You're jealous,' she says. Raising one leg she places a foot, shod in a spike-heeled shoe on your shoulder and scratches your cheek with the heel. 'You hate it when you hear me with them, don't you? When you see me being a very bad girl. But it gets you off, I bet.'

Easing the car into a parking spot, you then apply the handbrake. 'I really don't know what you mean, ma'am.'

She winks at you and then climbs out of the car. Walking behind her tight buttocks as they sway inside their tight wrapper of soft leather, you push a trolley holding her cases and laptop. At the terminal, she checks in and then returns to where you stand. You put your chauffeur cap back on.

'Remember to do all your chores, my little man,' she says, before leaning forward to peck you on the cheek. You blush and your urge to resist her wiles, to dislike her selfish character and to oppose her petty tyranny, suddenly collapse under the gravity of her beauty and sweet, sweet smell. This is why the chairmen of the board know you are safe with her. Why they rewarded you with a position in her service.

247

She straightens your tie and then scrapes a shred of fluff from the front of your blazer with a long red nail. Of late, she seems to spend more time saying goodbye to you at the airport. She lowers her voice to a whisper and stares into your eyes. 'One of these nights . . .' she begins to say, and then stops herself from finishing the sentence. 'Sometimes, it's not so bad having you around,' she adds.

'Thank you, ma'am.'

But her expression suddenly changes. 'But don't think I'm going soft. If you ever, ever, ever fuck with me, I'll have you destroyed. Understand?'

'Of course, ma'am.'

She relaxes again and exhales her minty, lipstick breath across your face. 'Don't let that bitch of a maid from next door in the apartment. I've seen her making eyes at you over the fence. I might complain. The slut.'

'Don't be ridiculous,' you say.

'Wish me luck, then.'

'Good luck, ma'am.'

'Put some bloody enthusiasm into it. Honestly.'

'Ma'am, I hope you have a safe and rewarding trip,' you say.

She pinches the skin of your thigh between her lacquered nails until you cry out. Sullen-faced, she then teeters away from you towards the departure lounge, pulling her hand-luggage behind her. You watch her walk away. Despite an announcement giving out flight information, you can still hear the heels of her shoes as they strike the stone floor. You watch her, and listen to that sound, until she disappears from view.

NEXUS NEW BOOKS

To be published in January

DEMONIC CONGRESS
Aishling Morgan

Eighteenth-century Devon. Old Noah Pargade is a wealthy yet cur-mudgeonly miser who marries the nubile and game Alice Eden. As anxious to avoid sharing his wife as he is his wealth, he makes sure she is enmured in his desolate old house on the moors. Fortunately for young Alice, there are enough young bucks in the vicinity whose advantage it is in to take pity on her. Noah's fears are well-founded, as Alice is able to continue her cheerfully sluttish goings-on. Especially when the swash-buckling John Truscott returns from his foreign travels, and quack doctor Cyriack Coke, replete with a cartload of bizarre colonic devices, visits the county. When the truth becomes plain, old Coke is forced to take drastic measures.

ISBN 0 352 33762 1

CHALLENGED TO SERVE
Jacqueline Bellevois

Known simply as 'The Club', a group of the rich and influential meet every month in a Cotswold mansion to slake their perverted sexual appetites. Within its walls, social norms are forgotten and fantasy becomes reality. The Club's members are known to each other by the names of pagan gods and goddesses, or those of characters from the darker side of history. Two of them – Astra and Kali – undertake to resolve a feud once and for all by each training a novice member. After one month, the one who's deemed by the other members to have done the best job will be allowed to enslave the other, finally and totally, for the duration of the Club's activities and beyond.

ISBN 0 352 33748 6

PRIVATE MEMOIRS OF A KENTISH HEADMISTRESS
Yolanda Celbridge

Graceful young heiress Miss Abigail Swift founds a new academy to teach Kentish maidens discipline and ladylike manners. She meets the stern, lovely matron, already adept at the art of a young lady's correction; the untamed Walter, longing to become a lady; and the surly beauty Miss Rummer, who keeps the local gentlemen on their toes. Visiting Paris, Abigail learns from the voluptuous Comtesse de Clignancourt that English discipline makes for French pleasure, and triumphs at the masked ball in Dover Castle by introducing her perverse but well-tested methods to royalty.

ISBN 0 352 33763 X

To be published in February

JODHPURS AND JEANS
Penny Birch

Penny Birch is currently the filthiest little minx on the Nexus list, with 14 titles already published by Nexus. All are equally full of messy, kinky fun and, frankly, no other erotic writer has ever captured the internal thrills afforded by the perverse shamings and humiliations her characters undergo! In *Jodhpurs and Jeans*, Penny returns to the world of human equestrianism, and also takes part in a very bizarre game of paintball!

£6.99   ISBN 0 352 33778 8

LOVE-CHATTEL OF TORMUNIL
Aran Ashe

Powerfully erotic fantasy fiction by the author of *The Handmaidens*. *Love-Chattel of Tormunil* continues the tenderly written erotic epic of *The Chronicles of Tormunil*, which catalogues the exploits and odysseys of outlanders, body-slaves, milk-slaves and soldiers, all versed in the Tormunite ways of tender SM and bondage.

£6.99   ISBN 0 352 33779 6

THE CORRECTION OF AN ESSEX MAID
Yolanda Celbridge

Rescued from degradation, young and naïve orphan Sophia joins the House of Rodings, a maids' training school deep in the Essex countryside, dedicated to the worship and correction of the naked female rear. She meets a cast of submissive and dominant females, all adoring or envious of Sophia's voluptuous bottom, and thrives in the complex ranks, rules and punishments of the House's hierarchy.

£6.99   ISBN 0 352 33780 X

If you would like more information about Nexus titles, please visit our website at www.nexus-books.co.uk, or send a stamped addressed envelope to:

Nexus, Thames Wharf Studios,
Rainville Road, London W6 9HA